*Judy,
much love and support to one of my favorite writers and friends*

Socrates is Dead Again

Nancy

Nancy Avery Dafoe

Pen Woman Press

Copyright © 2022 by Nancy Avery Dafoe
Cover illustration art Copyright © 2022 by Matt Cincotta
Cover background art Copyright © 2022 by Katie Turner

All rights reserved. No part of this book may be used or reproduced in any manner whatsoever without written permission from the publisher, except by a reviewer who may quote brief passages in a review.

Cover design: Lucy Arnold
Book Editor Coordinator: Lucy Arnold

Library of Congress Control Number (LCCN): 2022911765 (print)

ISBN 978-1-950251-10-0 (print)

First edition
Printed in the United States of America
BISAC: FICTION/Literary; FICTION/Metaphysical; FICTION/General

This is a work of fiction. Names, characters, places, and incidents are the product of the author's imagination or are used fictitiously. Any resemblance to actual persons, living or dead, is coincidental.

Published in the United States by
the National League of American Pen Women, Inc.
PEN WOMEN PRESS

Founded in 1897,
National League of American Pen Women, Inc.
is a nonprofit dedicated to promoting the arts.
1300 17th Street NW
Washington, D.C. 20036-1973
www.nlapw.org

"And of all these things the Albino whale was the symbol." Moby Dick, Chapter 42
Herman Melville

"A writer is a reader who can't control himself and therefore writes." The New Yorker,
October 1, 2011
Jhumpa Lahiri

Also by
Nancy Avery Dafoe

Unstuck in Time, A Memoir and Mystery on Loss and Love
Naimah and Ajmal on Newton's Mountain
Murder on Ponte Vecchio
Both End in Speculation
You Enter a Room
An Iceberg in Paradise: A Passage Through Alzheimer's
The House Was Quiet, But the Mind Was Anxious
Innermost Sea
Poets Diving in the Night
The Misdirection of Education Policy
Writing Creatively
Breaking Open the Box

Dedicated to writers working alone or in concert trying to make sense of living in this world; to my wonderful Pen Women friends; to poets Gwynn O'Gara and Jo Pitkin; to my influential professors William Rosenfeld, Samuel Fisher Babbitt, Mary Lynch Kennedy, and Karla Alwes; to Janine DeBaise and Mary Lynch Kennedy who offered to write endorsements for this novel, and to my daughters Colette and Nicole who are my first audience; to my husband Daniel who has always believed in me as a writer; and to readers everywhere who are brave enough to jump into a text and make our words live again. Thank you all.

Socrates is Dead Again

One

2:11 AM Texts

Drew Levin, Ian Frost ... (5)
5 recipients

Marshall Funkhouser
APOCALYPSE! TOTAL
DEVASTATION! HE'S
GONE! GERD IS DEAD! MMS
2:11 AM

Drew Levin
Marshall, Gerd dead?
No indication of how
or why? Accident?
Nothing about this
seems possible. No way
Adrian Gerd Wahl
is gone. Too young.
Far too vital. MMS
2:11 AM

Tom Hayes
Why doesn't anyone use his first name? How did his absurd nickname Gerd stick? Murdered? Suicide? He must have offed himself. His work revealed him to be more than mad. MMS
2:12 AM

Drew Levin
Please! Gerd pronounced Khurt. Norwegian. I find his work some of the sanest I've ever read, Tom. Not mad; true, unique. MMS
2:13 AM

Marie Rollins
Tom, S.T.O.P! A great man is dead. A literary giant lost. Can't sleep. Can't think. Horrifying. MMS
2:13 AM

Drew Levin
Not possible.

I just saw him.
Talked with him.
Can't be true.
What could have
happened? I can't
accept this. MMS
2:13 AM

Gillian Keating
OMG. I just
saw this news.
How? I mean,
Why? WHY?
Have you heard
any more, Drew? MMS
2:14 AM

Marshall Funkhouser
Yet, here we are,
reading about his
death in the ether,
middle of the night
or morning, left
wondering. Left.
Stunned, not yet
able to mourn. MMS.
2:14 AM

Ian Frost
Nice pun, Marshall.
"The rest is silence." MMS
2:15 AM

I couldn't text again that night after reading my friend Ian's comment. What response could possibly follow Ian, Hamlet, and Shakespeare in one line? And Gerd Wahl's death shocked us all. That is how it began. Our search, not just mine. Even though I, Drew Levin, had interviewed the famed writer, not Ian. I would attempt to offer Adrian Gerd Wahl's words mixed with my own as some kind of insight, yet I already knew there would be no definitive answer. The paucity of information suggested suicide, and suicide takes answers with it.

"The rest is silence" in the middle of the night, a group of my friends texting with each other yet still separate, alone. We were all characters in our own novels in progress and also in each other's budding works, too. Few of us had yet decided if we were going to end up being maximalists or minimalists. We were not a collective, but all too aware of the presence of those who came before us, those who contributed even without their say. It was as if I had assembled all of the writers I knew from central casting to answer the question of "why?" More precisely, the questions because they are far more numerous than any answers.

I was devastated and not alone in feeling decimated.

As Gillian Keating texted, "why?" That was our prime directive. For all of us—all envious, full of our hard-acquired hubris of identifying as "writer" yet left uncertain about our work. The suspicion is that we were, after all, slightly ridiculous in all of our seriousness. We knew what we wanted, and Wahl had it all. We were obsessive fans of the great Adrian Gerd Wahl, a writer with everything; everything that each of us desired, a man who inexplicably appeared to have taken his own life.

Two

Julia Reads Her Lover's Response

February 13
Julia,
Pablo Neruda's poem to which you referred suggests "lake" speaks a language that man no longer hears, as if we once held that capacity. This statement, or implied question does not so much offer cynicism but, rather, demands pragmatism.

    Nothing in Adrian's last letter spoke of his love. At least, not on the surface. Julia Alexander shook her head, her long, silver looped earrings softly touching her face as she turned her head from side to side again, reproducing the feel of cool metal on her neck, distracting her. She took a deep breath. When she first reread the letter, she had lowered her head in dismay, then fell into a rhythm of distractions. I'm strange, she thought but not as strange as Adrian. Her eyes left his words on neatly folded paper, but she continued to feel the weight. For a moment, there was nothing but emptiness. In that crushing instant, she let her pen roll across her open palm and watched the instrument fall.

Seconds earlier, Julia had examined the envelope, then turned the paper over hesitantly even though she was again anxious to reread Adrian's responses to her. Each time she thought of him, Julia used one of his names or nicknames that best suited her feeling toward him at the moment. Adrian was reserved for their intimacy although everyone referred to him as Gerd, a most unfortunate name. He never seemed to notice the oddity of his Norwegian Gerd as a medical condition. She wondered sometimes why she had persisted in their affair in the midst of such difficulty. Admitting that the exercise of writing letters was rather primitive, even quaint, she had always liked the feel of paper, something tactile as essential to their relationship. Of course, his habit of not answering his phone unnerved her. Who didn't answer his cell phone when the number was registered as a friend, if not lover? Suddenly, it was in front of her: what he had really thought of her. Even after all the times they shared, she allowed insecurity to speculate that he had not loved her at all. She wondered what had happened to her self-esteem of late, all that she had worked so hard to create.

Adrian Gerd Wahl was not an easy man to like at times, much less love, but that, she was sure, was an opinion only held by those few who knew him too well. To his adoring fans in the literary world, he was compelling and generous, ruggedly handsome, simultaneously superior and down to earth, but then, no, she thought, he drew her in, too. Wahl harbored the kind of duality and mystery in his face to which both men and women were attracted. If he acted indifferently to fawning or even love at times, his perceived apathy only made him all the more alluring.

The writer's conference, that monolith called the Association of Writers and Writing Programs (AWP), where she met Wahl, started for her as they all do: filled with promise, her nerve endings tingling in anticipation; language stimulating cortical areas of the brain, vocabulary entering on one of the higher floors as if they were all transported to inner workings of a thesaurus from street dictionaries below. On the escalator in the conference center, she noticed a writer she knew going down. Stopping herself from putting up her hand in order not to appear foolish, or worse, eager, she looked up again.

"Julia, I didn't know you were here!" an old friend from graduate school stood above the escalator on the landing, moving right and left as people tried to maneuver around him.

"Oh, yes. Nice to see you, Richard." They exchanged a perfunctory hug before moving into the stream of the erudite without seeming effort in the way one watches a ballerina pirouette across a stage, feeling the natural, balanced movement like wind or water, all awash in interiority, yes, that word beloved by too many attendees. But Julia was also aware of bleeding toes from practice sessions, from unnatural competition.

"Are you looking or just browsing?" he said, shifting the strap of his briefcase to his other shoulder. It must have been heavy with a new manuscript, Julia imagined.

"Just browsing. I'm fairly content teaching where I am."

"Oh, you're in the distinct minority, then," he said, slightly bumping into her as the crowd thickened near one of the doors to a workshop. "Which workshops are you attending, or are you offering one? I didn't see your name."

"Drifting in and out of ones that sound promising. Not presenting this year. Are you looking for a new position?"

"Curriculum Vitae on hand, and yes, I'm on the hunt, but first I want to catch this reading," Richard took out his conference brochure and ran his finger over the small type searching.

"Listen, I will catch you later," Julia said, as she left Richard trying to figure out which reading held the best prospects for new job connections. Julia turned her head to look back and see Richard still trying to figure out where he was going, the college writing job search on display or in process everywhere at the AWP, as lines were added to or deleted from manuscripts, books promoted, successful careers and books manifest while the less successful writers clamored, politicked, practiced flattery, and feigned control over their circumstances.

On an impulse, Julia decided to remove herself from the stream and ducked into a room where a discussion was already in progress. One of the presenters looked up and gave that eyeball scolding for her late entry.

"The interiority of the work. . ." Julia heard as the speaker continued, but she looked down at her phone and noted the number of emails she had yet to respond to, her attention already outside the room. So many writers whose paths had been diverted, stalled by realities of trying to make a living while writing, families or individuals uprooted and leaving home. For all their attempts at showing their talents and eminence, clear-eyed cynicism caused pretension to fall away and drift through rooms like dust in filtered sunlight.

***

Julia remembered even the light blue sweater she was wearing on the late afternoon she met Wahl, ordered from a company named POETRY, before her quest turned dark and bitter like coffee sitting in a cold metal pot too long, aftertaste still on her tongue when she got up suddenly, needing to escape. They had collided dramatically, straight out of some movie script.

She was in the massive but crowded conference arena reserved for the book fair. Filled with over-caffeinated writers in Boston again, Julia looked past the booth of Lost Horse Press when suddenly, someone shoved past her, nearly knocking her over. He was catching her. Adrian Gerd Wahl's large hands, she recalled, were well used to labor, unlike an academic. They could have belonged to a carpenter or street fighter. She noted skin abrasions, slight tears, healed scars. She saw his hands before his handsome face. When she looked up, she didn't recognize the man as the famed Adrian Gerd Wahl, but then he was not quite as well-known at that time, still making the talk circuit, his most recent tome only just released. She hadn't even read his previously lauded work yet.

"Well, hello." Teeth showing, perfect, and intelligent eyes, she observed.

"Hello. Is this how we're going to keep meeting?" She adjusted her sweater and had no idea why she decided to try to be funny, but he laughed.

"That's up to you."

"Let's get out of here," were her words to him. Still feeling the suffocating effects of too many writers in one locale, she wondered why she decided to be so bold. What made her think he would agree? But he did.

"By any means," he responded. His words surprised her again. "By any" rather than "by all" as he parted the crowds naturally and without seeming effort. The two of them moved down the escalator, his fingers still lightly touching her elbow one step above her as if their connection already depended upon that physical, electric link between them.

Down on street level, she reached for his hand and pulled him into an Asian restaurant she had spotted earlier on her way to the convention center. Leaning over their small, round table, resting chin on her upturned palms, she allowed herself to stare at him indulgently, take in his eyes and the smile that threatened at the corners of his mouth but did not fully open. He returned the intense focus. "You somehow look familiar," she said after they ordered, realizing she was being more than flirtatious.

"I've been to too many of these, so you look familiar, as well," he remarked with more than a hint of playfulness in his deep voice.

"I'm not recognizable," she laughed, "but your voice; I'd love to hear you read."

"How about hearing me speak?" Good, she thought, a sense of humor. I like this man.

"That will do." Before they had finished the Miso soup, she knew she would sleep with him, an idea which was entirely unexpected for her at this early stage, not a conclusion she typically reached. If she could have described herself before that day, she would have said "cautious or reserved," but she showed none of those instincts with this man. Only later did it occur to her that the woman Wahl probably fell in love with that afternoon was a fiction, a character playacting in rehearsal, practicing dress-up for an act without a script.

***

Not liking the feeling of pseudo anything, especially in herself, Julia picked up his letter. Examined it again. There had to be something more hidden between his lines, a subtext she had failed to decipher.

Neruda's poem to which you referred is "The Lake," and it's a Caleb Beissert translation, in which Lake Rupanco speaks. Translated, these lines in Beissert's version use the word "idiom," causing me to hesitate, in that an ideal word in the last line is "idiom," and feels rather like a translator's choice. "Idiom" opens up other associations that a word such as "dialect" does not, yet this duality suggests the problematic nature of translations in which the particular "genius" of a language is peculiar to that language and not necessarily translatable with implications and innuendo. Do we know Neruda's intention there? Beissert could make the claim that he knew, but I would still wonder if Neruda would agree.

With translations, we are not always certain what diction was the poet's choice and what enters discussions via translator's decisions. I can't imagine a translator choosing my words for me; someone replacing my carefully selected symbols with facsimiles, deliberating which one out of the many possibilities best suits his or her interpretation, rather than mine.

Our back-and-forth volley across metaphorical nets provokes me, and now I only have energy to serve up a few Galway Kinnell lines from his poem "Daybreak," in which the

11 | Socrates is Dead Again

heavens' stars sink down into mud. Please don't take this as insult. I'm just not inclined to compare our relationship to stars tonight.

Kinnell's poem followed. Julia tried to laugh, but her snort was not warm or generous. Those last lines, "sink down in the mud," she stifled her exhale mid-way so it sounded more like an extended hiccup. That was it. Adrian didn't even sign his letter to her. It was his last missive to her. The famed Gerd Wahl could write a thousand pages of fiction but only a few short paragraphs about some other poet and translations to the woman he purported to love, and what he did write might as well have been part of a lecture on idiom or one on polemics in some obscure college course. Worse yet, his letter could easily be construed as a devastating insult. Not the stars. . .

She wanted to be angry. But she knew the man well enough to sense his mercurial moods and voices, one reserved for lecturing, one for publicity, one for his dogs, one for social events, one for writing, one for their quiet time together, one for ironies he found in everything, one for guises he assumed at various moments of life. Why had he chosen his lecturer's voice for her? She reexamined flow of the changing dynamics in their relationship in seconds.

If he was insulting and exasperating, he could also be the most intriguing human being she had ever met, and this had once made her promise to give their strange but variously intimate and then distant relationship some latitude. How far she was willing to let that line stretch she never got to decide, but it seemed that every time she watched her tolerance expand into new territory, she recognized it might be too late for pulling back. She was not used to being taken for granted.

Understand, she had pursued him initially but then he acted decisively. No one could understand their relationship from outward appearances. Sometimes texting her in the middle of the night, Gerd expected her to respond immediately. He required an unusual level of commitment, an expectation that made it more difficult for her to make good decisions about parameters.

The tight community of literary writers and readers had been speculating for some time, in print as well as in public, about the mystery women in Wahl's life, and Julia didn't mind that he seemed to want to keep their relationship a secret, "private," as he said, but if inquiring minds and gossips really knew what loving Gerd Wahl was like, the mystery of the man might disappear. No, not the mystery but some of his allure. Harder than it looked. That night, like those many nights since she met him, she felt exhausted by conflicting tensions, pulls in polar directions which threatened her composure, a quality that had taken years to acquire.

As she reread his last letter, Julia couldn't help wondering whether there were—no, of course there must have been other women. He had affairs during their long absences, but she could not imagine those other women meant more to him. There were always women coming up to him at book events and social occasions: beautiful women flirting and trying to tempt him with their intellect because he was not easily won over by mere physicality. Aware she was not a beautiful woman, Julia, nevertheless, felt their connection was secure whenever they were together, but as soon as they were apart, he seemed emotionally reserved. Why did he write to her as if she were one of his students sitting in some lecture hall halfway across the country where he was only temporarily passing through as guest lecturer?

The reason she left him, an action originally weighed as temporary had become permanent, devolved into tortured regret. No, regret wasn't quite the right word. Her action, her decision on that fateful night had been a terrible mistake but one she could not alter. He, too, had made a decision that was unalterable.

One of his previous statements must have held a clue, she was certain. Another found line left uneasiness in its place: the phrase about "matters." She had either inadvertently avoided or deliberately turned away from something critically important he had said or written. He had given them to her: all the signs if only she was capable of reading well.

Only after he was so suddenly, so terribly gone, Julia was able to confirm the most terrible truth: she loved him without reservation. Yelling out loud in an empty room, she just wanted another chance. Repeat. Do over. She would drive to his cottage, run to him like some schoolgirl with a mad crush, but there was no path forward.

The immense cruelty of his final act beat her as savagely as fists he never used. First in her subconscious, Julia felt a shift into conscious thought: the idea that any mystery about a death is a story about a life.

Three

Man and Myth

"He was Ahab." That was what I told my darling Angela after she finished her shift at the hospital, her shoulders hunched from working long hours, her mouth pinched tight when she slammed our door. I should have been offering her a cup of tea or coffee, taking her coat and hanging it up for her, but I was too caught up in my theory, thinking about myself and Wahl. What could an interview with a dead man do for me?

"What? Who's Ahab?" Angela stood looking at me in her blue scrubs as if she weren't sure who was talking, then she dropped her coat on our dog-chewed overstuffed chair just inside the doorway. "Drew?"

"Wahl. Wahl was Ahab.

"Oh."

"Yes. A little complicated."

"I'm too tired for this. Can we talk about this later?"

"Of course, you're tired, I know, but just a quick response. What do you think about my basic premise? The analogy?"

"I have no idea right now. I'm going to bed." Her back already turned to me. She seemed sad, not simply tired.

Everything in the rearview mirror now. I'm trying to recall if she shook her head in disbelief with me or with the fact that the famed writer we both admired was gone forever. I was stunned by his action, but Angela appeared to take it harder than I expected. That disconcerted me; I'll admit. I had no idea she was so invested in a writer who was not me. I wanted to work through my theory of Wahl as Ahab, but Angela wasn't having it at the moment. She looked almost as if I had somehow caused this tragedy instead of merely reported it.

When I tried to bring up my ideas about the man and myth after her next shift the following day, she definitely shook her head. I did not imagine it the first time.

She said, "I don't want to talk about Wahl as Ahab or even talk about Wahl today," as if my idea were garbage.

"Why? I thought you liked his work?"

"Exactly. Too much. It hurts."

If she would have heard me out, I was going to say that Wahl's great white whale was nothing less than story itself, all those mythic constructs. That's what the great writer was chasing. Maybe I would end my feature on him with this analogy. I recalled after my first interview with him, I disliked the man yet worshipped the writer. Yet, after all this time, I was no closer to discovering Wahl than I was on that last night diving into Skaneateles Lake. I still can't believe I jumped into that dark lake. A night of "shifting and confused gusts of memory" as Proust wrote, according to Wahl, because I still haven't read Proust although I intended to.

Adrian Gerd Wahl, the writer I interviewed, not once but twice, the one who would change everything for me, the one with the strange name, was an arrogant genius, an obsessive and meticulous writer whom Melville would likely have recognized as both flawed hero and half-madman in his quest. I don't know if Wahl was mentally ill, or we just had to view him that way in order to make sense of his last actions.

I could call Ian, the least judgmental of my writer friends, and talk to him about my idea for the feature story. No, I couldn't call Ian after stealing his interview with Wahl. How much damage had I done to our friendship? My act was certainly forgivable but then, I never knew with Ian. Perhaps I had done the unforgivable.

He was gone. Wahl sacrificed himself for something, I believe, holding a mythical search above all else, and for that, too, I admired him. Maybe admired is not the right word. I have no idea why this famous writer took his own life. I didn't know if he was looking for monsters or a monster within. Since Angela wasn't listening, I had to toss those half-formed thoughts around in a vacuum, playing with endings for my feature that was not yet written. The weight of the unwritten was suddenly more burden than opportunity.

It hit me again: I was the last one to interview the great man. Sweat broke out in a cool room; people were going to be reading my account and looking for something significant, and I had no idea if anything was there for them to discover. So much in the balance: if nothing original or compelling was found, then I would be revealed as fraud. As possible rescue, I started thinking about fiction. If I invented a scene, who would know? There was no great writer preparing to dispute my view of events.

Suicide would never make any sense to me. A mystery without answer: was it possible that Wahl left any clues of his intent? I tried to consider what I would leave of him for his readers. Already weary from nothing more than speculation, I decided, in the least, I was not going to posit a list of questions as I was doing with myself. Readers, my boss would be expecting answers. I had to find a way to shape Wahl the man as distinguished from Wahl the writer, yet portray both. Just considering the task was daunting enough, let alone from two, wildly different interviews and perspectives. Let his words speak for themselves. I would simply quote him. Yet, there was a problem with that approach, too. I had to go through several notebooks and try to decipher what Wahl said and what I said. Damn, it never is a good idea to be drunk and try conducting an interview.

Without being aware of it, Wahl was the center for a group of my writer friends. When the center does not hold, "things fall apart" as Yates then Chinua Achebe penned. Ian would be proud of me for my allusions. But I was quoting Wahl there, not Ian. My good friends, all writers, Ian, Gillian, Shwetak, Marshall, occasionally Tom, all followed Wahl, read his books, reviews, his every utterance. Too many of us competing for an editor's notice, only to receive that blank stare, that unanswered query. Somehow, I suspected that Adrian Gerd Wahl knew he was the center of a lot more than to my friends. Yet he removed himself.

Ian, the one who convinced me I needed to attend next year's AWP Conference with him, could recite long passages from Wahl's novels. I once asked my friend, "How do you do it? Recite Wahl so effortlessly?"

"Read him again," he said with a half-smile. "Then again and again. Repetition." As if that feat was actually easy.

We bought the great Gerd Wahl's novels. I went paperback. Ian bought hardcovers. I tried to get Ian's copy signed by Wahl at the start of my last interview with the man but carelessly left Ian's book somewhere, Wahl's cottage most likely, on that last night. I didn't even have the courage to tell Ian that I'd lost his book. Hopefully, he would forget, but not likely.

Even my non-writer friends loved Wahl, but most of my friends happened to be writers. Almost all, except my best friends, Angela and Henry. Angela is a nurse, but she's a prolific reader. Thank goodness. Henry, well, he's my dog, and I'm guessing here, but I think if Henry and Wahl had ever been introduced, Henry would have drooled all over the big man just like Wahl's own princely dogs.

My proxy friends, friends of friends with whom I hang out, Tom and Marie, Ornal and Ellison also read Wahl, that solitary writer standing in opposition to community. I think there has to be a dissertation in there somewhere. If only I was back in grad school and not trying to survive in the world. We were ready-made as paradigm for that ridiculous theoretical discussion about authorship, still with one foot in the MFA programs from which we emerged relatively intact. Tom, I was not sure how long I could appease Ian by hanging out with Tom, a man too often cruel and self-centered, and it sure looked like he was into something serious, maybe even heroin. Why was I even thinking about Tom?

Circling back to Wahl because he was the man with everything who gave it all up. I assembled this cast on my page to answer one central question: why? And the irony was not lost on me that this story was all in retrospect, me telling, them telling, telling and telling, upending the central tenant of "show, not tell." That suddenly made me smirk, thinking Wahl would have approved of another broken writing rule, the way he annihilated the expected and stuffed rules into his worn fedora. "Do not mix verb tenses or mix them wildly," he once said.

Flipping pages absently then intently, I'm tried to remember my conversations with Wahl more precisely. No, more than remember. I wanted to reconstruct those moments, bring them to life. Wasn't that the writer's job? Something Wahl said must have indicated what he was thinking in terms of taking his life, but all I could bring forth was how generous he was the last time I saw him. How odd it was for him to be so open and unusually kind on that last night. Wahl was not known for either quality, particularly with journalists. I should have been amazed at how we got drunk together and talked as old friends, closer than many people I have known for years.

"Every story should be as alive as its human facsimile." Was that something Gerd Wahl said? I wondered if I wrote those words in my notebook or repeated what Wahl related. To be honest, those statements could have been mine but not likely. Unfortunately, a bunch of notations from my last interview with him were highly confusing because we both had too much to drink, as I'd confessed. I searched my notebooks and memory bank, making notations before falling asleep that night. Narrative was the one who walked away. I'd already started thinking in dangerous terms that Wahl was my story as if he somehow belonged to me.

Examining my barely decipherable interview scrawling, I came across the word "craft" underlined and the sentence beneath it: "Everyone advises writers to show, not tell, but I'm telling a story." I have thought about Wahl's remark a lot since I began relating everything.

I'm pretty certain my notes show Wahl was speaking, and I wrote his words verbatim. Never write about writers. Broke that rule myself. I always thought that other writers were the primary readers for books about writers, too, and they are good readers. Wahl's books broke open rules. I knew them all, too, even if I hadn't come out of the Iowa Writers' Workshop. My MFA was still worth something. In my jumbled notes about an impossible evening, I was certain I could find Wahl the man, not simply the myth. But the harder I looked, the more I doubted he had ever been with me.

"I'm going out for something to eat," Angela said as she entered the room, interrupting my train of thought.

"Want me to come?"

"No. I'll bring you back something." Then, she was out the door. When had Angela started disappearing or disconnecting from me?

Without agonizing over the sudden shift in our relationship, I returned to my musing. Maybe I tried too intently to recreate a scene I could not bring out of my inebriated state. Curve and strange slant, dropped letters gave me a pretty good idea I was in bad shape when they spilled across pages. Have to admit I was a little desperate then as well as now. Some of the lettering looked as though written by another hand. It seemed unlikely that Wahl had written something in my notebooks. There was a magazine deadline looming and professional expectations. I knew I would create an interview even if Wahl was not present. I possessed enough imagination and craft to make people believe Wahl was talking, sharing his secrets before taking his life.

Who could question my words if there was no one left to verify? I recognized the lapse as advantage. But the prospect of getting at the man behind the illusion was the reason I had set out on this quest in the first place. I did not want to give it all up. Even if I could trick others, I could not fool myself.

I didn't want to get into a weird and pompous lecture on social constructionism, but I may have to rethink this whole idea about discourse communities after what happened. My friends and I were merely epilogue in Wahl's story, but we were at least an extended one. Wahl was gone. Is gone. I had a conversation with the man that lasted all night and into the next morning, and he remains clouded like my brain that fateful evening.

Ultimately, Wahl was alone. Even in my presence, he was solitary. I imagined him reaching up out of those dark Skaneateles waters, neither in panic nor fear. I knew that he was not afraid at the end. Maybe for the first time, he was unafraid. At least, that was how I intended to portray him--unafraid.

A statement on my page in all caps: "I am Ahab." Then he leaped into Skaneateles Lake on that inordinately dark night. I jumped in after. I realized I had no choice. Quoting Melville, I guessed, made him giddy. From what I remember of Melville's novel, however, I hoped I was Ismael, the one who survived.

Four

Raining Poets in New York

Tom Hayes is walking down the street in the rain. He is relating his presence in first person. Raining all morning, threatening to continue in that vein, like a bleed out; cold, cold, drenching rain soaking into fabric; even tourists in for the weekend had decided to get off the streets temporarily and duck into nearby shops or restaurants, but I'm on a mission, and push past the misery of chilled to the bone, rain somehow worse than snow even though it was that time of year when snow was more likely, when I look up and notice something extraordinary. He switches point of view because it is his story to do as he pleases.

Streets were filling with poets as if the sudden storm had simply deposited all of them, bringing in writers from distant states and continents, carrying them over oceans and land mass in dense clouds until saturation with them crafting words and their elaboration was too heavy. Rains fell and writers descended, landing on their feet mostly, although a few were huddled and crouched, their eyes looking up and out at pavement, at me, at each other, surveying the landscape, details of the grating, while keeping mental ledgers, paying careful attention to all of it. Not a banker, hedge funder, or stock broker in sight. Those cogs in the machine had gone into offices and cubicles and left poets out in the rain. But here they are not in ruin. All the poets are easily mistaken for the homeless maybe because there is some cross-over.

And there is one crossing the street and moving toward me, his yellow, long nails like a bird's talons, hooked over a cart he pushes. His eyebrows unruly, leaving for distant ports, my God, his brows are long, his hands a landscape of wreckage, moss-covered and torn open by fallen rock, hair falling out although strands that are left reach his shoulders.

"Hello." I have no idea why I speak to him. He moves past me, yet notices my existence, wheels of his grocery cart staggering, an old piece of something once white wraps around them; I can't help thinking that it looks like toilet paper, though I don't believe it is because the wrap appears far too resilient. His clothing calls up a fishmonger from another day. He turns his cart and comes back my way, stops and stares. Phlegm knots in his throat, and a glop is deposited in front of my feet. I look at expectorant. We are fixated on one another. Challenge or insult? I dig a couple of bills out of my jeans, the last cash I have available, and stuff the bills into his torn shirt pocket. I don't know at that instant if this is a suicidal act or my first truly generous one in a long time. He allows me to touch him which surprises me as much as him.

Maybe I should rethink the offer, but, what the hell. It is only money, not mercy, even if they are the last dollars I have. He looks shocked. I'm a little shocked, too, having given up on myself, but I am also pleased, not known for my kindness even to myself. He looks puzzled before rolling on, his feet like the wheels of his cart moving into weather as if he has a destination, a purpose. I want him to make it. Another poet soul.

On the other side of the street is a Jack Kerouac look-a-like which seems odd because Kerouac was a good-looking guy in the 50s, but this contemporary Kerouac appears as out of place as the woman who is squinting and looking up and down the street searching for something missing in her stripped stocks. Tattoos run from her bare shoulders down her back to her exposed thighs. She is inked all over and exposed but unafraid.

With her poem composed, Zdravka follows a train of thought to the nearest bus stop where Garner—I like the names I give them—stands observant. Cameron and Liz are both working on a new collection and trying not to discourage the other with what they really think about creation. That kind of honesty might end their relationship, and they are still too attracted to one another to let go this early. Manuel is on his way to work as a dishwasher but inventing beats, accompanying a poetic line that will startle and surprise with its originality and assonance, sweep over the city like hot breath even if the city never recognizes the contributor, and he smiles. Liz thinks he is flirting and plans to use that image in a short story she is in the process of writing.

There is Tom Hayes, yes, now in the fucking third person, in the midst of this storm of ragged poets, and he feels hopeless and poor and lonely yet oddly exhilarated at the same time. Exhilarated to be at the end. It doesn't take a doctor to tell him he is close, but for this moment, for all these incredible moments in the pouring rain even when it finally turns to snow, he loves this fucking city and everyone in it—if only for an instant. This too shall pass.

At this moment, Tom thinks of Adrian Gerd Wahl, and something clicks. He doesn't know if the snot on his nose is from laughing or crying, but he doesn't even need a shot or snort or pill or drink. But he does need a cigarette. Thank God or the gods sitting on the chaos of an indifferent universe that he has not given away every last cigarette. He inhales deeply and with some strange satisfaction.

Five

Interview Disaster

[April 15]
Spring but already unusually warm. On the way Upstate, I found the four-hour drive fairly uneventful until I spotted a dead coyote alongside the highway. I pulled over and got out even though everyone was whizzing by along Route 17. At first, I thought the animal might be a German shepherd, and I wanted to make sure the dog was dead and not badly injured. I have a soft-spot for canines. Maybe it's the way they relate to humans, follow us, love us unconditionally. I didn't have a plan as to what I would do if the dog was injured, but I would have to do something.

On closer examination, I could see the animal was a coyote and a surprisingly large one. Struck but only a glancing blow, enough to knock its body to the road's shoulder, not hard enough to disfigure it. The accident must have happened only a few minutes earlier because the crows weren't even on the carcass yet. The coyote seemed like a creature out of another era, not fitting my image of our technologically driven age, and I didn't think there were any outside the Northern Adirondacks. But unmistakable, this creature's mouth curled in a snarl even after death or perhaps because of death. I would have hated to meet the live animal on a road at night alone. For some reason, coming upon this dead animal seemed like an omen and made me more nervous than when I set out to interview the great Adrian Gerd Wahl. I got back in my car, having accomplished nothing but a sense of dread.

All the way up from the city, I began noticing roads lined with carcasses, more deer than anything else, but there were dead skunks, raccoons, opossums, what looked like remains of a cat, feathers suggesting birds: a cornucopia of death. I kept expecting lush greenery and beautiful wilderness and got carcasses and refuse tossed from speeding cars. There was beautiful wildness, too, if I stopped obsessing about the dead.

My stop to check out the coyote remains didn't cause me to be late; in fact, I arrived at Wahl's cabin on the lake earlier than anticipated. Adrian Gerd Wahl met me in his doorway.

What I knew before meeting him was that Wahl was brilliant and difficult, an intellectual, but I was more than curious.

Wahl shook my hand and invited me in rather cordially before he ascended his throne, an overstuffed, distressed leather chair looking out through large picture windows with a view of the lake. He sat slightly hunched with one foot dangling off an ottoman and the other flopped carelessly over that brass-tacked, accented hassock. He was too large even for his furniture but not a heavy man. His cabin was casual but still spoke of money even in this homey setting. It was not only his indolent posture; I decide even before he spoke. I had spent a good chunk of the advance for this *Music & Culture* interview on a cashmere sweater/sweatshirt to look the part, and he greeted me in a worn green and black flannel, long-sleeved, that looked like it had been handed down from an eccentric uncle, elbows threadbare, cuffs beginning to fray, and collar flopping like a dog's ears with head stuck out the car window. His jeans are from another era, that supple, old loose pair that settles in for the night. I half expected him to pull out a crowbar or lift up an axe in a kind of paradoxical, urban Paul Bunyan caricature.

Wahl looked like a man who loved mutts but had purebreds and like a writer so sure of himself he no longer had to meet anyone's expectations. Something about his casual appearance was irritating. I am immediately discomfited to the extent that I'd forgotten to take detailed notes, or any notes at all, upon my entrance. I found myself backtracking before I'd even begun. What happened before I walked into this room? I was already trying to retrace my steps because I didn't have my tape recorder out, nor my mindset ready. Reverse course.

When I walked up uneven stone steps of his doorway, I noticed he nearly filled the door's frame, tall and daunting. He certainly didn't look chiseled but strong enough to best most. His dark brown hair is flecked with gray as if sea salt had sprayed and gently descended upon him. His beard is full but not unruly or long. Oddly, it struck me that he could have been a king but never a prince. I wrote that sentence down, finally committing something to paper.

"No tape recorders," he said firmly as I was placing mine on a side table. "Let's just talk."

What did I mean regarding that king, no prince comment? That Wahl was not climbing any longer; he had reached the top. He was good looking in a rough way that suggested he didn't care, somehow making him more arresting. Eyes? Blue and intense. Unusual to have such dark hair and blue eyes, I thought and found myself looking away from him as if I was guilty of something or embarrassed by staring.

His cabin was big enough but not grand, and even though the location on Skaneateles Lake was probably pricey, his abode was not the kind of place I expected. In fact, when I drove up, I almost went to his neighbor's house on his right. Now that home was palatial. Why Wahl chose a fairly obscure, Upstate New York country setting in the Finger Lakes area rather than NYC where his legions of fans and publishers dwelled, I would have to guess, unless I decided to ask him. Okay, I would ask him. I then recalled he had once written that he had a love affair with New York City but stated the affair was the kind of ardor that required distance to sustain. That was another possible question, but I didn't want to cover ground that had already been examined by others. Rethinking my questions before I asked them was not a promising start. Backing up again, I had to concentrate to remember his first words to me.

He stood in an open doorway, and I stumbled going up the steps with my hand out. "Drew Levin. Thank you for—"

"Yes. Come in."

I tried to take a few mental notes, but several minutes passed before I wrote down the words: stacks of books, newspapers, looks like copies of *The New York Times* and *The Atlantic*, and an old green glass lamp, like you'd find in one of those early twentieth century lawyer's offices, providing dim interior light even though the sun was shining brightly outside. Windows faced the lake which was down a steep bank. No curtains on any windows, and I could see the lake was about three-quarters of a mile wide across from his cabin. The large, open room looked cluttered but comfortable. Evidence of dogs apparent even before they began to sniff me. He called them, and the Labrador retrievers obediently sat at his feet before two stretched out.

I wanted to ask him why he didn't go by the somewhat less ridiculous name of Adrian rather than that unfortunate medical acronym Gerd, but looking at him face-to-face, that question no longer seemed possible. I already knew Gerd was pronounced Khurt. He waited for me, offering no suggestion that things would loosen up, as if he enjoyed my discomfort. Before saying much of anything, I was already losing track of what I wanted to do, how I wanted to conduct the interview.

I detected both his audacity in the way his words finally tumbled out quickly and the disinterest he showed in me, a lowly writer from a magazine his editor made him promise to court in the inevitable public relations campaign that accompanied any successful book being promoted instead of shelved by one of the big-name publishers. Gerd Wahl had a publisher who actually paid authors in advance. Gerd was holding court, in more than one definition of the word, and I felt like a frivolous jester.

INTERVIEWER: Nice place you have here.

GERD: [*Chewing on black licorice, he offered me thick, rubbery candy which LMW politely turned down. He was talking with licorice in his mouth and only somewhat self-conscious about it. LMW waited for black saliva to start dribbling out of the corners of his mouth, but it doesn't.*] I quit smoking recently and need something as spurious agent. This really doesn't do it, you know. [*LMW looked up to detect black stain on his teeth but saw nothing. He wished Angela, even Gillian could be there. He considered asking if he could take a picture right then but wisely decide against it because he was settling down and remembered his questions only to forget them again. And, yes, he wanted to tell Gerd that he could tell the man was still a smoker. The odor of tobacco lingered in the cabin.*]

INTERVIEWER: Where would you like to start?

GERD: Where do you want to start? [*Without waiting for LMW response, he began popping names like Ivan Boh, Paolo D'Iorio, Martin Fricke, and other contemporary philosophers. LMW struggled to keep up, uncertain of the works or men Gerd was discussing. Fumbling with tape recorder, LMW forgot that Gerd asked me not to use one. He stopped discussing Martin Fricke and looked at me as if drilling into my brain.*] I don't like tape recorders. Maybe we could have a conversation instead?

[*LMW wanted to drop names on him, too, but he suddenly couldn't remember names of his own family members, let alone contemporary writers and philosophers, and here Gerd was seamlessly drawing connections through metaphoric associations, artfully navigating this one-sided "conversation," this self-aggrandizing trope. But instead of anger, LMW stumbled literally and metaphorically, trying to impress.*]

[*LMW remembered why he started down that road: Wahl lessened you by the minute, until you feel like rolling over on the outdated but still somehow chic rug covering wide plank old wood floors; you, meanwhile, hoping he rubbed your belly like* he would one of his champion dogs. Within a few minutes, LMW felt rather than knew Gerd Wahl had made it, the pinnacle, top of the cultural heap, a man who had achieved fame and stature by his own definition and others simultaneously.]

[One of his three dogs, a powerful looking chocolate lab, put its head on the arm of the chair Gerd was sitting in, and the big man stroked his dog's muzzle lovingly, adoration of the animal for his master too close to everyone else's. LMW didn't ask him to launch the interview with a litany of contemporary philosophers; suddenly realizing he had to bring this whole thing back somehow. LMW should have started with questions about the famous man's dogs. Sufficiently intimidated, LMW started seeing myself in the way Gerd must view him.]

LOWLY MAGAZINE WRITER: I think people would like to know what platforms of social media you prefer: TikTok? Twitter? SVOD? Snapchat? Instagram? Pinterest? Reddit? Caffeine? Facebook? Google Plus+? Orkut? [*LMW realized after it spilled out that the seeming preference of hate groups for Orkut might be off-putting to Gerd.*] Tagged? LinkedIn? I could go on.

GERD: Please, don't. I'm not a social media animal although we're all social animals to lesser and greater degrees, depending upon the person. [*He glances at his dogs as he says this.*]

LOWLY WRITER: [*Momentarily nonplused because he had a whole line of questions related to social media and video website use that was going to frame part of my article. Campbell probably had this in mind, too. Ridiculous, struggling writer was already trying to figure out a new angle*]: All right. Let's talk about how you feel regarding all the adoration, you know, that over-the-top praise you and your works have received during the past few months and that last *New York Times* review, or should I say exaltation from critics? [*Foolishly, smiled here.*]

GERD: Over-the-top? Exaltation? Is that how you, or someone else told you to characterize reviews of my work?

LMW: [*Correcting the inadvertent or perhaps consciously construed insult, LMW tried not to respond to the direct insult hurled back.*] Effusive, perhaps, is the better word. I do write my own questions. [*Too defensively, LMW realized he was in trouble already. Thought Gerd might get up and leave at that point, but then LMW remembered it was Gerd's house.*]

GERD: Good for you. I don't read reviewers or reviews, effusive or otherwise. I wouldn't give interviews except my agent and publisher request it. The business end of the process.

LMW: He requested you do an interview with us? [*Tried not to sound incredulous here but that was bubbling to the surface.*]

GERD: You needn't sound so surprised or sexist. Both she, in this case. She lets me know the slant of a piece before agreeing to it. She thought your magazine would be fair and interested in what I have to say.

LMW: I am. We are. [*Calming down, LMW decided this could turn out fine.*] You write sections of your work in counterpoint. Would you care to comment as to why?

GERD: No.

LMW: Many readers struggle with your narratives' anachrony. Have you considered the difficulty this way of telling presents to readers? [*LMW shouldn't have used the word "telling."*]

GERD: I woke up and was five years old, then became a weary old man before settling into 44 again. Time being, according to the wonderful Pascal Quignard, as "this concatenation of sempiternal causes."

LMW: [*LMW understood only a couple of words in that last statement.*] But it requires a lot of your readers.

GERD: Living requires a lot of readers and non-readers. A facile examination does not really seem worth the effort.

LMW: You have concerns about how you will sound in a review or interview? Is that why you prefer not to give interviews or have anything on tape? [*What was LMW saying? It was as if he had lost his mind.*]

GERD: If a writer starts worrying about interviews and reviews, well, that writer won't write much of anything, at least not anything of worth. I would, however, like to be quoted accurately. If you are not able to do so without a tape recorder, then. . .

LMW: [*Writing furiously and worrying himself into near paralysis, LMW hoped for nothing more than a review (of the very nature Gerd spurned) for the better part of the last nearly ten years.*] Let's talk about the success of your work. After all, not all of your readers are as familiar with your allusions to other writers, but your response to readers' praise, their adoration, however, is something that everyone wants to know about. It's human nature.

GERD: Ah. Human nature and mass consumption; we're leaving philosophy to delve into that lower realm, with or without benefit of a Freudian bridge between the id and ego, leaving off the super-ego for now?

LMW: [*Becoming frustrated by his lack of control over the interview, LMW felt like standing up and yelling.*] By all means, let's leave off the Super-ego.

GERD: [*He caught my sarcasm and refused to address it or responded by dismissing it entirely.*] If you want to hear about my responses to effusive, that's the word you chose, correct, my responses to praise?

LMW: Yes, praise.

GERD: I will probably want to couch that rejoinder in some type of defense mechanism, and then we're talking about repression, denial, displacement, perhaps even projection. My response, if you are looking for honesty and brutal separation of public persona from private one, then you will have to make some decisions about, oh, I didn't even mention sublimation and this "workaholic" activity of producing tomes rather than novellas to deal with, let's say, repression of sexual or aggressive feelings. That could probably be worked into an article, sounding raw, unmasking the public persona, particularly once we get into a conversation in any way related to sex; something people will want to know, right?

[*LMW took notes rapidly, thinking that now he was going to get something good, something at least of a sexual nature, so much so that he could already see the bonus on his feature story when Wahl suddenly stopped talking.*]

LMW: Yes?

GERD: Something along those lines?

LMW: [*Who was nervously sweating through his new cashmere sweater.*] I think readers would be very interested in your take on sexual or aggressive feelings about writing or your ideas about those."

GERD: [*He laughed cruelly.*] Of course, those aren't my feelings at all, rather a series of ridiculous suppositions, but I could talk about Freud all afternoon because he essentially framed the 20th century's psychic landscape for us unless you want to argue that it was T.S. Eliot, a poet rather than a psychologist who—"

LMW: [*Trying not to show his disappointment at the sudden veering, LMW decided for some reason that interrupting was acceptable.*] I was really looking for your personal feelings about the subject.

GERD: So, your readers aren't interested in Freud or Eliot or my appraisal of their influences on the 20th Century?

LMW: [*Clearly anything was game once you accept the invitation.*] It is not that their influence isn't important, but I'd rather come back to your own work. It's not considered realism or at least not a term I would use to describe it. Postmodernism, certainly.

GERD: Now you're the reviewer. Postmodernism is your classification of my work, I see.

LMW: [*Nervously fidgeting with pen, LMW became concerned that Gerd's interest had turned aggressive.*] I think it may be uncategorical, but we are in the postmodern era. [*LMW realized this was not the word he meant either, or one that fit. Gerd seems amused for the first time.*] I mean, rather, it is difficult [*difficult? LMW couldn't come up with a better word there?*] to neatly define your fiction; perhaps the preferred word is metafiction. [*He was momentarily pleased with himself but should have stopped at "uncategorical" when Gerd was smiling.*]

GERD: [*With obvious sarcasm.*] Metafiction? In which I am self-consciously parodying myself and my work, as well as the age. There, you've categorized everything without Sisyphean labors.

LMW: [*Sensing he was being mocked*] I didn't intend to be so definitive because it's certainly not that—

GERD: The larger question is why we feel the need to label everything and everyone? Compartmentalize in order to feel we understand that which is beyond our understanding.

LMW: [*Now LMW was sure he was being insulted.*] Did you set out to try to write the great American novel?

GERD: [*Laughed again but bitterly.*] The great American novel has already been written for the time and place in America in which it was set. Melville, Twain, Faulkner, F. Scott Fitzgerald, John Dos Passos, Toni Morrison, Baldwin, Updike, Cormac McCarthy, Roth, too many to list, really, a ridiculous exercise and one I would not attempt.

LMW: Not trying to reduce it, but do you think Whitman set out to write the great American poem? [*LMW had no idea if he was trying to show what he knew or just divert his growing frustration.*]

GERD: Of course, but at the time Whitman wrote, that exercise was, perhaps, still possible. America was this wide land of seemingly infinite possibility but "smaller" in the way that encapsulating the nearly infinite still seemed possible.

LMW: We're trying to orient ourselves and place others in our conceptual schemes in some pattern that makes sense. This allows us to position ourselves. What pattern do you see yourself and your work fitting?

GERD: Let's stop for a moment. What is the question most often asked when we are introduced to someone new?

LMW: What do you do? What's your job? [*For a few seconds, we were actually engaged in an unscripted dialogue.*]

GERD: As in, your occupation, your economic status, your category, so we can immediately set you in your place and move on. What do you do?

LMW: Well, I'm a writer. [*After recognizing that Gerd probably meant the question as rhetorical, LMW didn't want to think about how long it took for him to say those words without feeling like a fraud, but now that he was earning a paycheck from it, he felt he had every right.*] I don't have your connections in publishing; however, I haven't had the level of success that you've found, but— [*Why did LMW disastrously insert himself here?*]

GERD: My connections allowed my work to be published? Perhaps you will make those connections. [*As if on cue, the big chocolate lab started jumping around his master. The two yellow labs were still rousing themselves slowly, stretching and yawning, almost human in their expression of fatigue or boredom. Gerd stood.*] I'm sorry. I don't have any more time for this. My dogs need a walk. I do, too.

[*Varg, the chocolate lab, lifted his large paw and held it suspended until Gerd took it then released it. They weren't so much shaking hands, however, as holding hands, connected in some more intimate way. It was as if the big dog sensed Gerd's discomfort and was providing his master a way out.*]

LMW: Oh, your dogs need a walk? I could go with you.

GERD: Ah, Varg, it's the struggle. [*He was moving toward the door.*]

LMW: [*Desperately, LMW tried not to take the cue.*] The struggle?

GERD: The labors. "Ask him a question."

LMW: Excuse me? I'm not following. For success, for recognition?

GERD: Beckett. The question: "Ask him a question." [*He could see LMW was searching for the connection; the great man leaving the idiot behind as he moved to the door.*] This human want, this lack, seemingly filled by adoration from people you do not know nor will ever know, and for that matter, care nothing about. I think we are done here. Travel safely.

LWM: [*Finally standing because Gerd's back was now facing the door.*] Adoration from others, which you seem to have in abundance. How does that make you feel? I mean you're in a position to be able to compare a kind of before and after success response, and I'm sure many other writers would find your comments intriguing.

[*Gerd shook his head of curly hair without turning. LMW could see how it might have appeared to Gerd that the fool in his house didn't even listen to what he was saying. And just like that, the great Gerd Wahl was at his side door to escort said LMW out. LMW realized instantly that he'd blown it. The great writer had started to divulge a moment earlier, and LMW had mistaken his cue, or had bored Gerd, or insulted him. LWM came into the interview too confident, with questions that were too pat, ready for preconceived responses, and Gerd was not going to comply.*

LMW should have known that the solitary writer does not suddenly and willingly join community and provide preconceived answers.]

Before I leave, I'm curious why you don't give more interviews or longer ones? It's an opportunity to get your opinions out there. [*Ridiculous implication was that Gerd would reach more people through LMW interview appearing in Music & Culture magazine rather than the ones Gerd had captured as a best-selling author.*]

GERD: Whatever I want out there is already in my books if people care to read them. Please do quote me.

LMW: [*Now flailing hopelessly in the doorway because Gerd was descending his steps with his dogs out in front.*] But your books are a little long for most people, and an interview affords an opportunity to reach—.

GERD: [*Suddenly turned to stare at LMW.*] Reach the people who don't read?

LMW: [*Ouch.*] At least the people who don't read tomes. [*At this point, idiot writer wanted to sock himself. Everything coming out of his mouth ended up as an insult or sounded plain stupid, but it was as if he had no brakes and his car was careening out of control.*]

GERD: Admittedly, my novels are long, too long for many, but then, I'm not writing for the many. Look, my dogs need exercise to avoid becoming destructive. I wish you good travels. If you have further questions, text me.

LMW: [*Who realized that he had gotten nothing at all from the interview except dismissal.*] So, when can we meet again to continue our conversation?

GERD: Was it a conversation? I didn't realize. Oh, have you ever seen the depth of devotion in a human being such as a dog displays? [*He was walking away with his dogs leaping around him.*]

LMW: Dogs, I know; my dog is a mutt. [*Gerd said nothing more as he headed up the bank and across the road to a field.*]

***

Start over. As I came back to myself, my panic rose. Adrian Gerd Wahl had shut the literal and metaphoric door on me. Strange thing, I wanted to be out of his presence even more than he seemed to want me gone. I got in my car hating and fascinated by the man, swerving as I made an abrupt left turn. In that maneuver, I instantly thought about Faulkner's Benjy at the end of *The Sound and the Fury,* howling as the carriage veered left. I wanted to let loose one of my own primal screams, but no one would hear it. Gerd was deaf to anything that came from my asinine mouth.

The fact that I had to face my editor with these few, ridiculous notes was enough to make me cringe, my heart palpitate irregularly. Then I had an image of Angela and her envy that I'd been in the great man's presence and come away with what exactly? In all the time I had been working, I had never failed so miserably before. Sixth grade all over again after Arnold Beesmer knocked me down with one punch to the mouth that I likely deserved.

And what would my writer friends and colleagues think? I had already planned on communicating to those beyond our little magazine about my interview with the Great Gerd Wahl. This interview was intended to be my launching point for the rest of my career, a possible move to a new magazine with larger circulation and better pay. How would I tell them all that I had failed? "He is an encyclopedia," they would say, "and you did not even manage to open the first page of Volume 1?" And I would have to admit, I hadn't even gotten to the front matter.

Ian, my tall friend not easily dismissed in his orange pants and black, curly mop of hair, the man who looked like you imagined a poet should look, was the one who should have conducted this interview with Wahl. Ian knew it before I came into the room to tell them I had gotten the assignment. Ian would be vindicated, his low opinion of my skills validated. He wouldn't even have to say anything at all, which made it somehow worse.

Gillian and Shwetak took their cues from Ian, and I couldn't blame them. I was done at the magazine. Campbell would stand there with his mouth open in amazement at my incompetence until he found his voice in order to fire me. I wanted to fire me. Ian would have come away with something amazing after his interview with Wahl. He would not have tried to inject himself and his insecurities into the interview. Yes, my friend Ian would have drawn out the great communicator from the insulated man. Ian, with his quiet demeanor, would have put Gerd on stage, rather than himself.

I had been looking too far past the interview, past the man to my own anticipated accolades for a piece of writing that was hypothetical. I understood at that moment that the interview had been about my questions, my framing the man and anticipating his answers rather than conducting an honest exploration of ideas. Wahl saw through it all immediately. I had been exposed.

It was not bad enough that I had been exposed before Wahl but before myself.

Unfortunately, self-knowledge does not lessen the sting of shame. It was not merely my failure at the interview or at my job; it was awareness of my own inadequacies as a writer. Wahl couldn't possibly know the desperation I felt to have my work recognized. There was no common ground between Gerd and me, and all of that had been brutally laid bare. Ian, Gillian, Shwetak would have something to say about this disaster.

Worse yet would be their pity, but Angela was the only one I could count on for sympathy, and even then, I was not certain. She knew my tendency toward self-aggrandizement. Somehow, I had managed to conduct an "interview" that was at once reductive, insulting, and hollow, not an easy task when talking to one of the most buzzed about, brilliant American writers on the planet at the moment. My only defense was being over-prepared. I tried not to think about what had happened, worked to push every word I said to him out of my head with music blaring from the radio. But no song, no distraction could lessen my humiliation which grew larger with each passing mile.

By the time I reached home, I had worked myself up into a frenzy like some hysterical kid. I don't remember exactly what I said into his message machine, but I begged, pleaded, and once I let it go, there was no erasing that painfully pitiful message that stood as testament to my shame. He would be able to play it over and over. Mercifully, Angela was not home at the time to witness my disgrace. No one would hear those agonized, ridiculous pleas but the most famous contemporary writer in the country, and I groveled before him.

Six

Sleeping with the Enemy

Tom Hayes turned off his iPhone and rolled over in bed. His flinging arm hit a table lamp, a modern, angular type that Marie's mother had given her. "Shit," he said out loud as the lamp fell to the floor breaking. Expletive mirrored his earlier text to his writers' group.

"What did you break?" was Marie's muffled question from under her pillow.

"Nothing. Shit."

"Really? That's your comment tonight of all nights?" Marie adjusted the pillow back over her ear, not yet realizing her mother's lamp was shattered. "I heard something crash."

"It's nothing. My favorite ashtray." Tom thought that would appease her momentarily. He recalled Marie's text again. He would have reacted to Ian's last comment, too, but didn't read it. Although Tom liked Ian from years back when they were in grad school together, there was something off-putting about a guy who could do everything better, Ian, he meant, not referencing

Gerd Wahl, who obviously did everything better. As Tom leaned over and tried to pick up ceramic fragments from the rug, he could not stop thinking about Marie any more than he could put Wahl out of his head. Now there was Ian in the bed with them, too. Acutely aware that this woman with whom he had been texting was next to him in their double bed with an old and lumpy mattress that was crowded with writers real and imagined. Tom found it difficult enough trying to sleep on any given night, let alone on a night in which the bottom fell out. Having great difficulty trying to pick up the shards of lamp from the bed, he stepped down.

"Shit!" His big toe found a shard, deeply embedded in the carpet.

"Again?" Marie asked from under her pillow. She pulled the sheet tighter around her.

How the hell could he not even afford a new mattress or a better apartment? His friends, nearly all of them writers, published or working desperately at that goal, even if they could not make a living that way, and Marie Garcia Perez idolized this man, this Gerd Wahl. *Why don't you use your real name for your handle anyway?* Tom was ready to shout at Marie Perez, make her clean up his mess. It's not as if he hadn't done this before. She should be used to picking up after him by now. Marie Rollins was the ridiculous pen name of the woman who was always about to walk out on him. Marie idolized Gerd Wahl, a real-life character who apparently killed himself, and at that moment, Tom did not care. And now his Marie was fluffing up or maybe punching her pillows because her action was too deliberate, because she always slept with two pillows like some princess in a fairy tale, before turning away from him again, shutting that chapter of her life, he suspected.

After the nasty job of retrieving broken lamp and cleaning his wounded toe in the bathroom, Tom momentarily rested his hand on top of one of Marie's journals which covered his nightstand. Why were her journals on his side, too? He never thought of Marie as a writer even though she kept notebooks around their cramped apartment. They never talked about what she wrote. Was it his fault that she didn't discuss her writing? He suddenly remembered that the first time they met, she was scribbling in a notebook. This being with whom he lived never mentioned what mysteries could be found on those pages of hers. He suspected her of writing inane stuff about work, probably, and some complaint about him being late on rent again, at best. At worst, there could be notations emasculating him, referring to him as being a quick fuck or a bad one. His sudden anger with Marie had something to do with his inability to provide any help with the rent. No, that wasn't it. It was because she no longer loved him, and so he decided to hate her.

He would get another job soon, but even if or when he did land a full-time job, it would be impossible to find time to write. Marie used to ask him about his writing but not lately. Then again, he wasn't working on anything at the moment. He was simply trying to come up with an idea worth his time. Where did the great Adrian Gerd Wahl get his ideas anyway? All Tom needed was one original idea, and then everything would be different.

"He had everything, and he, he kills himself." Apparently, Tom said his criticism of Wahl out loud. Tom tried to convey amazement, but disdain was all that came out.

"What?" Marie opened her eyes but did not lift her head. "What did you say about Wahl?"

"Nothing. Nothing of importance." He felt safe. She still had not noticed the lamp in the darkness of their room. She must have been half-asleep when it fell, he decided, but then, there was the old rag rug which muffled the blow.

A streetlight, one that had been out earlier, inexplicably came back on, breaking through narrow slats in the blinds. "Half of those fuckers on Twitter are idiots, you know. Ornal Aude, Ian's stupid friend. And now, here we have it. Lights come on when we don't need them." Again, he was talking out loud. Fortunately, Marie scarcely heard him.

"Shut up, please, shut up," Marie said, facing the opposite direction and curling into a ball like a mouse or mole. Hot, even with old, window-style air conditioning unit going full blast, they had to have sheets on the bed. Tom kicked them from his side. Marie was already wearing a long nightgown. There was nothing more to cover up.

"Please? You tell me to shut up and then add, please?"

"Okay. Just, shut up," she hissed.

"Much better," he said. Better to switch to internal monologue, he thought. *Living in Queens instead of Manhattan with rent overdue, no new prospects, no book contracts, no publisher, between jobs, an unfaithful, at least in thought, ice queen and a dead guy in my bed on a hellishly hot night. Yes, I thought I'd be at this awful point in my life after all of the expectations.*

But his fraught relationship, lack of career, lack of accomplishment wasn't at all where he thought he would be. When he had won the Faulkner Award in high school for two years in a row and a Whitman Award in college, got a scholarship to the University of Iowa Writer's Workshop for grad school, he imagined that accolades would never stop coming. Instead, he was stuck in an apartment that was ridiculously small in a low rent, no character building with subway stops too far to walk easily. The worst? He was sleeping with a woman who didn't love him.

Finally, he stopped panicking from the lack of work and failure to meet bills because he found medications that provided at least temporary relief, but then he had no cash to buy them again; circles began winding tighter, choking him even in those last moments. Marie didn't approve of drugs, reducing him to sneaking it like some street addict. How he hated this woman at the moment, hated her because he still loved her.

Trying to imagine having Wahl's life, Tom realized that he couldn't conceive of something as stupid as suicide, not when the guy had everything.

Give me five minutes of his life, Tom thought, wrestling with his old pillow. *I would have gone to Europe, partied on the Rivera, stayed in a villa on the Amalfi Coast, jetted back to New York for summer, and yes, and slept with gorgeous models, one after another, or maybe the three of us together.*

What was Wahl thinking? What a waste. He could have bought a yacht, maybe a baseball team and fired a manager, *picked up free agents and won a World Series for his club. And he could have purchased Nicole Kidman's nearly 4,000 square foot condo in lower Manhattan. Screw all that.*

He would have hosted a roof-top cocktail reception for writers and entertainers, attended Vanity Fair's party in Cannes or New York, found himself in little photos pictured in magazines, one more event where they paid him tribute.

He wouldn't waste either fame or fortune like Wahl. It wasn't solely that Wahl made a different choice, but that Tom Hayes had never been allowed those options, not one of them.

Tom watched Marie's slender shoulders rising and falling in slanted darkness, and he knew she was either dreaming or silently sobbing for Wahl, not either of them, not for unfair distribution of wealth nor talent, not for the loss of their unborn baby, not for the widening gulf of division between them. *It wasn't his fault that her father killed himself when she was a kid, nor that she had to work two jobs because he would have picked up a second one, too, if that asshole hadn't fired him.*

Marie wasn't always this way, he reminded himself. He wasn't the one who turned away every night. If all of that hadn't been the case, he might have leaned over and kissed her, smelled her lavender-scented black hair, felt around for her soft breasts, made love to her as he used to, but her tears were for Adrian Gerd Wahl, not him. Tom was suddenly soberly aware that he now hated as well as poisonously envied the famed dead man. Tom allowed this jealousy to burrow in as if he was a mere mole. He knew the mystery was not Gerd's death but what had happened to him. *Why didn't they all recognize that Tom Hayes was the real story?*

Seven

Marie Buys Little Gold Fish

Hanging by a thread in the display window, gold fish earrings caught my eye as I passed a shop on the corner. I have walked or driven by this little store a dozen times and never really noticed it before, never stopped to discover what was inside. When I saw those earrings, I knew that I had to have them even if the price was more than I could pay. To be honest, I had already told the clerk with his diminutive mustache to wrap them for me before checking the price.

"It's a very good buy, Madame," he says, smiling wide, his teeth crooked and stained, but he has nice eyes, very gentle. "Real gold." On his head, he wears a red fez topped with a Yankees baseball cap. The thick air is pungent with incense sticks slowly burning.

"You mean gold plated?"

"Yes, yes," he says, appearing as if I was the only customer to have ever ventured into his store. It doesn't really matter to me if they are gold plated or painted, but he wants me to test the excellent adherence to the surface by rubbing my finger across gold. "It conducts warmth," he says.

The earrings looked exactly like I imagined the little gold fish painstakingly created by Colonel Aureliano Buendia, making his living in such artistic manufacture before melting them down and organizing some thirty-two uprisings. Much more, they reminded me of you, Gerd, because you wrote about Buendía's little fish, with memory and loss of it alternately tying us down and trapping us, in your story "Citizens and Foreigners." I read that story three times. Each time, I discovered something I had not noticed before. I should tell you that I've felt like a foreigner here in this city since I arrived. And I live with a man I no longer love. No, I live with a man I've grown to hate. I feel intensely alone when Tom is in the room. I should tell you I loved following your obscure references to all of those other writers in your novels, like finding the right pieces in the 1,000-segment jigsaw puzzle that consists almost entirely of sky and sea. Blue, deeper blue, deepest blue. Tom said that you were pretentious with your quotations and myriad allusions, but Tom believes everyone is pretentious without recognizing it in himself. Yet, I don't want to talk about Tom or think about him, either, and I'm afraid he's hooked on something, Xanax maybe. It's not really a guess. I found pills spilled under the bed. I tried to talk to him about them, but he angrily denied everything. There is no honesty left between us. He's in denial about everything.

I asked him to leave, but I feel the weight of guilt. What if something happens to him? I can't care for him anymore because he is pulling me in his undertow. Did you leave anyone behind you who is suffering from that guilt because you decided to take your own life, Gerd? You must have hurt someone the way Tom has hurt me. My father, too, made that decision, and you cannot imagine the suffering in his wake. Perhaps you can. Perhaps you did not care.

If you had been my lover, Adrian Gerd Wahl, I would have forced you to be honest with me. I want to think you would not have taken that gun out and ended your life. Perhaps you would have shot me first, ending both of our sufferings.

I am finding it more difficult than usual to make my way out of this labyrinth of melancholy. Last night, I reread a section of *One Hundred Years of Solitude* because you loved it, too, and I wrote down one of the Colonel's lines in my journal: "Tell him that a person doesn't die when he should but when he can." I wondered if what you were telling us, when you made the decision to end your life, was that you died when you could, but it was not what should have happened. I don't believe either the Colonel or you.

A person doesn't die when he can, or we would cease to exist as a species. More likely, you were telling us nothing directly because we did not register in your life even as your devoted readers. Tom, and I'm sorry to be referring to him again, but he only left a short time ago, and I'm not used to leaving him out of my life entirely yet. I still find myself thinking about him coming home, yet he unkindly called me a "Gerd whore," and I suppose I was your fan, but I never had the opportunity to let you know. Tom can be terribly cruel because he is hurting himself, the worst kind of pain. Even understanding that makes it no easier to deal with him. At the end, Tom said I wanted to fuck you. He is in deep trouble, very deep, but I wanted to talk with you rather than him all night.

There are so many questions I wanted to ask you before I ask you to put your guns away. I suppose you would tell me to read your work, your novels and essays, your speeches. I have. Every last one, yet so many questions remain. What do any of us answer for each other?

If we made love, it might have been only because we were both unbearably lonely. Somehow, you had discerned this empty place inside of me. I don't know if you would laugh if you knew this, if you would find me pitiful and my own writing terrible and amateurish, like Tom said. I do know you wouldn't like Tom.

I was only six years old at the time Emile ended his life. Emile was stocky and strong with large hands that held me as he twirled me around until I was dizzy with giggling. Mother would scold him for swinging me too high, but he knew I loved it and would not let me go. I felt safe with him. Such delusion. Mother said, "Emile, you will pull her arms right out of her sockets," but you never did. I didn't even know what my sockets were then. My arms are still fine. Emile called me his little muse, rubbing his black whiskers. Mother said he should either shave off that stubble or "grow a proper beard." I didn't know what a muse meant either but sensed it was something good. My father had dark hair and rich brown skin. He wore white shirts when he went to work. That is nearly all I remember about him clearly except that I loved him. I can still see the contrast of his starched shirts on his dark skin. I don't know if he was an honorable man, but I felt it. Still, he must have known what his action would do to me, to my mother, to my aunties and uncle. For too long, I felt hollow and that has revisited me after your actions, Gerd.

Mother did not speak of him for years afterward except at the very end before her own death. Mother and I never spoke much after my father's death, I'm sorry to tell you. I think Emile damaged us, put us past healing. Unless I stare at an old photo, I can't even picture my father's face, but I loved him unequivocally. That is the strangest thing to know. I'm no psychologist, but I can imagine one stating that I'm merely projecting my need for a father's love on a memory.

Gerd, I read that you lost your father when you were only 9. It was an accident, I recall reading. You didn't want to talk about it, I could tell from that interview. Sometimes they pry things out of you, and you feel less for having said words out loud. When my father died, I thought the end of the world had come, and my mother, as I told you, was never the same. She must have smiled sometimes, but I can't remember her laughing after she found her husband stretched out, neck broken, body dangling from a beam in grandfather's tool shed. I remember she was calling her husband for dinner, and Emile didn't come. She had started to yell and get angry or perhaps impatient because dinner was growing cold, and who can eat cold lamb? "Fat congeals," she said, when she opened that door the rest of the way and put her pretty hands over her mouth to stifle screams that kept coming as grandmother and grandfather ran up to me, covering my eyes. I saw only your shadow before grandmother shut the door. I fell. I had dirt in my mouth, and later, Mother talked about miasma. I had to ask her what that word meant, and she wouldn't tell me. It was only much later that I discovered the definitions and implications. I fell into layers of meaning. Grandmother washed my mouth, but dirt was still there, and I touched grit between my teeth with my tongue, tried to pry it out, as I lay in bed and listened to my mother endlessly sobbing.

How terrible it was that Emile climbed up on that stool, fastened a rope around his neck, and tossed that thick knotted braid over a beam above his head. How terrible it was that he looked out an open door and could see clear down the valley, past crab apple trees, past grandmother's cement statue of praying Virgin Mary and ceramic frog in her vegetable garden, past faint images of my mother and me that he must have carried behind his eyes, and kicked back with one foot the little gray, sturdy stool, the one grandmother used to pick apples, tipping it over. You might have wanted to change your mind in those last moments, Gerd. Someone should have intervened and put the little step back beneath your feet. If I was taller, I would have lifted my father down myself. I would have caught him before he fell, and I would have taken his rough hands, walked with him inside the house to dinner waiting, cooked lamb still warm. Emile did not even leave a note.

But we never knew why, and I struggled with Emile's unnatural act even as I struggle with why you made that choice. I wonder, Gerd, if you had had children like Emile, I would like to think you would not have ended your life. Who found you? I question the scant evidence they report. Someone must have tried to revive you. They gave up too easily. I wondered how long it was that you lay on the floor, bleeding out, before a neighbor came over to find out why your dogs were barking? Your dogs could not have been in your house. You wouldn't have done that to them. I'm certain of that. You must have thought of them. It is strange to know that people you didn't know think about your dogs, too. I imagine you would have been kinder to your dogs than my father was to his only daughter and wife.

Those creating the reports must have been certain there was no one else in the room with you. There was no sign of foul play. Yet, I could have believed you were murdered. There is so much irrational hate and envy in this world, but I could not believe you took your own life. And I will never know why. I cannot understand, after reading the clarity of your voice, the sanity in your prose, such wisdom in your essays, that you would make such a choice. Then, after your death, everything must be a lie if I can't align what I thought I knew with what I know now.

I imagine the gold earrings dangling from my ears as the salesman wraps them. I want to touch them like totems.

Nothing personal on your part, you might say, particularly since you didn't know me. That is the curse of fame, I imagine: strangers feel as if they know you. I have this striking image of you in my head, one more pronounced than the visual of the man who left me, and I now realize that idol, that semblance has nothing to do with who you really were. Perhaps I created this other you out of loneliness and the feelings and ideas that your stories gave me. I will tell you that your stories allowed me to discover some invisible thread linking us. Yet, now I find these were not threads at all. I must remind myself. We were in no way connected, and so I must sever these imaginary ties.

It turns out that you weren't writing for me or even imagining me when you created your art. I'm not a child. I am a rational being and knew that, of course, but I wanted to feel the connection your writing suggested. You weren't aware of me or any of your readers at all. I wanted to find out the next day that your death was a hoax, a publicity stunt or that they had found your killer, a jealous husband, a foul critic, a jilted lover. I would rather have had you assassinated, brutally murdered than discover you had taken your own life. But you killed yourself, and I am forced to replay the scene of my father's exit from this world, as well as your death, endlessly circling back.

I have to reimagine you in the past tense now, have to reconfigure my dreams not simply to be about events that have not happened but will never happen, could never have happened.

"Please," I say to the salesman with his two hats.

"Excuse me, Madame."

I ask this helpful salesman to take the little fish out of the box he has wrapped them in, first removing pretty gold foil. He looks at me curiously, then unwraps them carefully, and obediently hands me the pair of little fish. Without hesitating, I put the earrings in, attach backings, hardly fumbling with them as I typically do, and walk out of his store. A little bell rings when I exit. I hadn't noticed this signaling chime when I entered.

"Come back again soon, Madame," says the mustached man with two hats. "I have many more fishes for you." And I think of that old cliché: "plenty of fish in the sea," and I can't help but think about Tom even though I never want to see him again. I try not to imagine Gerd's last breaths. Instead, I begin envisioning my own.

***

A few thoughts on the great Adrian Gerd Wahl via text.
Marie Rollins

Gerd Wahl,
you would
pluck out
the heart
of my mystery,
you would
sound me
from my
lowest note
to the top
of my compass
Hamlet MMS
4:15 PM

Tom Hayes
Hamlet again,
Marie. Christ.
Quoting Shakes-
peare? And
here we are
navigating
this breakup
without a
fucking compass. MMS
4:16 PM

Marie Rollins
Without a
compass?
Love's not

Time's fool,
though rosy
lips and cheeks
Within his
bending sickle's
compass come;
Shakespeare MMS
4:16 PM

Tom Hayes
Hamlet again?
For the record, I
would not
pluck out
your heart
even after
I plucked you. MMS
4:17 PM

Marie Rollins
You have
not changed.
Sonnet CXVI.
Thank you for
reminding me
why I asked
you to leave. MMS
4:17 PM

Eight

Sleep Deprived

Angela nearly fell asleep near the bedside of a patient. An elderly woman with wisps of white hair standing straight up looked at her and yelled, "Are you sleeping? Nurse, nurse, I'm talking to you. Are asleep?"

"No, of course not," Angela said, startled and fully awake again. "I just came in to see if you needed anything."

"I need a lot of things. How about some decent food for starters and a nurse who doesn't fall asleep on the job? What's your name anyway, in case I decide to report you?"

"Angela. It's good to see you are feeling much better. You didn't want to eat much yesterday."

"Well, that was yesterday, and you're lucky I don't demand to speak to your superiors for sleeping on the job. I thought nurses were supposed to be hard-working."

Angela smiled although she clearly wanted to leave the old woman. "Would you like juice or water? I have to check your vitals in a minute."

"Whatever you come up with will taste awful, but I want a cup of coffee for starters if that is not too much to ask someone sleeping instead of doing what you're paid to do." The old woman's hair seemed to get wilder by the minute, flying this way and that without a wind.

Clenching her teeth, Angela realized at that very moment, with a most annoying patient, that she had been thinking about Drew and Adrian Gerd Wahl. Then, in another instant, she wondered what it would be like to escape forever, the way Wahl had done. No, that would never be her way. She would always worry about the effect on others. Wahl should have thought of that, too.

When she got home, Angela resisted going straight to bed after kicking off her shoes in the corner. Drew was awake and making coffee. She heard him before she saw him.

"You're up unusually early," she said, peeking into their galley kitchen with its ugly mint-green cupboards. She had meant to paint them but never got around to it, and painting anything was not up Drew's alley.

"Thought for once I'd welcome you home with a nice fresh cup of java instead of snoring in your face. You've been working some tough, long hours. I've got some toast for you, too. You need sustenance."

"Thanks," she said as she took the extended cup from Drew's hands. She must have sighed audibly.

"Look, Ange, I know I've been a bit obsessed lately, what with this deadline and"

"And Wahl killing himself after your interview."

"Yeah. That, too."

"I guess I've been a little on edge lately, too," she said, remembering she loved this man standing in the kitchen with her bathrobe around him.

"Just a little." They both smiled, which put them at ease.

"So, how are you going to approach this feature story? Do you know yet?"

Drew gestured as if gathering everything in his outstretched arms. "I thought I'd assemble all of my friends in one small room, ask their opinions, watch them fight it out, until the last one left standing provides me with a great lead."

"Maybe not the best idea." Angela pulled over a counter stool and sat, dangling her feet. "How do you even keep track of them all? I mean, Ornal is with, oh, I don't remember. Tom and Marshall know each other from—I know, but I just can't remember how you met Ornal. Sorry. I saw her only that one time."

"Ornal? She and Ellison are together, at least I think they still are. I have to confess; I've never read anything she's written, but she's a poet, and Ellison is going to be the next big thing."

"You should interview him if that is so. And how do you know Ellison? I know about Tom."

"Ellison is Marshall's friend. Ian's, too. Marshall and Ellison teach together, at college. Well, really, Ellison is Marshall's and Scott's friend. They all used to go to reading events in the city together, and one of those open mic readings is where we met."

"And you know Marshall from?"

"Ian. Everyone kind of runs through Ian if I'm being honest. Ian and Tom were roommates in grad school, you remember.

Marshall and Ian worked together at city college for a while before Ian came to *Music & Culture*. And you know Ian and I have known each other since we were kids.

"Were you good friends back then?"

"Everyone was Ian's friend. He's that kind of guy. You wanted to be his friend, so you made the effort."

"And Marshall and Scott are lovers?"

"Yeah. Ornal used to work with Scott, and she met Ian before she met Ellison."

"So, Ian and Ornal were an item once?"

"No, just friends, Ian says, but I have the feeling he meant more to Ornal than either of them lets on."

"Ian needs to find a good woman."

"Yes, he tells us that all the time. Maybe if he spent less time talking about it, and actually doing something to meet someone."

"I don't know Ornal, but I like Marie, and no one ever talks about her. She's smart and thoughtful," Angela said suddenly, trying to show greater interest in Drew's writer circle.

"She's great but moody. Mostly, Tom shows up without her."

"Do you wonder why?"

"Really, I don't get what she sees in Tom." Drew pops the toaster early and butters the bread, handing a slice to Angela.

"Thanks. Does anyone?"

"Maybe Ian understands, the guy is pretty tolerant in general. If Ian didn't include Tom, I don't think the rest of us would. Marie met Tom right out of grad school, so he was likely a bit more stable and less self-centered."

"Which is a good thing."

"A very good thing. Do you mean Tom or Ian?"

"Tom, of course. Ian is stable."

"Of course, but Ian has got to be pretty sore at me. Looks like what I did was betrayal even to me."

"Don't be so hard on yourself. Ian could have spoken up if he had really wanted the Wahl interview. They could have given the job to him if they thought he was the best person to tackle that role."

"A done deal by the time he found out." Drew shrugged. "I didn't turn it down or suggest Ian would be the better candidate. I probably should feel a little guilty."

"Don't. You can't be a journalist and feel badly about the people who don't get your breaks. And Shwetak you met at work, so he really only knows—"

"All of us because Shwetak is like the nicest guy I've ever met, and everyone likes him, including Gillian, a lot."

"Does that mean he has a chance with Gillian or none at all if the competition is Ian?"

"Don't know yet. Ian and Shwetak are close, but Gillian is the only one who decides that particular contest. And what makes you so sure that Ian is the favorite here? I seem to recall her talking about Shwetak a lot."

"I don't know. I just suspected because Ian is."

"Ah, what you didn't want to say before. Ian is good-looking and talented."

"Well, I'm sure Gillian finds Shwetak to have both of those attributes, too. And you're all fans of the great Adrian Gerd Wahl."

"Naturally. Are you ready for your quiz?"

"Oh, no, please. I need a map with their names and associations first, and I'm afraid I've already forgotten all the questions."

"Complicated."

"Yes. Life is."

Nine

Hit-and-Run

Being a highly intelligent animal comes with disadvantages as well as the obvious traits leading to ascendancy. Varg, Adrian Gerd Wahl's favorite Labrador retriever, had long ago figured out how to turn the door handle using his snout then push with his paw at the opening crack until he could shove the door, which was seldom locked, open. Keener intelligence gave him special privileges with his master, and it also gave him greater freedom. Doors that swing open for Varg shut on the snouts of Viggo and Viktor, not lazy dogs but practical. The yellow labs whined, more out of habit then desire, for only for a few moments before settling back down on the rug next to the stone fireplace where their fur and bones soaked up the warm glow.

Sometimes Varg hunted squirrels in the morning; at other times he simply wanted to get away from his legion and sit alone on the dock, looking out over the water in the way his master did, watching early vapors rising like aliens. He could sense tensions and releases in the air, in some way grasped life and death scenarios played out all around him, even on a seemingly peaceful early morning to the unobservant, like his animal fellows in the cabin.

A few years earlier, Gerd Wahl made his way through a maze of breeder's pens and past puppies wrestling and rolling on the ground. The big man first noticed two yellow fur balls that would soon be named Viktor and Viggo. When Wahl approached, the two trotted over and leaned against the large crate with soulful eyes. Varg was the last pup chosen out of the litter from champion-bred sire and dam, but Gerd could not take his eyes off the chocolate lab. That pup's immediate reaction and quick responses to both verbal and visual cues would have made him the one to go home with Gerd, but the breeders were eager to ensure companions for their dogs and keep pups together where possible. Never intending to take home three pups, Gerd changed his mind and left with a full crate of yelping pelage that quickly quieted on the long car ride, the pups eventually entangled in one sleeping mass.

It took Gerd merely days to train the chocolate lab and only a few weeks to train Viktor and Viggo. All three were quick studies, but Varg was almost scary in his responses, Gerd thought. Varg's attention to detail was more precise than a lot of the human beings he'd known. Man and dog formed a deep bond, and it was not long before Varg had made himself the leader of his pack and the intuitive favorite of the writer.

If Gerd had really thought about the power of these hunting dogs and their need for regular exercise, he might have turned around before arriving at the breeders' kennels, but by the time he recognized how much work the dogs were, the solitary writer had long since grown attached. Fortunately, the farmland on the other side of the road from his cabin belonged to an obliging man who had no objections to Gerd's three big dogs running through his fields as long as no corn was planted in that section. Winter was best for running the dogs over fields covered with anywhere from a few inches to feet of snow, and the dogs could tire themselves leaping and jumping, temporarily disappearing in soft snow under their large paws. Varg always returned upon first command, and the other two followed his lead. Gerd had no problem letting them have unleashed free reign.

"Viktor, Viggo, come!" Gerd never had to command Varg.

When they were young, Viktor was the most destructive, surprising Gerd on a daily basis with the ingenuity of how the pup could take apart things that did not even have the semblance of segmentation. There were dismantled pillows, stuffing from an old chair, separated and chewed baseboards, torn newspapers, magazines, and books—one that was actually quite valuable, a first edition, shoes and sandals that became half-digested snacks, lamps that were overturned and separated into parts, fraying rugs that became long tangles. Almost everything was fair game for restless pups. Gerd eventually learned how to run them near the point of exhaustion, and they would settle down like old hounds at his feet.

Varg, however, never engaged in willful destruction, as if all of the chaos was beneath him, and the two brothers never challenged the clearly dominant dog after they arrived home from the kennel. Over the course of the last couple of years, Gerd began leaving Viktor and Viggo with the neighboring farmer while he was away on trips and taking Varg with him, except when Gerd flew.

On one particularly calm morning after sunrise, Varg left his master's bedroom, the only one of the three labs to have that access, and stepped outside. Within a few minutes, he was on the trail of a squirrel down by the water's edge that, if it had seen the big dog an instant later, would have been a trophy brought back to be laid on the stone doorstep at Gerd's feet. Instead, the squirrel had sufficient time to race for and up a tree with Varg's hot breath gaining.

Eastern gray squirrels in adjoining trees chattered angrily, raining down a cache of insults on the dog's head, from the safety of two tall pines; one squirrel, in particular, felt immune to the dangers below, having escaped multiple times. Their population had been culled by the three dogs in recent summers, and the bushy tailed rodents were naturally bitter or so it seemed to Wahl when he looked up to witness their scolding. Although Varg narrowly missed catching that troublesome squirrel, the big dog inadvertently flushed out an orphaned fox kit in the undergrowth that had also been keenly eyeing the loudest rodent. The young fox had been about to pounce or otherwise would never have gotten that close to a charging Labrador, and the chase was on with fox racing up the embankment toward the other side of the road and potential escape into the woods beyond open fields. Varg gained on the kit and was about to fatally engage the small canid at the precise moment a passing car struck the fox and Varg instantaneously.

Narrow and sinuous, the lake road presented particular driving problems, but cars and trucks often sped through, anyway, especially early in the morning before there was much traffic and the summer tourists were still sleeping. Dismantling the fox, almost knocking the kit out of its fur, Cadillac Escalade struck only a glancing blow to the chocolate lab, startled driver unable even to swerve. As casual as the collision was with the 5700-lb. machine, nearly missing Varg by inches, the Labrador was dealt a fatal blow.

Slowing the car too late, the driver turned to look in her rearview mirror and realized she had hit a dog and not a man. "Just a dog," she said out loud, then continued on, her day starting off much worse than planned.

Up even earlier than usual, Gerd was preparing his coffee when he thought he heard first a muffled, unidentifiable noise and then a dully registered, thickened skidding sound. Although it was probably nothing, something triggered Gerd's distress reaction, but his reason fought it off. By the time he finished his first cup, opened the paper, and Viktor and Viggo were standing by their dishes waiting, panting, Gerd looked around for Varg. He yelled for the big dog once in the cabin, and then saw the narrow slit between the screen and doorway to the lake. He knew it had been opened by his stealthy, smart animal.

At first, Gerd casually shrugged even though other reactions were taking form. Varg had done this kind of thing before. Still with feigned calm, Gerd walked over to the door and whistled for Varg a couple of times. He waited. Nothing. Slipping on a pair of old loafers, broken in the first summer he bought the camp, loafers positioned for easy exit from the porch, Gerd nearly stumbled as he pushed his other dogs away from his feet then shut the door on Viktor and Viggo.

"Stay," he said unusually sharply. The two reacted to the change in his tone and crouched submissively before Gerd walked down toward the water, stumbling and sliding a couple of times on the wet moss grown on rocks and near tall, bent grasses. He called again for his favorite companion. Caution had given way to escalating urgency. Viktor and Viggo were reacting again, barking in intensity and pitch from inside the cabin.

Looking up and down the shoreline for a few minutes and out over the water because Varg was a good swimmer, Gerd quickened his pace. As he struggled up the wet hillside, he had a profound uneasiness descend, slap him down as if trying to suffocate him, but he fought it heroically. Then he raced toward the road, his heart beating faster with each leaping step until he knew before he got to the scene, before early morning sun sent shafts of slanted light between thick growth of old trees, before cause and effect could be calculated, before he saw the chocolate fur matted and stiff, before he knelt to hold Varg's huge head in his hands.

"Still warm," he said softly, cradling his friend as man curdled himself around the animal in the road. Only when another car honked and swerved, did Gerd take notice of where he was again, finally lifting the heavy black body and carrying Varg home.

Ten

"Legendary Literary Writer Dead at 44"

My life changed the moment I interviewed Gerd Wahl, but let me return to the instant I read that first chilling headline. I jumped onto Huff Po to read more about Wahl, checked out various editions of news, blogs, and Twitter. After texting with my friends half the night, I finally fell asleep.

    Angela left for work earlier than usual, so I had to talk to someone about what had happened to the great writer. Our further speculations led to no new information: my friend Ian with his conjectures about Gerd's possible murder, and Marie angry with the rest of us, especially Tom, for texting about Gerd at all in the middle of the night. With the ascent of morning, I wondered if anyone had discovered new information that would put our fears in a new light.

    Ian Frost, Tom Hayes (6)
    6 recipients
    Drew Levin

    Texting not

Tweeting about Gerd to avoid all the random idiots. Any one heard anything new? MMS 8:24 AM

Tom Hayes
Gerd not a character limited guy like the rest of us. Or was he really a dinosaur incapable of changing to survive? MMS 8:25 AM

Ellison Espada
Limited? Hardly. Tom? What does that say about the "rest of us?" Wahl was

not a "dinosaur"
unless you
are referring
to his stature. MMS
8:26 AM

Marie Rollins
Insecurity via
Social Media.
It's like
Wahl's
listening.
Somehow
disrespectful. MMS
8:26 AM

Ornal Aude
Paranoid?
He's listening?
How'd Wahl
get us to read
more than
350 pages?
We're hard
wired and
programable. MMS
8:27 AM

Drew Levin
We're in the
Program Era,
not programmable.

75 | Socrates is Dead Again

There's a
difference. MMS
8:27 AM

Ornal Aude
You obviously
feel compelled
led to show
what you
know. MMS
8:27 AM

Drew Levin
Audible sigh.
Sorry, Ornal.
Gerd is
gone. I still
can't believe
it. Somehow
surreal. MMS
8:28 AM

Ornal Aude
Devastating.
Do we ever
really know
anyone? MMS
8:28 AM

***

    I had been hoping Ian would jump on, and we could have some kind of intelligent messaging, but instead, I felt trapped with an angry Tom and Ornal. I knew none of us, however, were intending to be disrespectful; clearly, all of us admired Wahl, but I imagined the conversation between Tom and Marie or Ornal Aude and her lover Ellison after those at-odds couples climbed into bed together after tweeting or texting. Thank God, Angela, my love, is not a fan of Twitter and only seems to text to tell me what time she is getting home. I appreciated the fact that Angela's not another writer with whom I have to compete or constantly weigh my work achievements against. And those other writers, all of Ian Frost's friends, too, because he is the one who introduced me to them. I only really knew Tom and Marie before, then later met Gillian and Shwetak, those last two my workmates. I'd seen Marshall and Scott at a few events and when I was out with Ian, also meeting Ellison and Ornal around that same period. The fact that Ornal was from another planet, as she claimed, really dictated her relationships. Like I said, I was glad Angela did not tweet. She'd have confirmation that I am more of a weirdo than she probably already suspects.

Not much more about Wahl's death in the news or posts yet but lots of speculation. I don't know what I thought I'd find, but I couldn't stop obsessing about Wahl's death either. Rumors already started considering suicide, but early reports weren't stating anything except he had been found in his home in Upstate New York. You can tell when it's a suicide, however, because of the paucity of information in news reports. Still, suicide didn't fit, not with my image of Wahl, not with the man I knew. Let me correct that: the writer I thought I knew. Someone with too much to lose to take his own life. The fact he had everything the rest of us wanted, yet still killed himself didn't add up. He was entirely too logical, too grounded. This was an assumption made from reading his work which I decided needed to be separated from the man who created those words.

It occurred to me, not that he died at 44, far too young, particularly once you get past the age of 30, but that he was noted as legendary and a literary writer in the same headline. Right there, I knew something. There was another paradox at work in this world. I couldn't be nonchalant, though. *I knew him, Horatio,* or at least I thought I did. Why? Why was the word that kept leaping out, if not from my mouth, then from the page or the ether? Maybe I should have picked up on something from that second interview in which we talked at length, but then again, I was recovering from too much of a good thing that night. I considered the idea that maybe I had not known him at all and had to be careful because the inference was out there that I did. People were convinced I was now the expert on everything Wahl. So much depended on it, and my feature story was not even written yet. Word had gotten out (thanks to my colleagues and our magazine publisher) that Wahl had granted me a second interview, beyond a rarity. It was better that no one except Wahl knew the reason, and he would not be talking. The inference was that Wahl and I had become friends.

Although "everything" was at the speculation stage, people were bound to weigh in on something they knew nothing about. What I didn't know was how to classify what I felt about Gerd's death. His death was shocking, that I know. But I hadn't reconciled information about the loss of the writer with the living, breathing, larger-than-life man I sat and talked with, not once but twice, at length. I drank with him until I forgot everything and had to stay overnight at his lake house! I had his story, his words, his gestures, and yet suddenly felt as if I knew nothing. At the same time, I sensed my anxious, guilt creeping around. Death would only further add to Gerd's legend.

A couple of centuries ago, at 44, a man would have lived a long enough life. Today, 44 was considered a young man, far too young to have exited this world. And what had he left behind? Was there another Wahl original story in a drawer some place in that cabin of his, tucked away where some cop on the scene wouldn't know what he had as he bagged and stored? Those last Wahl pages could have been dismissed as nothing more than physical evidence to be placed in an innocuous box and left to rot in police storage. I started to get really agitated thinking about those likely pages Wahl left behind. I had to go through my notebooks.

Within hours after the announcements of his death, Gerd was joining ranks with immortals, and you could sense more accolades coming. I began adding up how many writers had killed themselves: Hemingway, Plath, Romain Gary, Klaus Mann, Richard Brautigan, William Inge, Hart Crane, Nerval, Olle Hedberg, John Berryman, Charlotte Perkins Gilman, Iris Chang, Carolyn Gold Heilbrun, John Kennedy Toole, and damn, if I had written *A Confederacy of Dunces*, I never would have contemplated suicide, but then I most certainly would not have ever thought about suicide if I'd been any of the rest of them. I almost forgot about Jack London although his death might have been accidental, but unlikely. Hunter S. Thompson with the funniest god-damn suicide note, one of the best ever written. Anne Sexton, Tom McHale, Spalding Gray. But Spalding Gray was different, I decided. His suicide was the result of a brain injury sustained in a car accident in Ireland, that injury causing loss of acuity. It made sense on some level. Virginia Woolf. I think I listed her already. Was I going to incorporate those who might have killed themselves, but evidence had not conclusively proven it, like Randall Jarrell walking out onto a freeway? Already losing track, and here I was tossing together poets and prose writers, too many of them ended this way. I stopped my morbid, mental count. Other people in other occupations killed themselves, too, I reminded myself. Ex-military, doctors, policemen, oh, there were definitely occupations that held higher rates of self-inflicted deaths than writers.

There was, however, this creeping suspicion that these intellects knew something the rest of us didn't. But I decided that thought to be illogical and dangerous, and I pushed the idea back down. Wahl was a giant in our sphere and now there was this absence, a sudden vacuum created, a black hole of sorts that could pull us in. The threat of whirlpool-like attractions seemed entirely possible. What about the wider culture because, let's face it, writers and serious readers are a very thin slice of the larger pie. It was entirely possible that people outside the writer/ serious reader bubble were not even aware of Wahl. I was used to reading about and talking with other writers and hadn't considered an equation in which the famous writer's loss was not felt in the least by the vast non-reading public. For the moment, however, I couldn't get past my own morbid speculation and curiosity that had not yet hit anything close to grief.

There would be inevitable conjectures: what might he have achieved if he had lived to be 80 or even 65? Then I began looking at his death from another angle. Doubtful anyone would write about how fortunate Gerd Wahl was never to have contracted Alzheimer's disease or dealt with his own impotence, sexual or intellectual. He would never look spent and haggard, past his prime. He would not end in a nursing home with no one to visit because all of his friends and family had long since passed away. We seldom discuss the good fortunes of the dead.

His face was suddenly in front of me, his wry smile. I started wondering what he was thinking in those moments before he ended it. He had to have remembered our conversations. Even if they weren't real conversations to him, they were to me. Yeah, I wanted to know if he thought of me before dying. Sounds egotistical and ridiculous, but I felt I had made some connection with him. On some level, I hadn't stopped thinking about him since I was granted that first interview, whether I wanted to or not. Even if Angela wasn't also a fan of Wahl's, I would have been obsessing over the guy. But she was a devoted one. I kind of loved her for that, too, even if her fawning over Wahl drove me a little crazy with jealousy. At least I could be honest about my unhappiness with her attraction to him.

Gerd seemed too grounded for such an act. No, that wasn't right either, but I couldn't believe he was the kind of man who would kill himself, but then again, I'm not sure if there is a "kind" of suicidal person. Suicide is one of those choices that does not add up. On another level, there was the whole, how could someone who has everything give it all up? I guess I could understand those who end their lives when they are in prison for killing their entire family, that kind of demented, depressive madness. But what Wahl did was unforgivable.

Adrian Gerd Wahl was gifted, brilliant, according to everyone I talked with, hugely successful, and seemingly in charge of a life most of us could only dream of in terms of independence, fame, fortune, respect, fawning fans, and, perhaps most significantly: real accomplishment. That last part got to me. What Wahl had attained was what all of us were after: creating something memorable, something of worth, and then he does the unthinkable. There was the persistent question, since we were all going to die anyway, why leave early?

Angela had dressed in darkness and left for work, but there was a note tacked to our refrigerator under her favorite, handmade magnet, a weird photo of Gerd in one of his cool hats. I've tried wearing hats like Gerd's, but anything other than a baseball cap looks entirely ridiculous on me. She'd made her magnet out of a picture of Wahl from magazine clipping, and her note read, "Bad headache. Can't believe he's dead. Went for a walk. Didn't take Henry out." Angela Mazziotti, my Angela, this woman I have been in love with forever, was infatuated with Gerd, and from my point of view, her devotion was a little puzzling. She wasn't a writer. Angela was a reader, as I've mentioned, probably a better one than me. Apparently, all of the readers in the world weren't already writers.

All of this musing got me thinking about Angela and why I was permanently hooked. She was not the most beautiful woman, but sometimes, looking at her, I was sure that was true. I think it's her confidence, her self-assurance without any awkwardness or arrogance. And her relentless kindness and compassion are weirdly sexy.

Even if I couldn't stop thinking about Gerd, I didn't want her to do the same. Jealousy is not a trait I wanted any part of, but I had to acknowledge the worm in me. I started wondering how long this would go on, her mourning Gerd; even if she'd had only one night to digest this news, I was ready for her to be over him. I had a headache, too, but I didn't have the luxury of leaving easily. Of course, she worked longer hours than I did and at least twice as hard, but I was used to her coddling me. We were seldom home at the same time, but then, I thought maybe that was one of the keys to our lasting relationship. We didn't tire of one another (at least I didn't) because we infrequently saw each other.

I had Henry to attend to. Thank goodness, I had Henry. He was already nosing my arm, nudging really, getting my elbow sopped, pushing me to let me know he wanted me to get up and get going. Dogs wait for no man in the morning.

I started out walking my dog around the block. Well, walking is not exactly what we set out to do, or at least I intended to take him for a run, but he had other ideas about six minutes into our jogging: Henry quit and sat down on the street with me pulling on his leash and him lowering his snout, making it looked like I was trying to yank my dog's head off his neck from the point of view of passing motorists. Thankfully, there weren't many people out yet. It was scarcely light. One real advantage to walking my dog this early was getting to see the city when New York was somewhat quieter, kind of surreal. Naturally, a lot of New Yorkers would say this city is always surreal in the way we accept the abnormal as normal or routine, even events as terrible as murder, as unsettling as suicide, as relentless as life.

A woman in a Hybrid Escape slowed, still at an hour when a car could slow down and not be rear-ended, and looked at me with this kind of sneer that I'd get from my mother whenever I did something really wrong as a kid. Come to think of it, that's also the look I get from Angela sometimes. I must inspire women to great heights of derision. I immediately stopped strangling Henry and smiled at this stranger, nodding my head as if to say, "Yes, you caught me in the act, but I've come to my senses, thank you," ridiculously patting my mutt's head. Even felt false to Henry. He looked up at me: "You've got to be kidding with this bit. This pat on the head stuff; nobody's buying it." That woman did, however, and drove off. I looked down smugly at Henry.

Henry, however, implied with that tilt of his head, "Some people are perfectly fine with my actions. So, watch it, buddy." Then he scratched himself vigorously, knowing full well that I never carried through with my threats, even implied ones. Okay, time for a new flea collar or that stuff in a tube that Angela says I should buy instead, but it feels like I'm slowly poisoning not only fleas but my dog. I finally managed to get Henry back over the curb and on a sidewalk. He seemed to think that streets were perfectly acceptable places to roll around even with all of humanity moving past. Of course, that is one of the things I love about Henry and dogs in general: they seem oblivious to imminent danger and death unless danger has four legs and looks like another dog, then the fur on their backs stands straight up and we're in for it.

I'm obsessing over Henry, I know. Because Henry is the sort of dog a guy like me would have, accidental and slightly silly but smart enough, this little unidentifiable breed of a dog got dropped off on my building's steps, howling until I let him in because he licked my leg when I opened the outer door.

"He could've had rabies," Angela said after Henry's formal adoption was complete. By formal, I mean that I took him to a vet, got him shots and dewormed, and he was full of worms, the vet tech said. Rather than be impressed with my resourcefulness, however, Angela questioned his constitution. "He could be sickly and die on you." She always resorted to extremes when talk came to issues of health which didn't seem like a good stance for a health professional.

"He's in remarkable shape other than having worms which are now gone," I stated in triumph.

Henry licks my toes after I take my socks off. Angela says it's because he likes the taste of salt, and my feet are sweaty and stinky. She always adds "stinky," but I'm pretty sure it's because he reveres me.

My darling Angela made it clear when she finally moved in with me that Henry was my dog, my responsibility, and I hate to say it, but he hasn't grown on her. Of course, that might be part of the reason I like this mutt so much, at least most of the time. Then I'm thinking about Wahl's dogs. Even focusing on Angela and Henry, Wahl intrudes on my thoughts. What was he thinking with his terrible last act? He should have at least considered what his death would do to his dogs.

We'd both had too much to drink last night, and I mean Angela and me, not my dog. Henry is tired of being patient. Every morning, he jumps up on my bed in exasperation and starts panting and whining in my face. I needed a higher bed, I decided, envisioning putting the thing up on stilts. Certainly, it would help if the mattress wasn't on the floor.

Only when Henry was breathing heavily and dripping his saliva on my arm did I notice that Angela had already gone that morning. I didn't panic because it was her habit to get up without saying a word and get ready for work without waking me. She really had awful hours, on weekends, too. I couldn't help the fact my job had a later and more compassionate start time and respected man's need for regular weekend vacations. We'd had that conversation about nurses and the disrespect reserved for them by the very public that most needed them.

I was thinking about all of that, not Gerd for a moment, when Henry dropped his leash on me. That little metal part on the end actually hurts when hitting bone. He's that smart. After giving me time to get my shit together, he goes and knocks his paw against cupboard doors until his leash falls. I find this trait endearing and smart, but Angela says it's freaky.

She is quick to point out on many a morning, "He's your dog. Take him out!" So, in a fog and often still in darkness, I throw on some kind of clothing, and I'm not sure what I'm even wearing until I get back to our apartment, and, on Mondays, Angela's not terribly useful day off, she is often standing in our open doorway with her hand over her mouth laughing, apparently because I'm wearing one of her sweaters.

"I've got my own jeans on," I say in my defense, but I have to look down to make sure. We're both pretty damn skinny. Angela will then give me a hug, and we might actually have sex before anyone's had a proper breakfast, including Henry, who lets us know by scratching his dinner bowl repeatedly during our delightful and unexpected session.

"Why do you love that mutt so much?" she will ask.

"I don't love him. I like him, a lot," I always respond.

All right, I love this mutt. Angela has accused me of loving Henry more than her, but when I try to explain different types of love, she says something like, "I'm not talking about fucking. And I certainly hope you don't want to fuck your dog. I see the way you look at him with such reverential love."

At which point, I get defensive and pretend anger to distract by throwing something across our infinitesimally small space, and I only manage to make her annoyed. She curses at me half in jest, picks up whatever I've thrown, and I hope the object of her pseudo anger is one of my things because that will make the next conversation easier. I finally take Henry for another walk to get out of her way. Henry has more exercise when we're fighting. I think he intentionally causes discord between Angela and me, knowing outcomes will somehow be favorable to him, and he might spot one of the bitches he likes around a corner. Of course, he likes every bitch he meets. I have to remind him, however, that we're more likely to run into another male and everyone has to get their hackles up, cross to the other side of the street if it's a big dude.

Half-way down the block, I start thinking about the fact that I don't really love Henry more than Angela. It's simply that he never berates me, loves me unconditionally, well, sort of, except when I'm dragging him down a street like this morning. But I can't stop thinking about something else either. That's this unsolvable yet disastrous problem about suicide: people who commit the act it would seem do not stop to consider all of the people they are affecting. I can't even imagine what Wahl's family or close friends were going through if I felt this crappy over Gerd Wahl. Death is permanent, but when a choice, we are all left at edges, dealing with dread that you can't easily take back.

Suicide makes me angry and then down right depressed, but I have a dog and dogs have a way of making you forget important stuff again and concentrate on picking up their doggy poo and watching them try to scratch their rears and poke their heads into every disgusting thing that smells on the street or door stoop, yanking you all over.

Henry is about as different from Gerd's three championstock Labradors as any dogs could be. Only thing I had that Gerd didn't have better and more of until a couple of days earlier was Angela. And then I think about those gorgeous, obedient specimens that adored their master, bowed at his feet like the rest of us fawning writers before the great man.

My God, I suddenly remembered, what happened to Wahl's dogs? Perhaps he killed them, too, moments before taking his own life, and I felt sick, ready to puke in the street, but I didn't. Not the magnificent Varg? He wouldn't have killed that dog, but then Adrian Gerd Wahl shot himself. Nothing seemed off limits. Hurriedly, I made my way back to Angela, feeling disoriented but grateful to be going home. More than that even. I was grateful to be alive.

Eleven

Rough Flight

Celestine had arranged a reading/speaking tour at the end of February involving six cities on the West Coast, and Adrian Gerd Wahl pushed past his perpetual reluctance to fly in order to board the plane, follow his agent's plan, be the good and generous writer about to embark on marketing his own work as expected. It was what every well-published writer was doing, but he told himself he didn't know if he could keep doing this. Sales were never his strong point. This activity was, in fact, something he hated with a simmering boil at first but had become white hot.

Although he had first class seats, paying for the extra accommodation himself, the space around him felt restrictive. Buckling and unbuckling his seat belt three or four times before loosening the strap again, he tried stretching out, his legs too long for even the extended enclosure, shutting his eyes in an attempt to sleep, but he could hear someone coughing, sneezing, the plane's engines. There was a baby in economy class screaming, however faintly, he could still hear her; those seemingly desperate cries found him, jangled a nerve. One of the flight attendants handed him earphones, and he placed them on in compliance before deciding what he wanted to hear. The flight attendant returned and stared at him before catching herself, smiling flirtatiously. C'mon, he thought. You must see bigger celebrities than me every day. Unfiltered perfume descended; cabin air dense.

"Are you comfortable? Can I bring you anything else?" She continued to stare.

Was she pretty? Yes, but not his type. What was his type? Uninterested, he shook his head in response then closed his eyes again. Still, the buzz of the plane produced a sensation akin to wasps. Rubbing the back of his neck, he gave up trying to sleep and pulled out a notebook, turning pen over and over in his right hand, amazed that it refused to produce a single word. There was nothing. Not even a forced description of emptiness. For an instant, he admired those artists who could draw, sketch a chair, back of a woman, a glass, fingers holding a cigarette, but his hand felt large and clumsy. His teeth suddenly covered in fuzz as he passed his tongue over them. There was a toothbrush in his carryon, but he didn't want to get up, much less make his way to the narrow little canteens they called restrooms on a plane. He really wanted a cigarette even though he had given up smoking some time ago. Yes, he really wanted a cigarette. That long slow draw played out in his imagination.

He caught the eyes of the flight attendant on him again, causing him to turn away and face the window. By the time they were climbing over the Rockies, his head was pounding through the back of his skull, his throat parched despite the water he kept pouring down it, and his eyes felt wired open as in a horror movie. *Clockwork Orange,* he thought, nauseous when the shuddering began almost as if he was standing on the ground above a tremor, an earthquake belching from Earth's center. At first, he imagined it was his own body's reaction to nerves, but then he heard other passengers wake and stir suddenly, a bald man across the aisle pulled the hurrying flight attendant's arm and demanded loudly, "What's going on?"

Steadying herself by holding the back of the seat, she shook her head dismissively as the captain's voice entered the cabin: "We're experiencing a bit of turbulence; we'll see if we can't climb out of this." All wide assurance in that velvet voice but a slight strain could be perceived in the clipped end of words. Gerd felt the plane ascending, tilt suddenly, his ears popping even as he practiced exaggerated swallowing. Gum. He had forgotten gum, those ear infections from childhood kept returning to remind him. Plane shuddered as if in pain, unable to free itself from torment. Again, the aircraft lurched unnaturally, and everyone was awake now, asking questions, chattering in agitation, a few kids crying, likely their ears hurting. A woman one row up from him reached for her husband's arm. He could not see their hands but the tendons in her arm viewed between seats told the story. Tension on the plane rose with their ascension in the atmosphere until a sudden flopping motion like a boat come lose from moorings sent a shock through the passengers, and it was quiet, fear spreading like contagion.

An image of a red and white bobber in rough waves came to Gerd, little buoy slipping under, struggling to surface, pulled down, reemerging as if gasping for air, yanked beneath water until lost, plane choking before drowning, he thought as a woman's sobs broke through his clear image of bobber on water, pilot now too busy to reassure passengers, some of whom had begun praying. Flight attendants buckled into their seats, as well, looking up in order not to meet eyes of anxious passengers. Their averted stare betrayed them, he thought, and the lines of strain in their necks, even the backs of their hands showing evidence of tension. With each lurch of the plane, Gerd felt the tight knot in his throat loosen, his lungs expand as if he had begun swimming underwater by swallowing sea water as naturally as a porpoise, and his long-standing panic blew away like sand across tarmac, individual grains flying one at a time and then in sudden whoosh in a cloud dense with the last particles. Calm, he thought of a line in *Godot:* "The English say *cawm*." He smiled although he felt guilty for his sudden ease, knowing that others were suffering around him now.

Then the plane found an altitude where winds no longer punished it, whatever storms were converging had been passed through, and a sigh of relief was audible from some two hundred passengers, except for Wahl. He tried to be generous for them. They still had to fly over another range of mountains, he reminded himself.

When they landed in San Francisco, the congregation broke into applause. They were going to survive after all; some of the passengers hugged one another before releasing each other in embarrassment. Gerd witnessed their joy, detached, as invisible panic raced back in a gust across concrete runway and directly into him. They had landed.

Twelve

Julia Tries to Save a Life

When she was only 18, she knocked on my door at the end of the long hallway in our dorm, the one where freshmen were camped, and said she came to talk because my roommate, a girl she knew from high school, wasn't in her room. I would have to do for her, because otherwise, what was likely to happen next was on me.

"I'm going to kill myself tonight," she said in the same tone one used for such mundane statements as, "I'm going out for pizza." My first response was attempted flight, but she stood in that narrow passage between the rest of the too-small space and my doorway, backlit by hall lights. She appeared in shadow and as ghostly.

The last thing I wanted was to be involved in some disturbed girl's life story or try to prevent whatever it was she was intending to do, but in that moment, I was already in it, surrendering to her story. I backed up, and she entered my dorm room.

I turned the desk lamp on to shed a little light on that dim scene in order to give her a face, but she moved around as if she was familiar with the dark, standing, then roaming corners of the room the whole time, feeling the air with her hands, and I kept wondering if I should call security but needed an opening to do so. I guess I wasn't used to suicidal confessions or even strangers imposing themselves.

"Why do you want to kill yourself?" I asked too logically.

Incredulously, she laughed. "Why would I not want to kill myself?"

"There is great beauty in this world," I started clearly enough.

"And grotesqueries that implode such beauty in cruel ways."

For every impassioned plea I made for the symmetry and grace in the world, the inherent worth of the individual and living, Meredith, and I had forgotten her last name, the first-year student who carried herself like a wiry young boy, retorted with a matter-of-fact counterpoint, pulling me deeper into the place where she was psychologically located, then shifted to past tense.

There a mother left her daughter to pick up a man in the streets, a man who smelled of liquor and sweaty clothes but who carried a wad of bills before depositing them on the Formica table at the center, looking the child up and down while her mother undressed in an adjacent room, shooing her kid away, but there was nowhere to go.

"The kid went into the bathroom, the only part of that apartment which had another door, the bedroom merely closed off with a colored sheet hanging from the opening, and she sat on cold, broken linoleum while she listened to muffled voices rise and fall in waves and short electrical pulses, the man now knocking on the bathroom door without identifying himself, and the kid compliant because she didn't yet know any other way.

"He forced the door the rest of the way once the kid started to close it on him, his hand up her second-hand dress, exploring the little girl's body which was frozen, rigid, when her mother stepped out for a few minutes, the man told her, to get some drink for them with the money he had given her. And when the mother finally got back, the door to the bathroom was shut, the child squatting naked and bleeding, squeezed between rusting tub and wall.

"'Put something on,' said her mother when the man left, and her mother had to use the toilet. Although the girl didn't kill herself that night nor the next because the idea of suicide had not been formulated, she knew that she had fallen and would keep right on descending. She's still falling," Meredith said.

"But it was the man not the child, not her fault," I protested.

"My cousin was a pretty, no, a striking girl and she was going to be in the movies. She modeled for a department store, taught herself how to stick her fingers down her throat to initiate a gag reflex and throw up after a meal, so she stayed skinny and desirable," she said. "I loved her clothes.

"They were making a movie near where she was living in Houston, but it was a non-equity production, no union actors, which was good for her, she said, because she didn't have enough to pay union dues. She practiced her lines until she knew several parts by heart. When it was her turn, she gave the performance of a lifetime, even her spine seemed to tingle with delivery. There was silence at the end of her audition because they had not expected this polish, this charisma from a local, but then the director called her over, and she was prepared to accept the part, trying to look nonchalant and keep her heart from betraying her as he took her small hand.

"'Not bad,' he said after a moment of squeezing her palm, 'Not bad at all, but you're too big-boned, kind of horsey, really, for this part. But I might be able to fit you in as an extra.' He let her hand go and turned to his assistant. 'Can you find me a girl we can stand to look at for this role?'

"She cried all night, then called at 3:00 a.m. and asked me how she could throw up her bones.

"I laughed at her at first because I thought she was kidding even in the middle of the night, or morning.

"Later, when she got into smack and crack and other drugs, she would call and sound completely incoherent, but I tried talking her down only to have her hang up without telling me where she was. That went on for a while.

"When they found her, she was propped up against trash bins in an alley, cut up pretty bad and unconscious. They got her to a hospital where she regained consciousness and told them her name, gave 'em my number, but by the time someone got around to calling me, all they said was, 'She passed.'

"Not even, she passed away. She was lucky, really. It only took her 23 years to get out."

"And you want to kill yourself because your cousin was murdered?" None of this made any sense to me.

Meredith smiled. "You're too literal," she said unkindly.

"Not always," I protested, trying to defend myself. "Someone you knew and cared about died horribly, but that does not make the whole world horrible."

"Someone was raped; someone died in an alley; someone was motherless, and they are all one. Don't you get it?"

"I'm not one for riddles," I said, getting angry that she was intruding on my evening, making me feel awful, and condescending at the same time. "Wait, are you talking symbolically?"

"No, literally." She threw herself on my bed and stretched out as if she meant to stay the night. "I'm fucking exhausted, and you're too slow for disputation."

"You don't have to insult me."

"Yes, I'm afraid I do."

For her sake, I tried to make an argument for staying in the world. I hadn't read Socrates nor any of the other philosophers at that point. I had yet to take the History of Religion course that provided the non-answers to the big questions except the ones we still don't know. I resorted to crying, sat down and curled up with a cramp in my gut. It was a last resort that I was almost entirely unaware of.

"Really? You're crying. I'm telling you that I'm going to kill myself, not you. Don't be a child."

"I can't help it," I told her. "I don't know what to tell you. I just started college, but I know there is someone experiencing joy and another in terrible pain at every moment in this world. Really, I don't know anything, less about life, and I wanted," I was sobbing at this point. Trying to articulate a full sentence seemed next to impossible. "I wanted to get a pizza tonight."

"All right," she said suddenly. "But, together, we're eating the whole fucking pie at once!"

She stroked my head, and I sat up straighter. We did order and eat an entire pizza in one sitting, and Meredith did not kill herself that night.

I thought for a long time that I had saved her life. I was arrogant and naïve enough to believe that I could prevent someone who wanted to take her life from committing suicide. How foolish I was. I honestly believed I could save another human being.

Thirteen

Tom's Self-Interview

Why hasn't any major publication interviewed me yet? All this talk about Adrian Gerd Wahl, and just because he died, he shouldn't be the only writer getting all the attention. By this time, I once imagined, the demand for features and interviews about me and my work would be coming fast and furious, just like the fortune. I would not want Drew to interview me, however, because he'd likely botch it like he has with Wahl. If no one will rise to the task, then I will do it myself. Self-interviews are in vogue, I've heard, or at least they were for a few minutes.

Q: What is it like to be famous? Is it difficult to deal with your legion of followers?

A: At this point in time, I have come to accept the interruptions and constant fawning praise. In the beginning, however, I resented the invasion of my privacy, beautiful women always outside my door.

Q: I could see how that would be a problem. How do you start a work of fiction? What compels you?

A: Aren't those two different questions? I'll try to answer them as you asked, however. I never start a work of fiction the same way. What begins one work seldom seems repeatable as impetus. My first novel began as catharsis (here I invent) after my brother and then my father died, and I don't count my mother's second husband as a father even though he told me to use that term. Second one arose out of a line that dropped from the ceiling like Annie Dillard wrote, or, at least Dillard quoting someone else. Inspiration for each work varies, a quality both exciting and daunting because there is that sense of randomness, rather than process, at work. The one I'm working on now hit me when I woke after dreaming. I tried writing down the images as narrative, but the whole thing came out jumbled until I began manipulating scenes to fit story arc. That's when dream and poetry collide.

Q: Do you think of yourself as long-winded?

A: Is that meant the way it sounds? Because I didn't agree to this interview to be insulted.

Q: Do you see your writing as part and parcel of the "Program Era?"

A: By that do you mean that my work is part of a social movement that is born in and cultivated by social media and the writing workshop era? If that is your question, then I would have to say that my work is definitely invigorated by this collaborative force and propelled to some degree by social media, the concept exploding in all directions around our writing communities. But in terms of initial conception and the style choices, I still want to claim some of those bygone attributes of the social expatriate, the isolated writer tapping away on quaint typewriter keys.

Q: So, you envision yourself a Hemingway? Want to claim the ability to escape your community at will yet be embraced by it on a whim?

A: Did I come across that way? Okay, maybe I do. I'm not sure we're as programmable as theory suggests, at least I like to think that I'm a bit more bohemian. I suppose I will go down writing about individuality even in the face of mounting evidence against solitary cry. Please, let's not get into a dialectic on "conceptual writing" vs. "peak language" here. I'm as conceptual as the next solitary writer.

Q: I'm not sure what you are even talking about now.

A: I would have thought you would want me to discuss, to some degree, technology's role in sustaining our writing communities, if such a concept exists, or is it an artificial construct which facilitates our vanities?

Q: Whatever. Do you see yourself repurposing language of the culture, or do you envision yourself as conceptual with your art?

A: How is it possible with a surfeit of language all around us not to be engaged in repurposing to varying degrees? People want to point to the genius of Shakespeare, but let's be honest: how many phenomenal writers came before him? And, didn't he steal from other writers, too? How about a question more directly related to me?

Q: I'll ask you what you would prefer to be asked: what does it feels like to be famous for your compelling, literary work?

A: Oh? I'm famous now? I like "compelling," though, so I'll answer that if only in the hypothetical.

Q: Since you're making up the questions, can't you make up situations, too?

A: I suppose the accoutrements of fame have become such an integral part of my life that I half expect someone to be taking my picture when I wake up every morning. I suppose that's a little disconcerting, you know, wondering about how you look at every weird juncture of your day, but really, I have no complaints. Fame allows me to reach a wider audience, provides me access to all kinds of, no, scratch that last phrase; sounds a little too indulgent.

Q: Aren't you concerned that your work will be seen as too self-reflexive, past post-modernism all the way to mental masturbation?

A: I thought we'd agreed to avoid insults posed as questions? Naturally my work is self-reflexive, and I think it would be impossible for anyone writing in this culture to fight against that sort of hyper-awareness of every word, every motive, every character that may be parodying or, in the least, imitating other characters already populating the contemporary literary scene.

Q: Why haven't you finished a major work since graduate school?

A: It has to do with lack of audience, lack of cash, lack of inspiration, simply lack.

Q: Like to offer to help these kids build their careers as writers?

A: I will be honest here (implying I haven't been before). The best advice I can give is, "Quit writing. Find work more productive or at least less self-defeating."

Q: Is literary fiction dead?

A: What kind of a question is that? I refuse to engage in hypothetical debates with you because of the closing of a few book store chains, a paucity of younger readers, an intellectual drain (or is it "intellectual die-off" taking place?). Besides, nearly every reader and writer has already participated in that hypothetical conversation.

Q: In light of your whining about the "20 Under 40 list," any other criticisms of it you'd like to offer our readers?

A: Since you've asked: There are an equal number of men and women on that list; blatantly unfair to the entire male population of this country, and now that I'm thinking about it, there were a lot of foreign-sounding names on that list; the whole list looks suspiciously politically correct, even subversive, and a statement on our generous immigration policy. I would prefer a list featuring many more white males ages 28—32.

Q: So, you're racist, sexist, and elitist, too? Well, then, could you offer your vision for a perfect "20 Under 40" list?

A: I'll ignore your slander. Naturally, I'm a bit biased on this account, but I think a list made up entirely of men named Tom who are 31 and living in NYC would be far more appropriate.

Q: Aren't you 32?

A: Not for another month and 2 days.

Q: Do you think that the Toms' list might be a little too inclusive since there are probably hundreds of Toms, maybe a thousand, who are 31ish and living in NYC?

A: They can't all be writers, can they?

Q: What would you be willing to trade for literary success?

A: Apparently, I've already addressed that question. Look around. And, you ask too many questions.

Q: How about paranoia? Who's coming up the steps?

A: It's only Ian Frost, and it's not my door. This is Marshall's and Scott's place. I'm just visiting, and Ian may be a threat but only the literary kind which, who am I kidding? Ian's hardly menacing. One published book does not make him the next Gerd Wahl. And, I've got a favor to ask him. He owes me.

Fourteen

How Drew Got His Plum

Look at me, my mother's darling boy, the first professional writer in the family. Really see me as what I am: a moderately decent writer who has led a pretty privileged life, and I had been given the assignment, after which the inevitable jaundiced eye surveyed me as I walked up to the counter inside our favorite little restaurant, a remnant of quaint before even this hangout became sophisticated. Sometimes we meet before work for breakfast and only occasionally before heading home if we get out early enough. I went to order an egg sandwich and hash browns, per usual, but my breakfast was already on the counter.

Gillian and Shwetak were seated together, but Shwetak moved over one stool to accommodate me, as if he had been saving my seat. He was always the most thoughtful. Ian was further down, on the other side of Gillian. We looked straight out of an episode of *Friends* without the complications and fun of sexual tensions; all right, with some of the fun of sexual tensions. Or, more precisely, we were like another version of Seinfeld only

Gillian wasn't nearly as promiscuous as Elaine, and the rest of us all thought we were Jerry. Even Shwetak was under that illusion, and he hardly ever delivered a punch line and was far too nice to be Jerry. Maybe Shwetak existed in "Bizarro Jerry" world.

I mentioned that I had just been texting with Marshall and Scott before I came. We discussed Wahl, of course. Marshall typically started us off.

Drew Levin, Ian Frost... (7)

Drew Levin
Wahl's death
feels like the
end of some-
thing bigger,
beyond. MMS
8:12 AM

Ian Frost
His death
feels larger
than one man. I
knew him,
Horatio. MMS
8:12 AM

Scott Williams
No more myths.
So, we
invented
one: Gerd Wahl. MMS

106 | Socrates is Dead Again

8:13 AM

Ornal Aude
Gerd was
human and
seriously flawed.
He was man,
not myth.
Perhaps
our under-
standing
of his work
would be
clearer if
we examined
with critical eye. MMS
8:14 AM

Tom Hayes
He exponentially
expanded it, his
myth, our
delusions. MMS
8:14 AM

Gillian Keating
Illusions?
or delusions? MMS
8:15 AM

Ellison Espada
Continued

information
about Gerd
shooting
himself.
We can
no longer
deny it. MMS
8:15 AM

Ornal Aude
Too many
writers'
insecurities here.
Not enough
about what Wahl
accomplished. MMS
8:16 AM

***

At some point, my friends and I had all been told we were good writers. No, very good with words, the sort of language that catches light on water, and that knowledge should have been enough, but it wasn't. Never is.

Gillian Keating is four or five years younger than the rest of us. Our crew from work had all the weirdness of friends being sometimes in competition with one another. We could have come out of the Iowa Writers' Workshop for our hubris although only two of us passed through those pearly gates. That would be Ian Frost, not me even though I applied. I told Ian I decided not to go, but he suspects I got turned down. I'm not sure why I have to lie about this undistinguished moment in my CV, but then, once the misunderstanding happened, I had to stick with the script. At some point if he bothers with even a cursory search on the Internet, Ian will have his suspicions confirmed.

We work for the same magazine, but the days of writers on the staff of a magazine sitting in an office have become archaic. In fact, print magazines are mostly dinosaurs, and we're in the process of going strictly online, but Craig said he'd need writers online, too. Craig Campbell, our esteemed boss, made the promise we would likely have jobs but hinted layoffs were possible. Then he said he'd keep us working as long as he could. Workplace promises aren't worth much these days. Ian has been the only one who never seemed nervous about the prospect of sudden collapse of his employment, Ian being the most resilient of all of us. One way or the other, Ian was confident he would land on his feet even in perilous situations.

I don't think working at the magazine is where we all became friends, however. If I had to pinpoint a precise moment, I would say Friday nights checking out bars and clubs where you could listen to music or perform a skit or read something you wrote. One night, we laughed at a comic and then stood clapping for an 18-year-old prodigy performing his poetry during open mic. Gillian, always brave, recited a passage from her work, and Ian read a poem he said he'd written months ago. Those evenings connected us, and Shwetak and Ian kind of fell in love with Gillian at the same time. Maybe I would have, too, but I was already in love.

From there, we haunted other poet houses in the city. Even Shwetak recited verse he had written after the death of his parents. His poem stunned an audience. I still remember that night. After Shwetak read, you couldn't hear a whisper. With their no heckling rule, the place was particularly inviting to poets and writers who were trying out something new. In fact, that's where Ian introduced me to Tom, Marshall, and Scott, and I think that's where I met Ornal and Ellison Espada, too. I tried to hang with my work crew, however, and Shwetak and I ended up in a corner one night when Angela had to work again. Shwetak was trying to deal with the incomprehensible, that horrific loss of his parents in an accident.

I cannot fathom the pain let alone the horror of Shwetak's story. "They were electrocuted on a bus in India on their way to a wedding," he said. "It's a long story or a short one, depending on who is doing the telling."

I tried very hard not to picture it. Strange that I want to ask him more about it but asking would be too horrible for both of us. I do know that Shwetak's been on his own for some time. I don't really know how he made a living here before landing this job. I don't know if his parents left him anything. They must have. Doesn't seem like a question a friend would ask. Unlike Ian, however, Shwetak appears nervous all the time. And with the talk at *Music & Culture* of downsizing, I think, how are you going to downsize from five? If they do, I am hoping they cut me rather than Shwetak.

Ian and Gillian and Shwetak kept going back to those poetry haunts, but, lately, I kind of backed away. Everyone knew that Ian, not me, was the hub of our writers' circle. To tell the truth, I'm not sure how that came about; I know that he connected people, and there were days when I didn't feel like being connected. I'm not sure if it was because I'd gotten the Wahl interview or because I wanted to spend more time alone with Angela.

Most of us had been freelancers trying to make a go as writers before we got actual jobs. That doesn't usually work out too well, freelancing, that is. My parents stopped supporting me two years ago, and I continue to remind them that independence is particularly daunting in this city, but not being native New Yorkers, they variously encourage as my cheerleaders and then ignore me. I figured that I could always go back to Wilkes Barre if life in New York ended up going south.

After getting the Gerd Wahl interview, I felt guilt. I happened to walk in at the right moment, as the call came in, and when Craig asked, I said, "I'll take it," before I even knew what "it" was. Life is all about timing. In fact, there's a similar story about timing as to how I met Angela. Sometimes, I'm one lucky bastard.

Ian had been at our rag a year longer than me. I try not to think about fairness since it's a concept without practical applications in our world, and there was no telling how long it would last—the magazine that is, let alone my new-found elevated status. I learned a while ago not to turn away from good fortune even when such fortune isn't deserved. Like I said before, that's exactly how I ended up living with Angela. There was some other guy hanging around her, and apparently, I learned from one of his friends later, Jeff was getting a drink for her and ran into some old friends, stopping to drink and chat too long, when I stepped in at the opportune time: the bar scene worked out for me, and Jeff became history.

Gillian is a writer, too, but her job title is secretary and office manager. Sounds reasonable to me, but I understand why she's angry. She helps out with both correspondence and accounts; in fact, she was as much a bookkeeper as a secretary and manager, as if we needed a manager, but ours was a barely adequately sized staff. She stayed on anyway. Campbell was not a particularly enlightened boss; in fact, as Gillian has said on more than one occasion, "He's a stone-age bastard" although I felt she was being too harsh, particularly since good old Craig had given me this assignment. I was beginning to see him in a new and very positive light, but I have to admit Craig was hard to like if for no other reason than he was ridiculously wealthy. He had enough left to him that he could blow tons on doomed ventures like writing about music and culture.

I didn't feel sorry for Gillian, though, because her situation made it one less person to have to compete with; of course, she could still write, but no one was listening to or reading her work except apparently Ian who sometimes critiques her stories, she told me. I try not to spend too much time reading other writers' work unless they are really close friends and even then, I kind of dread the task because if I hate the work, what am I going to tell them? If I love the words, well, they already know the manuscript is good. Much easier to be friends with an unsuccessful writer, a doomed writer, one for whom there are no prospects, or, better yet, a non-writer.

"What did you do to get it?" Gillian asked without waiting for formalities or hello, how was your morning? No questions at all about Angela or Henry. What was strange was that I was jealous of almost every guy around Angela, but Angela liked

Gillian and was always telling me to invite her over. They had only talked a few times, but they both liked each other. They clicked. I liked Gillian, too, for her bluntness and honesty, but those qualities could also get annoying pretty quickly, I decided, under present circumstances. Wasn't likely that I would ever invite Gillian over to my apartment, at least with Angela there.

"I don't know. Maybe the assignment was a punishment."

"C'mon. No one believes that line. He'll take another coffee with cream only." Gillian usually ordered for everyone because she knew our tastes well. A little unnerving. I think she ordered for me the first time before I even told her what I wanted. I'm not sure now, but my recollection seems to find her clairvoyant. That's the reason my breakfast plate was sitting there when I walked in.

Strangely, Angela wasn't ever sure what type of coffee to order for me on the few occasions we went out for breakfast. Usually, she was up and out of our apartment to work her nursing shift before I had even rolled over to hit snooze again.

If ever there was a poster girl for the Irish, Gillian was it. An abundance of curly red hair, freckles, quick smile, and piercing greenish blue eyes, she had that quick tongue, wit included for the same price. "A punishment for Gerd," she laughed, but then conversations got uncomfortable again because all of us knew that there was some truth to it. "Okay. I'll buy that. Not, you are the chosen one, but each one of us isn't." She looks around me to Shwetak. "We have a female, a, where were your parents from again, Shwetak?" All of us cringed when she said that, but she seemed entirely oblivious to potential disaster and insensible to Shwetak's feelings on the matter, or maybe not insensitive, merely uninformed. I suddenly realized that maybe she didn't know his parents were dead because the night he told Ian and me about the tragedy occurred before Gillian was hired. There was an older woman—maybe 60—working as secretary when I got my job, but she retired a few months later, mostly because she kept messing up billing. Not that she was too old, but apparently, she had Alzheimer's. That's one reason I'm not worried about my job. Craig actually hates firing people.

"India. Is it that difficult to remember? You've only got a couple of choices, really." Shwetak must get tired of our indifferent or subconscious prejudices spilling out.

"Sorry. So, we have a woman, an Indian." I look at Shwetak to see if he's wincing, but he is taking the remark in stride while he sips his tea. He is the only one in our office who drinks tea instead of coffee, and I think I've forgotten this fact a few times when it's my turn to pick up coffee because I sometimes come back with black coffee for him.

"Not an Indian, an American whose family came from India."

"Yes, then we have an Ian; see; now there's where things fall apart."

"Yeats," I said, but everyone ignored me. I liked Yeats, and I was clearly trying to deflect here, but I felt compelled to point out to all of them every time I came across an allusion. Okay, admittedly, I'm a tad insecure. Angela always acted as if she thought my uncertainty was fascinating rather than annoying, but I wonder if she was purely being nice. No, I know she is.

"I missed—I blew past my last deadline," Ian said softly enough that he would have been hard to hear except we were already waiting for his response. I almost didn't show up to meet them because I kind of hated to see what Ian's reaction would be to my new-found success. I actually preferred that he be angry to this response and was thankful that he was at least a couple of seats away. I couldn't see his face without straining my neck.

"Thanks, but that doesn't help me prove this." Gillian spoke with her hands moving around, and she nearly spilled her entire cup of coffee; as it was, she splashed liquid anyway, making small rings on the counter that Shwetak reached over past me and dabbed at. I guess he was either extremely neat or he didn't want Gillian to look as sloppy as she was.

"Which is?"

"Male, Caucasian, educated, wealthy: privileged by birth. Drew's an obvious choice if Ian wasn't the better writer, but I say, enjoy it, Drew. Must be your time."

"Well, thanks for making that clear," I said, finally leaning forward to look down the counter at Ian to see how he reacted to my comment, but Ian hadn't even shifted on his stool, nor did he respond. He was smiling at Gillian, though, and I felt a twinge of annoyance even if they were both my friends. "And who told you that I was privileged by birth? My family started with very little, at least middle-class sort of want. They were—and now I live in what could be easily misconstrued as a closet."

"Are we talking Freudian here?" Shwetak was actually trying to make a lame joke, apparently about my sexuality. I deliberately ignore Shwetak in this instance. I don't want to encourage his new-found confidence. What I wanted to ask was the question: who came up with the evaluation that Ian is the better writer? One published book does not give Ian instant credibility; or maybe it does. I have at least three books that are waiting for a publisher to wake up to the fact that they will sell even in a disappearing niche market and even though they don't meet the standard of 80,000 to 100,000 words, but then neither did Paul Harding's profound little book *Tinkers*, I want to point out, but then I remembered that Harding was an Iowa Workshop guy, too, and a damn good writer.

Gillian read my thoughts. "You know exactly what I mean. The first three automatically put you in the privileged category. At least here—"

There was a hierarchy although we generally operated as if class structure didn't exist. Ian was on the top tier, and I think I had recently made a shift to that rung with him, maybe even passed him with this assignment. Had to hurt, but I was tired of feeling for other writers. There were too damn many of them even among friends or more particularly among my friends. Every night, I was thankful that I went home to Angela but not merely for the fact that she was not a writer, too, at least not one that mentioned her work. Honestly, she would have had no time to write.

"You do realize that there is almost an anagram here: Gerd-Drew. We need only change one letter."

"What are you suggesting? That I got the assignment because of an anagram?"

"Of course not, at least not consciously, but who knows with Craig? So, what are you going to do with it? This plum? Gerd will rub off on you. We won't even be able to talk to you anymore." Gillian, as usual, was directing.

"Of course, you will," I said, secretly hoping that there was some truth to this prediction. "I don't think one interview is going to change my life, even an interview with the almighty Gerd."

"I don't know," Gillian jumped in again. "Gerd is very likely to change your life whether you want to acknowledge this shift or not."

"Disgusting, really." Shwetak ventured in here after looking like he was falling asleep for a minute.

"What?"

"You know. Our obsession with celebrity, with fame," said Shwetak.

"I wanna live forever," Gillian said, suddenly slipping off the stool, breaking into song, snapping her fingers and dancing next to the counter. No one joins in, and she stops as suddenly as she started, shrugs, and sits back down. I like Gillian, I've already stated, but I'll come back to that later. I was thinking about the fact that Angela was never particularly spontaneous, but she didn't annoy me either. Gillian might be thought of as attractive by guys other than me, but her hair was too wild really and she always wanted to dominate the conversation.

"Except it doesn't work like that," Ian broke in.

"Why not?" Gillian sounded almost mournful, but her words were clearly sarcasm.

"All right. Name the Poet Laureate this year," Ian challenged.

"What?" Shwetak was baffled by Ian.

"Play along." I actually wanted to see where Ian was going with this line.

117 | Socrates is Dead Again

"Kay Ryan," Gillian said, and I recalled the fact that I actually liked Ryan's concise, accessible poetry.

"She's been Poet Laureate for two years," Ian continued as if we hadn't spoken.

"No three," said Gillian and, of course, she would be the one who knew.

"No two and, like, a couple of extra months, and she's finished her term. W.S. Merwin was named to that honor," Shwetak corrected us.

"It's someone else now. Merwin's term's been over for some time," I said, fact-checking with my phone. "I know his poetry."

"I thought you didn't like Merwin's poetry?"

"Who told you that?"

"You did."

"Well, you can't believe everything you hear."

"You're a Merwin fan but not enough of one to know when he was the Poet Laureate, without cheating." Gillian had this incredible memory, and she seldom used her phone to look up facts, at least not in front of us.

"Your point?" I got around to asking Ian who had started this debate, purposely ignoring Gillian's last comment.

"How many of you have read Ryan's work?" Ian asked. We raise our hands like school children, which must have been a rather strange and ridiculous sight. "As I thought."

"We're all nerds and writers, so, again, what's your point?"

"We're not nerds or at least I'm not," said Gillian which made her appear only more so.

"No. Give me a minute. Where did you read her work?"

"I read one of her poems in *The New Yorker*," Shwetak boasted.

"When?"

"Last month."

"I think she's had a couple in there. Yeah, at least two," I said. "Come to think of it, I wonder how many poems she had published by that magazine before she was Poet Laureate."

"Does anyone know?" Ian asked.

"Before she was Poet Laureate, how many of you had ever heard of Kay Ryan? Really? She's old, you know."

"Well, over 60," I chimed in.

"Careful. Imagine what the youngsters will be saying about us in a few years," Shwetak smirked.

"Youngsters? Really? Did Gillian say that? Oh, sorry, that was Shwetak. Could have mistaken you for Gillian," I said, having fun.

Gillian cries out, "Is that supposed to be an insult? Do you think you are insulting Shwetak or me?

Shwetak yells, "66. Holy, she got a MacArthur Foundation Genius grant not too long ago."

"The Holy Grail," Ian bowed his head slightly.

How could we not know this? I wondered.

"You're all wrong. This is her 24th poem for *The New Yorker* since 1995.

Blows your theory, doesn't it?" Gillian said, as we all stared at her. "I did a little fact-checking myself."

"I feel like the Great and Powerful Oz has been unmasked," Ian remarked, staring in amazement.

"What theory?" I asked.

"He was going to say that the only reason *The New Yorker* published her work was because she was famous, but they were printing her poems before anyone knew who she was," Gillian said triumphantly.

"One point for *The New Yorker*." I held up my glass in a mock toast.

"No, one point for Kay Ryan," announced Gillian, who extends her sloppy coffee cup my way.

"Two points for you," said Ian, looking at her but pointing a finger at me. "You've got the Gerd interview."

Shwetak interrupted our thoughts. "What is it about him? Really? We know lots of great, writers. Why Wahl? Why was he the chosen one?" Initially, I wasn't sure if Shwetak was talking about Gerd or me. Then I realized that he was remarking on the fact there simply wasn't enough to go around.

"He's like one of the old-time pilots," Ian said casually, pulling his hand through his thick dark hair. In fact, Ian reminded me of one of those solo, hot-shot pilots himself.

Gillian smiled either at Ian or the thought of Gerd. "Yes, that's it. He's got that boy daring, the verve of a pilot in an open cock-pit, fearlessly launching into air; doesn't hurt that he's damn good looking, either."

"All timing," I said. With that remark, we fell silent, each one of us thinking about the writer we all wanted to imitate. Maybe Ian was thinking about the timing of my entrance at the precise moment Craig got the call. Maybe he was thinking about making out with Gillian. That's not right either. We were all thinking not about the writer we wanted to imitate but the one we wanted to be.

Fifteen

It's About a Lion.

Maybe It Should Have Been a Tiger.

Ian Frost, Tom Hayes . . . (8)
8 recipients

Tom Hayes
Needed him
to be example
if not immortal.
Gerd Wahl
failed us and himself. MMS
7:32 PM

Ellison Espada
Wahl, last of
the CONCEPTUAL
writers? MMS
7:32 PM

Ornal Aude

"It is Knowledge
of the unseen that
made it acceptable
for us to be blind."
Gerd's words, I think.
IDK. He was
mere, flawed
mortal after all. MMS
7:33 PM

Marshall Funkhouser
Always
mortal, but
we projected
our desires,
our hopes.
We have
been blind
before and
will be again. MMS
7:33 PM

***

At the Met, Ellison Espada stood back from a large-scale painting and surveyed his girlfriend Ornal who was looking particularly cute in her light blue sweater and black jeans, tight enough that the threads were starting to pull at seams. Her large, dangling, blue earrings were coordinated with her sweater. Additional tiny silver jewelry in her eyebrow, nose, and left ear made an impact statement, he felt. "Really, tell me what you see in this?" he asked her. She could wear anything or nothing at all and look great, he mused, objectively.

"It's not a Rorschach test, you know."

"Yes, but I'm curious; humor me."

"All right, but remember, you asked." Leaning closer to the art, then turning her head slightly first right and then left as if the light would alter perception, she sighed. "There is a man with a chalk-white face whose eyes have been gouged out of his head, but he's screaming with black teeth and lips and a black rose at his throat." Ornal now studied her lover as carefully as the painting. Ellison was always immaculately dressed, a New Yorker by birth, and thoroughly comfortable in his beautiful black skin, she mused.

"A black rose? You see a rose? Where?"

"At his throat. I'm not finished. He has no body only bloat for a stomach floating below his head that looms the way a Nazi might appear after angels were finished with him."

Ellison stared at her. "You see, that's what I mean."

"What?"

"It's always about a horrific man and a Nazi, even in an abstract."

"Not always. What do you see?"

Ellison ran his long, thin fingers over his newly shaven head. "Not a Nazi in sight."

They both laughed, a temporary truce. "No, not fair. I was honest with you," said Ornal.

Ellison backed up slightly as if to get a better view. "Paint is splattered like jumbled words on a page, clamoring, struggling, and always attempting to reach the edge of canvas, screaming for audience. Abstraction suggests something dark as you have also noted."

"You really want me to tell you what I think about your latest chapter, don't you?"

"I'm that transparent? Okay. I'm not arguing."

Ornal turned. "She turns into a lioness then eats all of the men in the village, one at a time, particularly enjoying their balls? Other than the inevitable feminist backlash that will be the likely result of a lioness who eats men simply because it amuses her, maybe your totem should have been a tiger."

"Why? What do you mean? A tiger?"

"I think feminists other than you will appreciate the reference to a tigress. There is something fiercer, more independent about a tiger, not a social animal at all, like the lion."

"Oh, no. She has to be a lioness." Ellison looked slightly confused though he leaned forward in anticipation of her next response.

"Why?"

"It's my story. Why would you replace her with a tiger?"

"You weren't listening." Ornal cushions her words with a smile. "As to animal totems, in Tea Obrecht's story *The Tiger's Wife*, the woman turns into a tiger, and although she eats a man, it is perfectly justifiable."

"I like her story, too, but I'm not interested in imitation."

"Not imitation, recognition of the totem"

"Is this your way of telling me to toss the story?"

"Not at all. You brought up the tiger. Let me finish. Everyone likes Obrecht's story. And there is *Life of Pi* in which the tiger Richard Parker, well, you know what happens. I think tigers are in vogue right now. Oh, and there's that John Vaillant nonfiction book, *The Tiger: A True Story*. And there's *White Tiger* which won the Man Booker Prize. Face it, my darling, lions are on the outs.

"I think you're cherry picking. Where are tigers in Wahl's novels and stories? Not a one. And you conveniently omit 'The Veldt.'"

"Gerd? He doesn't write about animals, making the comparison ridiculous."

"He has three dogs, and he has written about them in essays. Bradbury wrote 'The Veldt.'" Ornal could tell when she pushed things too far, but she found it hard to retreat.

"So, now I'm ridiculous?" Ellison could not help feeling defensive. If you couldn't get support for your writing from your girlfriend, what was the point? "And animals are symbols but more than symbols. Your criticism of my story is really that the lioness should have been a tiger?"

"Yes, Bradbury's kids sick the lions on their parents who have unfortunately stopped indulging their offspring."

"If I recall correctly, it's all a simulation in a science fiction scene," Ellison said. "The lions feast on the screaming parents in the end as we read about their kids having high tea while they watch engorged lions lick their chops."

"Horrifying, delightful," she laughs. "You need a tigress."

"God, you're stubborn." At that moment, Ellison was not sure if he loved or loathed this woman in the moment.

"And you're too worried about what everyone thinks. A tiger rather than a lion."

"Do you really think I care about societal expectations?"

"You went there," she said walking away. He pursued her. "I didn't mean it like that. Don't be so damn sensitive. Everything isn't about race," she said.

He turned to face her again. "Wrong. It's always about race for me and millions of other people of color, but you wouldn't know."

The last remark stung Ornal in a way the other comments had not, and she pulled her head up, and straightened her back. The couple didn't talk to each other the rest of the way home, even when they boarded the M Train when some guy tried to grab Ornal's ass, and she let off a string of profanities. Ellison either pretended not to notice the man until his abrupt departure or really didn't look at his girlfriend in the crowded car.

Then a young man reading a newspaper had turned to a page with an article about Gerd Wahl's death. Both Ellison and Ornal tried reading it upside down before fixing on one another.

When they got back to their apartment, Ellison shut the door to his study. He didn't slam it as she anticipated, but the closed door was symbol enough. Ornal was no longer annoyed with him but unsure of how to change the dynamic without appearing to be the one to submit.

No dill weed," she lamented, closing the spice cupboard. "We have no dill weed," she yelled.

"What about the other kind?" he yelled back, forgiving her the indiscretion. "We could share."

"None of that either. We're out of everything."

"Not everything," he said, popping his head back into their common space. They laughed. "Still mad?"

Ornal shook her head. "Not with you."

Sixteen

Feeling Like a Fraud

It's not likely Drew will be able to get anything original out of interviewing Wahl. He has yet to say anything to me about his landing this assignment. Yet he knows how badly I wanted it. Even Shwetak, who tries to never take sides, said, "Gerd interview should have gone to you, Ian." Am I the only person to address him by his surname rather than Gerd? Strange how his middle name, the least likely candidate, stuck. Parents should choose their children's names wisely within a culture. Every parent should try to imagine how that name will be perceived in various cultures since we live in a world in which even our names are examined from every conceivable angle and tongue. But Tom's comment about Wahl's name? Too far. He's an ass sometimes, just a vulnerable one, or I'd cut him off entirely. I can't believe I ever roomed with him.

Maybe I should give up Twitter and texting, for that matter. Social media has become a drain rather than a means of keeping community. Another night of nonsense. Kind of desperate out there in the ether. Always someone off the wall (pun not intended), especially on Twitter.

Let's face it, Drew is my friend, but he can barely keep the attention of Angela to whom I would definitely consider making love to, in almost any other circumstance. If Angela and I ever had the chance, I would have made that relationship work. She's smart and clever, and this rarity—she's kind. This whole friendship and loyalty framework is overrated because I've been thinking about Angela all night instead of the cosmic shift at work in which Drew somehow trumped me out of another opportunity that I believe I deserved. All right, I don't really deserve the chance to interview Adrian Gerd Wahl because here I am obsessing over and desiring a woman much more than my career or lack thereof. And one published, nonfiction book hardly counts, particularly one that does not even earn me even a modest living. Initially, however, that one little memoir put me ahead, gave me some gravitas and instant credibility in this bubble. It's what made Drew crazy: Ian Frost is published, but now Drew can turn it on me. The opportunity to get inside Wahl's head. I have already composed a list of questions and a subset, leading to some revelation. I so wanted this opportunity.

Want translates to nothing, however. I feel fraudulent sometimes, but I certainly can't reveal that to Drew or to Angela, even to Gillian who is my cheerleader at work, in case Angela, not Gillian, is interested in me more than she seems to be letting on. I caught her looking at me recently; at least, I think she was staring at me, but who knows? Maybe she was staring ahead without seeing me, or maybe she was looking at me and thinking, "What a weirdo." I used to be able to read women better. I used to have no problem with girls and then women, but one kind of paralysis seems to lead to another.

I try not to blame this inertia on the city because New York is nothing if not alive every second even when death is in the streets. But I feel like an alien here, a transplant, a foreigner struggling in a city of foreigners who all seem to feel more at home than me. After leaving Iowa, I expected life and career to come easily: jobs, rewards, and instead, there were lines and dismissals: lack of notice in a city that thrives on everyone being noticed for five minutes. Even publishing a book didn't do it. The one validation I thought I had amounts to nothing much. Of course, this rigged scale only seems so dismal in comparison to Gerd Wahl. If I try to stand on a scale with Tom Hayes or Drew Levin on the other side, I come out fine. Why is it always a competition with writers? Why can't we just be pleased for one another and leave it at that?

Drew always tells me that he turned down an opportunity to study at the Iowa Writers' Workshop, that enclave from which I seem to have emerged unbroken yet scarcely published. Then I picked up this quirky book, *We Wanted to be Writers* with its rather brutal, strangely funny appraisal of the workshop environs, those foxholes reserved for paradoxically smart fools and gargantuan egos. I wish I still knew that arrogant bastard, the one I used to be. I miss him sometimes. I know Drew's lying about the Workshop, but he still feels more truthful to me than my recollections as a student in those daily competitions. I want to tell my friend at work that I'm done with clashes over the imagined race, that he won, but then I'd be dishonest. It's impossible to be done with competition in this society in which competitiveness is not only economic but psychosocial. Even New York's beggars in the street are competing with one another. They get pretty freaking creative, too. Costumes of the beggar could be out of some Shakespearean tragedy. Yet, there is a real tragedy to it, as well, not lost to anyone paying attention.

But, damn, I wanted that interview with Wahl. Maybe only to meet him, listen to him, find out where his head is; then again, he would probably suggest that I could find that out by reading his work. I don't know if I even like his fiction, but it is compelling, and I had entered his latest novel, wandered in and couldn't find my way out for a while. His fiction, unlike his essays, unsettled me if I admit to it. Is that what all of us are searching for? A reader to wander in our words for a while and leave unsettled, still thinking about them, unable to leave those symbols behind?

With every page I turn, I'm confronted with another good writer, sometimes a great one. Who knew about somebody named Toni Mirosevich? But then, there is this essay "The Datura" that I can't stop thinking about, with images like notes on that jazz horn to which he refers. Or, let's be honest, who knows Brian Jay Stanley even though you probably should if you appreciate good writers? Brian relates order through disorder until my head is spinning with his "Taxonomy of Disorder." I don't even know if it's encouraging or disheartening to discover this many fine writers making towers, whole mini-civilizations with language at the going rates of poverty, maybe $15 for a blog post, $50 for a page. Unless you're a known entity, then you might be looking at $250 to $1,000 or more for an article or story.

Who knew that being good at this highly skilled enterprise would not be worth the price of a pair of shoes worn by a pro athlete? They pay athletes well because everyone wants to see them hit the ball further than physics would suggest the human body is capable of, of dunking a basketball by flying both vertically and horizontally as if from a loaded mechanism not from bones, tendons, and muscles. What do writers have to offer? "Words... words... words," as Hamlet said. Just so many words. Only the key to linking our humanity, past to our present, demonstrate our higher order thinking skills, separating us from what exactly? Apparently, writers are not particularly valued because people don't seem to read anymore, or at least the pool of readers is drying up.

Screw this whole idea of being a writer. There are only a few occupations that I find truly heroic, none of which I am remotely qualified for: a pilot, a firefighter, and a doctor, but only if the doctor is working in some remote clinic halfway around the world saving lives while someone is writhing in agony on a gurney, and the doctor calmly and steadily attends to the deep slices in the skin and muscle or sooths the fevers of cholera, or spasms from Ebola, operating through constellations of the body's ills and scars. And the pilot I admire, he's not a commercial airline pilot; no, he flies small craft or old clunky early types covered in cotton or cellulose. This pilot knows how to read the wind and horizon, flies without instruments, cheating death every time he lands in a storm; hell, every time he lands at all, his eyes and steady nerves his best instruments. Of course, I'm too nervous to take up flying, but maybe I will anyway.

Wahl is, or rather was, a writer, neither a pilot nor a field doctor, but he came across like both, all that daring with calm nerves, aloof as he soared over head. Writing was what we do; nothing heroic there in the community. Stayed up late, chewed pen tips, scrawled out words on scraps of paper before finding our way to technology, barely touching highly responsive keys where Hemingway once hunted and pecked on his Halda portable, the typewriter that recently went up for auction, as if somehow this ancient technology would still hold the old Hemingway magic of those abbreviated, virile sentences. Strange to think that one sentence is masculine and another feminine, but the comment feels true even if viewed as sexist. Thinking about Hemingway's typewriter made me want to go out and buy a relic even though I knew I would never use it. If I had the extra, I would have purchased his Halda at auction, set it up on my desk, and let it inspire me. Not Wahl. He would never have wanted Hemingway's typewriter or word constructs.

Wahl is no copy, and yes, he is heroic. Very few writers have this aura stick to them, and I was not one of the chosen few. To be honest, I was sure that publishing my first book would do the trick, relieve the pain of doubt that persists, but my barely noticed text sits on a shelf growing dusty and mocking me: "You thought publishing would lead to other opportunities?" Even ordering extra copies of my book seemed pitiful, waiting for a paltry royalty check. I would have made more in tips as a waiter in a restaurant on a given weekend night than I did on my book. All of this is so damned depressing that if I were inclined, I might have contemplated suicide, but I'm not inclined to think that way. I like living, even in all its ugly, unredeemable mess. I only want to know how I was more confident at 15 than at 30. No progression.

If, however, I forget about my insecurities for a few minutes, come back to the desire to reveal the enigma, those "old verities and truths of the heart, the old universal truths lacking which any story is ephemeral and doomed—love and honor and pity and pride and compassion and sacrifice," as Faulkner said or, rather, wrote, then I might find a way to live.

Would I have been a better choice than Levin? I wanted to know about Wahl's processes, either to humanize the legend or enlarge the aura built up around him. Perhaps, to destroy those myths entirely. That was the power of the interview, and Drew was never going to get it right. Would he know when to press the question and when to pull back before Wahl closed up on him? Not likely. Even if Levin does manage subtlety, I was not going to get those notes, and that was galling, wrong, but I had to accept it.

The New Yorker seldom, if ever, publishes fiction written about writers, but they would be the perfect vehicle for my portrait of a writer we were obsessed with, or, pardon me, a writer with whom we were all obsessed—all being part of that handful of writers and readers left in the world, but I can't help wondering if Angela is thinking about me right now? There is no reason on earth why she should be. Those two are practically married, but I remember her looking my way.

Why do women do that if they are happy with the guy? Guys are at least we're fairly transparent about it. Here I am singing Sinatra's *New York, New York*, and I can't carry a tune. Where is that Sinatra CD? Probably loaned it to Tom or Shwetak.

I had to admit my fixation with this highbrow rag *The New Yorker*. As if their editors were the arbiters of contemporary taste, held the definitions of literary worth. What makes it acceptable for them to declare writing and writers as off-limits? Do they think no one but writers will be interested in writers writing? Okay, maybe they've got a point, but who reads more than other writers? To be honest, however, I'm not getting any further with any of the other lit magazines either. I'm trying like hell to be practical, to forget theory, the high-minded stuff we were fed in college and grad school for years, and work on practical.

So, I'm in New York and nothing is happening, yet everything is happening around me. Maybe you have to be born here to get it or have it find you. But I know that's ridiculous, too. Still, I feel as if transplants like me never seem to fully fit in, but everyone here is a transplant if you go back a little; everyone and no one suits this city. It is. We are. It likely would have made no difference if we had gone to L.A. or San Francisco or Chicago. Maybe if I wasn't hungry, and I remembered that I hadn't eaten supper.

I dropped the metaphorical hunger and realized that I really was hungry. I grabbed my jacket and set out down the street. Already the smells suggested Greek cuisine for dinner, but I was craving Italian garlic at that moment; not pizza but those greens with whole chunks of garlic infusing them, escarole, yeah. I should stop thinking about food and women and about my lack of recent successes as a writer and focus. Gillian is crushing on me. But Shwetak is in love with her, and Shwetak deserves a break in this life even if it comes at my expense.

Seventeen

Stealing Gerd's Words

Turned out, I, Drew Levin had a secret longing. Sitting in the midst of papers strewn about, attempts to pull it all together: rejection notices neatly filed away. Not really. I never file nasty notes or even outright rejections. Rather, I put them on top of a bookshelf for a few days then toss them out. I knew that what I was looking for in this deluge of words was not accolades, nor the writer's life I thought I desperately desired but simply, banally, yet significantly, some kind of answer. When I dropped the pretense, in no one's company but my own, what I really wanted from all this craziness was what every other writer worth his salt has wanted. Gerd's frightening brilliance and insights, buried deeply in piles of his verbosity, like the innocent discovered underneath rubble from an earthquake, would finally reveal something of import. What was I looking for from him? I had read his last novel twice, and I intended to read it again because I was sure that I had missed another level. Everyone around me seemed to understand what I did not.

An early reviewer of Wahl's work had made an allusion to "The Emperor's New Clothes," but that critic received so many negative comments, fallout about his critique and obvious jealousy oozing out of his every sentence, the entire line of questioning Wahl's fiction was shut down. I still wondered, though. In the middle of trying to write two novels, I'd gotten lost and abandoned them; calling social services would be appropriate if such a safety net existed for symbolically lost writers. At least I wasn't showing my jealousy like Tom Hayes.

I had this dream, more like a daydream because I was directing it somehow, this dream in which I stole Gerd's undiscovered tome, the one he was still working on before his death, and no one knew about it but him. I was in his study, that chaotic and carnivorous room where his papers lay like virgins. Of course, I steal them, his words, but not for the reason they would all assume, not even for the reason I initially thought I would take them but for the fact of what I might discover. There was hidden nobility beneath my crass surface. I imagined how I would feel for that one instant in which I would assume possession of his words, his voice, and his ideas. If I had come up with something on that other level, everything might be different.

Spiders running on walls again, only this time, they are larger and running everywhere, threatening me even before my discovery. In this dream, walls are closer than I remember them being, wood rougher with long splinters broken away from surface. It is impossible to touch any object. I try to stay in the center of the room, but centers keep shifting, moving left, and my feet can't seem to find solid floor. Still, I push on, force myself into a position where I confront pages, those personalities as yet undiscovered, larger than I have seen before, stacked and ominous. Why threatening? If I reach back, I might see what I have created for myself.

They are mine now. I feel their metaphoric weight, not merely the volume of paper, and I am stumbling to try to reach my car before someone finds out that I have broken into Gerd's cabin by the lake, accidentally knocking over a candle on my hasty way out; perhaps it wasn't really accidental. Dreams seem both deliberate yet out of control. Backtracking through chambers barely articulated as thought. Freud would have a few words to say about my dreams, I'm sure. The fire starts in the library, taking off rapidly. Of course, on waking, I believe that I would have stopped and gone back to let his dogs out because even in my most corrupt, detestable state, I can't imagine allowing his beautiful dogs to burn to death out of my selfish desires. I like dogs, after all. I like Gerd's dogs even if they make mine look less than. I have trouble opening his door, and Gerd's champions are leaping at me along with flames licking at my face, when it suddenly springs forward, and I'm awake.

Angela slips into our bedroom and undresses slowly for me. This is another dream where I expect it to get good. We make love with his words, not mine, all over the room. She is quoting me, or him, but she believes the phrases, constructs she sees emerging are mine. Then, she is smiling horrifically: her face looks plastic and is changing shape. Now, even our lovemaking descends into nightmare. Gerd's words loom over us in amorphous but threatening shapes.

I wake again or reframe my conscious thoughts, shake my head, and fall back on the pillow. I can't find my way back into that dream. Who would willingly enter nightmarish visions? I never really felt the elation of possession or of understanding wrapped up in Wahl's words. No sense of fulfillment, and I'm left hollowed, not hallowed. Why return to this dream of stealing? It starts in envy and ends in horror again. When I self-consciously re-examine my words or thoughts that become full sentences, disgust keeps tumbling out of my conscious mind. I notice a profusion of "I"s beginning a pattern in some ego-driven language that suggests I am creator, actor, strategist of ruinous language, and I start thinking about how self-centered the English language makes us or permits us to be. Then I re-think: "to be" and Hamlet and actions happening to a man and not the other way around. This other stream of conscious eruption rather than natural flow has ameliorated my lust and greed. Where would it have taken me if I had followed that stream, successfully stolen Gerd Wahl's novel even in dream sequence?

Gerd turns me out before I can get far, an intruder in his kingdom not permitted to remain long enough to gain his trust, so I would never know. I was never allowed to be cognizant of having created words like that, what creation felt like and accolades for tropes, to experience some further measure of validation as writer, or what it was like to discover more in those symbols marking the page. I hadn't even found meaning in his words that were supposed to be mine.

This was not theft; it was recurring torment and one I could not share or confide in to anyone, even to my forgiving, benevolent, merciful Angela. I had a dirty secret after all.

Eighteen

Tom Calls in Ellison, Scott, and Marshall, not Ornal

What could I expect if I invited them over? Some kind of reductive "conversation" in which everyone is lauding Wahl again? Honestly, I couldn't take any more talk about how amazing Gerd Wahl was, how revelatory his work. If I could turn their attention to a new enterprise, my company concept? Possibly something might come out of the think tank I was trying to create. Marshall was the one I had to convince. The others would get behind Marshall if he found my proposal intriguing. I was not asking Ian because he's too high-minded, too critical of my ideas. There was also the distinct possibility he was seeing Marie.

After the absurdities of greetings, I launched: "I can't write anything longer than a few pages. Nothing worth shit. Not Gerd's work I'm talking about: mine."

"You sound a little desperate there, Tom," Marshall said, attempting not to laugh.

"I keep coming back to the night we found out about Wahl's death," Scott said.

"But we have to move on," I reminded them.

"Whatever that means," Marshall deadpanned.

No one spoke for a few seconds, which was long for a group of writers. I called in Ellison Espada, Scott Williams, and Marshall Funkhouser. I thought we would meet and brainstorm a marketing plan for me specifically and for them if it worked out, aware that this would appear rather self-centered. I had to figure out a way to make it seem as if this concept involved a group benefit. I did not invite Ornal, which was tricky, considering the fact that Ellison lived with her.

Ornal wasn't even attractive, with her boy-cut, blue and sometimes gold hair, her weird outfits, body piercings, and skinny boy body. What does Ellison see in her? Scott and Marshall, however, get along better than any married couple I had ever met. I was actually surprised those two weren't married yet since gay marriage is legal.

"Where's Marie?" Marshall asked.

Just when I had begun to form a plan, the image of Marie popped up. She is still gorgeous, sensuous, unforgiving, and a royal bitch from less than royal origins. Trying to get her out of my head where she was still dwelling, I thought maybe I needed to go out and meet someone new. But first, I had to have a place to live. Technically, Marie had already kicked me out, but she allowed me to stay in her place until I found another apartment. A temporary arrangement, she said, and I have to take the couch.

For some reason, I still listen to her. If our lives had turned out differently, I might have stayed with Marie. I don't remember exactly when I started to hate her more than I loved her. "She's not here. We're not."

"So, what is the big idea before us?" asked Ornal as soon as she walked in, which royally pissed me off since I had not wanted her. Ornal sure wasn't going to start leading the discussion. I shot a disapproving look at Ellison who acted as if he didn't know about her invitation, perfectly indifferent to my silent protest. I decided to be magnanimous and not kick her out.

"Look, I want everyone to be involved in conceptualizing. And I don't want to define the concept too precisely at first."

Scott tossed his flame-red scarf over my already overloaded coat rack by the door, looked excited rather than annoyed. "What exactly are we conceptualizing?"

"A writing/marketing/publishing group that uses social media to move our meme," I said before Ornal could start talking again. This much I had already worked out.

"Our meme? What's our meme? Come to think of it, what exactly is a meme, and how does one move one?" Ornal laughed.

Ellison shot her a mildly scolding look, as if that was sufficient when I wanted to strangle her. "Don't be bitchy, woman. Let him finish," Ellison said with far too much kindness.

"Look who's calling who a bitch," she shot back, for some reason looking at me.

"Whom," Ellison corrected.

"O.M.G.," said Ornal, "see what I mean? I have to live with this guy." She then did the unthinkable and pecked him on the cheek. Ellison smiled in triumph.

I decided to ignore everything that came out of Ornal's mouth. "You know those brothers Vegard and Bård Ylvisåker, Ylvis? Well, I was thinking we could form a group and market ourselves like that. The big idea that spreads from person to person via our web connections will also be our promotional vehicle for our product."

"Ylvis? I'm sorry, I don't know them, and admit I'm a little confused as to product," said Marshall, leaning forward from the best chair in the room, the one I had planned on sitting in until he plopped there first.

"That's why we need to brainstorm," I said, getting a little excited about the fact that at least Marshall showed interest.

Ornal jumped in: "Ylvis is a comedy group. I don't think you qualify. And what product could you possibly have that would interest the masses?" Ellison far too politely squeezed her hand.

"The product is our writing and our advice." I said, trying to bring everyone back.

"In other words, the big idea is that you're going to market a big idea with words about a product of words although none of us are comedians or musicians; we don't have a real concept to sell, and we're marketing a product that already exists in the billions on the Internet?"

"Ornal, will you please let the man finish one thought?" Ellison was taking my side, or I would have thrown them both out.

"Pinteresting," Scott said suddenly. "We could jump on Pinterest, have boards with categories for the project, and keep everyone apprised of our progress. I love Pinterest."

"That's one idea. Exactly," I said. "And we're not marketing a big idea; we're marketing our skills. The product is our ability to write well and provide instruction or advice to others."

"Ok, I love pinning, too, but I use it to get style ideas. I still don't see what you're organizing or collecting?" Ornal persisted. "How is our 'ability' a product?" Ornal, leaving Ellison, was circling behind me like a buzzard.

"Our social system of writers; our brand is our writer's collective." There was stunned silence for a moment. Marshall scratched his beard and chin, and Scott reached for his scarf as if chilled until he realized that he had already taken it off.

"Tom, I'm not exactly a social media illiterate, but I'll be honest here. I don't know what you're talking about," said Marshall. "The concept seems far too nebulous."

"Is this the moment where everyone gasps after discovering the emperor has no clothes?"

"That's it, Ornal!" I yelled, standing up just as she came around the back of my chair again. "Get out. Get out now! I never asked you to be part of this group, anyway."

Ornal's jaw dropped. Ellison, unfortunately, came to her defense. "I asked her to come with me! If that's a problem for you, then you've got a problem with me, too. We'll both leave."

"Apparently, it fucking is," I yelled.

"Let's go," said Ellison, turning for the door.

Before they left, Ornal looked back over her shoulder, "You're a fucking idiot, Tom, and clearly void of any real ideas.

"And you're a fucking stupid bitch slut," I yelled back, clearly past the point of return. Ellison pivoted in the doorway, took a couple of steps forward, then hit me. The force surprised me. I fell backward, and Scott partly caught my fall. One or both of us knocked over my books on the coffee table and upended the drinks. I was more emotionally hurt than physically. Ellison surveyed the damage without a hint of triumph. He stood for a moment longer, then left without saying another word.

Ornal opened the door again and stuck her head back inside, "I forgot to say, you're a misogynist, sexist pig," then she slammed my door, or Marie's door. At that moment, I was particularly glad that Marie was not at home to witness my humiliation.

Marshall extended his hand and helped up Scott first, and then both helped me to my unsteady feet. I could feel my nose gushing blood.

"She didn't need to be repetitive; I mean sexist and misogynist?" Scott said before asking me, "Are you okay?"

"Fine. I'm fucking fine. Son-of-a-bitch and his dumb fucking bitch." I rubbed my face, smearing blood, and felt for the couch to sit back down. My upper lip was swelling.

"There, there," said Scott. "Let's not lose our cool or disparage anyone further."

Marshall went to the refrigerator to collect ice and wrapped it in a dish towel that was hanging over the stove handle where Marie always put a fresh one. "Let's calm down. I think your idea needs a little more conceptualizing," he said, presenting me with the icepack.

"Well, that's kind of why I called you."

Marshall and Scott looked at one another and started laughing before abruptly stopping again. "Okay, we'll try this," said Marshall.

"What are you writing now, Tom?" asked Scott.

"I can't write shit," I confessed, gingerly touching the wrapped, rock-hard ice cubes to my lip and nose.

"We know that isn't true," said Scott. "Let's start from a basis in reality."

"No, it really is. I haven't written anything decent in ages, and every time I try, this hideous monster appears on the page." I looked up at Scott who was standing over me with a concerned expression. "Not Ornal. Only an empty page"

"Oh, that hideous monster," said Marshall sarcastically. "What do you care what Ornal says anyway? You get too worked up over her. I hate to say it, but it's almost as if you are in love."

"Absolutely not!" I protest then concede, "It's because she's, she's partially right," I confessed. Thank God no one referred to Marie kicking me out at that point, or I would have broken down like a baby.

"Stop worrying if what you write is the best piece ever written and focus on making it the best you can write that day." Scott was always helpful, but I didn't want to hear that.

"Why didn't I think of that?" My sarcasm was thick.

"Actually, that's not bad advice," Marshall said.

"Thank you," said Scott, who I could see felt vindicated.

"Sorry, I don't need advice right now." I had to lean back because my nose had suddenly become a font of blood.

"Oh, dear," said Scott, getting paper towels from the kitchen.

"I thought that's why you got us all together? For advice," Marshall took my head in his big hands and lifted it upright again. "You shouldn't lean back," he advised.

"Brainstorming ideas, not advice. There's a difference. Besides, I need some fucking dough. I've got to find a place to live."

Scott and Marshall exchanged glances. "Oh, dear," said Scott, handing me a fresh towel.

"No, I'm really, I'm broke, and I have to get out of this apartment." It was all I could do to keep from sobbing.

"This apartment isn't that bad," said Marshall.

"Marie kicked me out, but I'm still here because I don't know where to go, and I've used every damn excuse I can conjure up to get a little more out of my parents, but they aren't buying. They keep telling me they're on a fixed income, and I've had a great education at their expense. Is it my fault they adopted me when most people think about retiring?"

"I didn't know you were adopted," said Scott.

"Surprise," I said.

"I thought you had a job?" asked Marshall.

"Had a job. Lost it. Apparently, I don't have a serviceable skill and not any good friends."

"Really, Tom?" Marshall and Scott said simultaneously.

"Well, I mean other than you two."

Marshall took out a pad and pen. "All right. Let's brainstorm like you wanted, Tom. We'll figure something out."

Scott brightened. "Oh, yes, we will."

I leaned in. "I hate that bitch Ornal."

"We have already established that less than helpful fact," Marshall nodded, "but we need to move past grievances."

"She can be a bit of a pain," said Scott. I tried to smile but it hurt too much.

"Finally!" I said, my voice muffled through the towel.

"We need a website," Marshall offered "And an outline for what should be on the website, honing in on exactly the specific skills you or we are marketing as writers."

"And then?" I must have started to look hopeful.

"That's the hard part," Marshall said.

"What if she's right?"

"What?" Scott asked.

"What if Ornal is right, and I really don't have anything marketable to offer. I mean, I'm no comedian," I said.

"I don't know about that," said Scott. "You made us laugh today."

"Thanks, I think," I said, trying to wrestle out a thought.

"We don't need to be comedians. Look. We know how to write. Let's figure out a niche and start blogging about it." Marshall looked up with an optimistic smile.

"Don't you already have a blog?"

Marshall nodded. "Yes, but that's for my students. It's part of a course I'm teaching. I can't mix this in."

"That eliminates my next suggestion."

"Which is?" asked Scott.

"That we develop a site for the best curse and swear words and phrases in the city. But you can't be teaching kids on one site and cursing on another."

"I'm not sure," said Marshall, entertaining the idea. "If the site offered a perspective on how slang is driven by culture, perhaps a study in psychology and how language functions as emotional intensifier, leaning about how we flounder in communicating our deeply rooted passions, it might have some redeemable, even educational value."

"You're serious here, right?" I asked.

"I think so. And I believe I read that curse words have become the most commonly used words in the English language. We're talking lots of global repetitions. No reason we couldn't make this academic. It would still have to be unaffiliated with the college. I don't want to mix the two."

"I don't know," offered Scott. "I recall that there are already a lot of websites or pages devoted to this topic."

"And academics don't make," I said.

"Hey, I'm surviving," Marshall said. Scott patted him on the back. "Well, together we are surviving."

"Sorry. Maybe make it specific to New Yorkers. Like Brandon Stanton's *Humans of New York*, we'd have "Curses of New Yorkers. Feature individuals as well as individual curses."

"I like that," said Scott.

"Then we'd have to weed out swearing and cursing propagated by those who are not native to New York which limits the number pretty severely," Marshall mused.

"So, we're back to square one?" I asked.

"Swear one," said Scott without cracking a smile.

"Terrible language play," added Marshall. "Maybe only temporarily, though. The dynamics could apply to anyone passing through New York, so the website features curses heard in New York." The three of us sat motionless without saying another word for several minutes.

"Anybody have anything? Anything?" I asked.

"Isn't that from Seinfeld?" Scott offered.

Nineteen

Julia's Last Letter

Julia never mailed that last letter, and when she opened the desk drawer, her letter was there, startling. If she had sent that missive, would her last communication have changed the outcome, caused Adrian to reconsider, put his gun down? What would she have said if she had been in the bedroom and come into his living room to find that he had a gun to his head? Wondering if she could have somehow prevented the tragedy, she suddenly felt a chill again. He might have turned the shotgun on her first.

It was her letter not his. Still, she opened the letter tentatively. By the time she had written it, she had dispensed with salutations.

I wondered what you thought of the man who made quilt art out of old book covers, crudely stitching the fraying fabric? You looked long at them but said little. Did you like his artwork? Did you think defacing the old books was somehow wasteful? I am thinking about them still and you. Yes, I remember Florence.

Yes, I am hopelessly in love with you.

He had appeared at her door very early one morning, the call waking her. There was scarcely time to pack her bags because they had plane tickets to Rome, and immediately after landing in Italy they headed to Florence by train, all spontaneity, but it was fortunate that she had renewed her passport recently, she told him. On the plane, he confessed he hated flying as she listened to a woman in a seat across the aisle complain and then snore loudly all night. When they landed six hours later—the pilot said they had caught a tailwind—Adrian hurried her to a train, lifting her luggage then his own, stuffing the bags into crowded bins before they found their purchased seats taken by a mother and her child.

"These are our seats," she tried to reason with the unreasonable young woman, who acted as if she did not understand. Gerd shook his head at her not the mother and led her to a passageway between cars where they perched near steps; she was angry until finally resting her head on his shoulder. The conductor came around and took their tickets, motioning for them to take their proper seats.

Gerd was sometimes thoughtful of other people, but why not put her first at least some of the time, she wondered? After all of it, the night flight, the crowded day train, the fatigue and cramped quarters, the sticky hot smells of sweat, they were finally walking along the Ponte Vecchio, looking out over the bridge, past locks left by lovers. She wanted to place a lock for them, too, until he told her that those locks were damaging the old bridges. They stood staring at the brown river and across to muted ochre and reds in the buildings lining the shores, colors filtered by mist and time. When, suddenly, Adrian bent down.

She thought he was about to propose but instead, he held her face in his large hands and kissed her.

"Perfect," he said.

And then they flew home. She never mentioned her disappointment or mistaken assumption.

Reading her letter again, she moved from one beautiful moment to pain.

Last night in Boston, the snow wouldn't stop, but you left with your coat open and without your hat. I will hold it for you. I know you have others, but this was your favorite, I think.

The snow provoked, everyone sloshing through its deep, melting ice rivers. Still, it was an adventure at least in the sense we got our feet wet before running back inside for the warmth. I miss you.

***

It didn't seem possible that her letter contained so little substance, about that dream weekend in Italy and the other space in which they mingled with other writers from around the country at the writers' conference. Adrian could be gracious with people and, then, seem to despise or have an aversion to them. She wasn't even certain he did not feel that way about her at times. Even if she read her letter over and over, no revelation arrived, no questions were answered, and she leaned her head back in an agony of doubt. She should, at least, have sent that last letter. Why had she held onto it?

Suddenly, it became urgent that she talk to that writer from *Music & Culture* magazine, the one who got the last interview Adrian had given. Drew Levin, that was the man's name, she had written it down. That writer had interviewed Adrian. What more might he have to say? Oh, God, she thought, I've got to find him.

Before falling asleep, Julia remembered Adrian quoting Houdini one night while they were stargazing above Skaneateles Lake. He repeated the line. She wrote it down for some reason even though the quotation did not seem particularly important at the time. Getting up in the middle of the night, Julia searched, until she found that line: "Never have I forgotten the fact that 'life is but an empty dream.'"

Twenty

Ian Considers How the World Treats Us

Here we are again in the middle of the night, trying to figure it out, through the most ridiculous form of shorthand communication about why what we do is so important to us if not to anyone else. I already responded to Drew's comment, then threw out one of my own. Drew and I were always competing even when no one else seemed to be aware.

> Ian Frost, Gillian Keating, Drew Lev
> 8 recipients
>
> Drew Levin
> Thoughts
> on writing
> and what
> we do?
> Why? MMS
> 1:16 AM
>
> Ellison Espada

Ian, do
you plan
on staying
up all
night?
Because
this is not
a short
conversation. MMS
1:16 AM

Marshall Funkhouser
I'm not
up for a
dissertation
but texting
on existential
or pedestrian? Let's
go. Survival. MMS
1:17 AM

Drew Levin
Processing,
raising
questions,
meaning of
existence
or existential—
just life. MMS
1:18 AM

Ornal Aude
"Writing is
like sex.
First you do
it for love,
then you do
it for your
friends, and
then you do
it for money."
V. Woolf MMS
2:20 AM

Tom Hayes
Writing
nothing
like sex.
Not V.
Woolf,
incorrectly
attributed. MMS
2:20 AM

Ornal Aude
Google
would disagree
with you
about
quotation,
as well as
about

writing. MMS
2:20 AM

Tom Hayes
Have you even read Woolf? Doesn't sound like her for a reason. MMS
2:21 AM

Ornal Aude
Go back to insecurities. Prince Hamlet masks. Cleverness with language Feigning madness. Searching for truth. MMS
2:21 AM

Tom Hayes
Feigning madness? He killed himself! Gerd?

156 | Socrates is Dead Again

Hamlet?
Oh, quotation about writing and sex was French writer Molnar. MMS
2:22 AM

Ornal Aude
Have to have the last word, don't you? MMS
2:23 AM

***

The evening after they returned from Marie's apartment, Ellison said to Ornal, "Damn, girl, you have to stop provoking people."

"What? You should talk!" Ornal threw her bag across the room for emphasis. They both heard something break.

"You're going to get me killed one of these days."

"What? I'm not! Do I really? Not that often."

"Only all the time."

"Tom's a wimp. He couldn't hurt"

"I'm not talking about Tom. I'm talking about you. There will be some big-ass white dude who's going to insult you, and you'll get into it with him, and the next moment, I'm lying on concrete with my head smashed in, brain-dead or, if I'm lucky, just dead."

Ornal slumped on the couch's arm, her eyes welling, lip quivering. "God, I don't want you brain-dead or any other kind of dead." She dug her fingers into her palms.

"Then you've got to let go. Don't you think we attract enough attention as it is?"

"You mean?"

"Yeah, I mean I'm one smartass, good-looking Nigga and you're a hot, wired, feminist, white chick with blue hair and rings in her nose. That will do it for most. Could we just not provoke everyone?"

"I'm threatening?"

"Threatening as in, your confident, smart presence is enough to make a lot of men feel less than, and less than is a dangerous place to go with some individuals. You don't need to challenge them all on a daily basis."

"You don't want me to stand up for myself?"

"I do! That's one of the things I love about you, but you don't have to make every interaction a fight. You know, pick your battles, that's all."

"I do."

"Too many of them because we have battles that are important, maybe ones even worth dying for, but not everything every damn day is worth dying for."

"Not the one today, you mean."

"Definitely not that one. And c'mon. Tom Hayes? Really? That sad, drug-addicted mess. He's a relatively harmless misogynist."

"Harmless misogynist? Do you think those two words really go together?"

"I qualified it with 'relatively.' See, right now, you're trying to start a battle with me."

"I didn't mean to. I cause you a lot of trouble, don't I?"

"Honey, that's an understatement. You're like a cop car, constantly spinning red, then blue white blue white, sirens blaring, speeding down streets. It's a lot of excitement even for the dudes in the car but sometimes way too much. Too much."

"Is this our breakup scene?"

"What? Woman? What do you think I'm trying to do here? No. This is the slow down scene. I just want you to notice. I need some mental space to write, to think, to breathe, to live. How the hell am I supposed to, *'forge in the smithy of my soul the uncreated consciousness of my race?'*"

"So, if you get to be James Joyce in *Portrait,* who am I?"

"I don't know. You're an original."

"Do you really think you're the next James Joyce?"

"Hell, no. I'm no Joyce, nor James Baldwin whom I would much rather be, but I'd like to create something, anything of worth at this point. And I need a little quiet and calm to create."

"Because I'm such a problem, you can't even write?"

"Look, I know women have it tough, too, and have been stomped on in this country as well as all over the world, but you have to realize I face this white oppressive wall every damn day, and yes, we have to stand and fight sometimes, do what we have to do, and take whatever punishment comes, but not every damn day. That's all I'm saying."

"Because?"

"It's exhausting, and we can't fight when we really need to if we're always at war. And you scare me a little."

"I do?"

"I don't know if I will always be able to save us."

"I know I'm exhausting. I'm sorry I caused a scene at Tom's, or I guess it's really Marie's. I'm sorry you had to hit him. I don't know why Tom drives me crazy. He didn't want me there. I could tell the minute we walked in. He was the one provoking a fight."

"So, let it go sometimes, that's all. Why do you care what he thinks? Someone might even think you're in love with the guy."

"No! I don't really. I don't know why you love me."

"I don't either." He laughed.

Ornal jumped up, and he caught her before they both fell over, and then they were pulling off each other's clothes, reaching around one another, and covering their bodies with kisses.

Twenty-one

Gillian Asks Shwetak to Dinner On the Night Ian Asks Out Gillian

Everyone thinks I'm in love with Ian, and I'm not entirely sure on that account, but the man I am most interested in, if we don't consider the dead Gerd Wahl, is the most honorable and adorable Shwetak Misra. Whenever I think about him, I keep ruminating on the meaning of his surname: honorable, although a play on words in English comes embarrassingly close to miserable. I will never share this last musing with him. I'm sure he would not find it humorous. He is, however, the most honorable man I know, but I am certain that he thinks of me as nothing more than a friend. There is no indication in his gestures, his smile, or his words to suggest that he is attracted to me, but I'm persisting because it's my nature to be persistent in the face of long odds.

If this attempt at courtship fails, I might be risking the friendship, too, but I've never been one to shy away from disaster.

I don't know much about his family or history, but I recognize that there are cultural, ethnic, geographic, historical, and religious differences between us: nothing major, at least.

If I expected him to leap up and embrace me, I'm not sure, but I was surprised by his nonchalance about my proposal. Well, it felt close to indifference. I didn't say anything remotely clever, rather, asked him if he wanted to go out with me, like that night, and he said, "Sure." I didn't dare to tell him that I'd been practicing how I was going to ask him out for two weeks, spent another week looking for a new dress that would be short enough but not too short. It was blue, complementing my eyes, he told me politely. So, it turns out he noticed.

It would be lovely if this was the beginning of an uncomplicated and happy love story except the fact that Ian asked me to a new gallery opening the following afternoon, and I said "yes," until I realized that he meant something more than going as friends. Then everything got extremely uncomfortable when he heard that Shwetak and I were going to dinner the night before the opening. A significant amount of standing and staring, eye-avoidance, a couple of throat clearings, and unnecessary hand movements with coughing between the three of us ensued before I decided to say something. "I'm sorry, Ian. I thought you knew."

"Knew what?" he persisted in making me feel particularly awful because at that point I'm sure he knew exactly what I was talking about in regard to Shwetak. I looked at Shwetak for help but was certain he would desert me, throwing me into extended humiliation.

"Gillian and I are an item," Shwetak said abruptly, surprising me, Ian, and himself, I think.

"An item? Really, Shwetak? I don't know if anyone is using that term 'item' anymore, but good for the two of you."

Obviously emboldened, Shwetak responded, "Yes, they are; in fact, 'itemized' in reference to couples is one of the hip terms on various forms of social media."

"Ok. I'll take your word for it." Suddenly Ian started laughing, and then we were all laughing, Shwetak nearly doubling over and holding his stomach.

"What's going on over there?" Drew asked, passing by, but Ian, Shwetak, and I were in no condition to explain our suddenly weird circumstance. Drew shook his head, shrugged, and left. Ian didn't tell him either. I finally had to confess to Drew at breakfast one morning that Shwetak and I were an "item." He was far less interested than Ian, however.

To be honest, here, the love knot was Gordian, far more than either Ian or Shwetak knew. I was pregnant. Not with Shwetak's child, as I wish I was, because we haven't even kissed yet let alone slept together, although I think we would have a beautiful baby. In the future, when I do have Shwetak's child, I hope she has Shwetak's eyes because those lashes go on forever.

The developing fetus currently in the first few days of my second trimester is also not Ian's, but Ian Frost would make a great sperm donor with his brains and good looks, even if he's a little too tall and slightly hunched over, with oversized black glasses that make him look too smart, like the guy in movies the girl is supposed to fall in love with but doesn't. He doesn't seem to care about looks, but that's not the reason I don't fall in love with Ian. Sometimes you know you should be in love with someone but you can't do it. And then, there's that other guy, the one you definitely never should have slept with but got caught up in the moment.

Hello, son of mine; you're the product of a nearly forgotten past, a holiday fling with my old boyfriend, one who cruelly dropped me in high school by telling me he was sick. He said he couldn't go to Prom with me due to illness, then showed up at the dance with the girl with the biggest boobs in our class. Shannon had big hair, too. The rest I should keep to myself, such as how he said he didn't think I would come to the dance. He was sorry I saw him but not sorry for what he had done because he was in love with Shannon, and he had never actually loved me even though he told me he did numerous times. Ah, what am I thinking? I wouldn't really tell my child about this man who is his father, even in utero. I'm not sure what possessed me to have a few drinks with Seamus Brennan over the holidays then end up in his bed. He really hadn't changed at all, I discovered. Remember that guy everyone wanted to date in high school until they actually did go out with him?

I was surprised by Seamus's lack of emotional development, having stayed exactly the same as he was at 17, almost as if he was frozen in that hypersexual adolescent state of self-absorption. At first, it must have been endearing. Even false flattery gets you somewhere, and exciting, of course, all that energy. Then reality takes over. I don't know if I wanted revenge or for him to beg me for forgiveness, or if he was too hot to pass up in my inebriated state.

That's not exactly the way it happened, however. When I woke up with my dress on the floor along with the coverlet and sheets, he was already dressed and heading out the door.

"Lock it from the inside when you leave, babe," he said smiling irresistibly. "See you around sometime."

I started to look for coffee in his little flat but couldn't find any. I have to admit I didn't search too long, what with cockroaches scurrying back into hiding every time I moved a box. It didn't even look like he ate at his own place. I hadn't noticed how filthy it was the night before when he half-carried me into his bedroom. It's amazing how thick I can be. Of course, it was dimly lit, and I wasn't his housekeeper. He would probably make a good specimen for a scientific experiment. Unfortunately, I'd probably make a better specimen: the subject who does not learn from her mistakes.

Surprised, however, was not the right word to describe my reaction to finding out that I was pregnant: frightened, and stupefied come closer. What's more, I'm a good Catholic girl, or at least I was. The irony of it is that Seamus was my first and only sexual liaison other than that one guy a few years back, but he doesn't count because we were both drunk, and I never even got his name and promised myself that I wouldn't let anything like that happen again. It's hard to admit this to anyone, so it is generally something I keep to myself. I couldn't even tell my three brothers because they would have to kill Seamus.

I knew I was about to start showing even underneath these oversize jackets I wear at work. If Shwetak was ever going to fall for me, it was now or never. And it was not as if I hadn't thought about him that way. Really, I'd had a thing for Shwetak from the first day or at least the first week I saw him. What was puzzling and completely unanticipated was the fact that he said, "yes." I know it sounds as if I was trying to trap Shwetak into something. That would be completely, or at least partially, false. I fully intended to tell him about my pregnancy a few dates into our new relationship.

Spending a good amount of my time imagining dialogue with Shwetak in which I confess my pregnancy, and he lovingly tells me that he wants to raise my child as his own, I fell deeper into fantasy. Then I would have one of those awful conversations in my head where he says something like, "Oh, I can't believe you tried to trap me, you promiscuous whore, you." I realize that I should check to see if Shwetak is really Hindu or not, before I have these projections or decide to marry him, not because it would bother me if he were Hindu, but I should know a little more about his religion in order not to go around offending him. The worst part is, I don't need Shwetak to rescue me, but I'm only now realizing that I might have ruined a relationship with the one guy I actually want to be with.

Maybe I should quit work here and resign myself to going home to Brookline, but I don't think my parents would be thrilled, particularly with my belly extending like in *Alien*. And it would be a dreadful retreat. I try to imagine a scene where my parents accept me and my baby with joy, but that smacks in the face of reality. They were too damn glad to see me and my brothers leave after Christmas. My father said, "It's nice to finally have the house to ourselves again," about my mother and him enjoying each other, as if their children prevented them from having sex for 20 years.

Twenty-two

Drew's Second Chance

[Date: June 17th]
Notes from the interview: I determined to take better notes, beginning with more careful observations. His house (he called it a cabin) had been built sixty or seventy years earlier before the newer developments along the shoreline, camp style evident. There was, however, the feel of something old and solid in the wood beams, and I thought that Gerd's cabin would be standing after the new builds around it had succumbed to the next wave of development.

    I had to retrace my earlier steps. Before I even approached the great man's doorway, I noticed green everywhere as soon as I got out of the city and headed Upstate. Going through the Catskills, I entered a time-warp or the way you feel coming into a foreign country. The contrast of the crowded city compared to open space was striking with undeveloped hillsides, trees in such abundance that I suddenly wondered why we needed to conserve forests. Let the lumber companies have at it. By the time I reached Gerd's cabin on the lake, I felt like I was entering some immense botanical garden.

The man looked weary this time around, less intimidating. Gerd Wahl carried some sorrow about his shoulders and around the eyes, even in the way he held his large floured hands. [*Floured? What was this?*] The ego he manifested on my last visit seemed to have been pushed to the background.

GERD: Come in. [*He said warmly*] I've made bread.

DREW: You make bread? [*I tried not to sound incredulous but did. Of the various things I imagined this guy did to relax, baking was not anywhere on my list. This strange fact would definitely make it into my feature.*]

GERD: Only occasionally. [*The odor of fresh baked bread permeated the house, and the dogs were as excited as I was, only for different reasons. They were noticeably salivating.*]

DREW: Thank you for allowing me to interview you again. It's gracious. Whatever you want to talk about is fine with me. [*I meant this. I still couldn't believe that he called me back, bought into my half-sobbing plea to return for a better interview. He saved my job, maybe my career. Already, everything felt different than the first time, but it was still unsettling, even Gerd seemed like an altered man.*]

GERD: I can be a real bastard sometimes. Butter?

DREW: Ah, yes, I mean about the butter, and I happen to think you are very generous. [*He handed me a thick slice of still warm bread with melted butter on top, then set unbuttered slices on the tile for his dogs.*] How long have you been baking bread? [*I said this actually slurping. This was not on my list of potential questions, but I had decided to try freelancing with my asks.*]

GERD: Since early this morning. Sorry. Since I was 10; my mother used to bake because she loved it, and she taught me. As a chemistry professor, she approached baking as a science, but it came to feel more like a rite of passage, I suppose, but it is all about precise measurements.

DREW: You were close with your mother? [*The question immediately felt ridiculous. I superimposed another.*] Did you talk about science or philosophy or writing with her?

GERD: She was an amazing woman. We talked all the time about everything. I wouldn't know where to begin except to say that she was also a good listener. [*He smiled in a genuine manner that I had not seen before.*]

DREW: How old were you when she died? You were 9 when your father died, right?

GERD: [*He hesitated before responding.*] You can readily find that information other places, you know.

DREW: Yes. I didn't mean— [*I realized that I needed to come up with some better questions quickly. I glanced down at my notes in preparation for the interview. It was right there: he was 20 when his mother succumbed to cancer. She had a lengthy battle and must have been sick the last five or six years of her life, and Gerd would have been in high school about the time she got really sick. His father had been killed in a car accident when Gerd was only a boy. He was, I suppose, an orphan at 20, but he looked as if he had always been alone. I decided to try a new track of questions.*] I find myself wishing I had created your characters. Have you ever had that experience? Wishing you had written a character conceived by someone else, one from a novel you admired?

GERD: Many times. I used to fantasize that I had written *Ulysses*, drawn Stephen Dedalus or Bloom out of the air fully formed rather than pulled Stephen from his younger self worked into that torturous being in *Portrait*, though he's far less interesting to me in Joyce's expository, semi-autobiographical earlier novel. But Molly is really the character that I go back to and wish I could have written. She is also the unfinished character in Joyce's work, double entendre not intended.

DREW: [*Of course, it would be Ulysses, another almost unreadable tome, but I had finally finished that novel on my third try.*] *A Portrait of the Artist as a Young Man*? [*I wish I hadn't said it immediately, fearing that stating the obvious would annoy him to the extent that this interview, too, would be over before it began. But he was far more tolerant this time.*]

GERD: [*He ignored my obvious need to identify more precisely.*] Holden Caulfield, perhaps, the antiheroic Ulysses, the less contemplative, vastly undereducated but, like Dedalus, wandering around NYC as opposed to Joyce's Dublin for a day, shrinking from the contemporary monsters he meets. And Orhan Pamuk's Kemal Bey who wanders around the world searching for items to place in his museum of innocence. It's not his best work but—

DREW: *The Museum of Innocence.* [I nearly yelled it out loud.]

GERD: [Ignoring my outburst] But the Pamuk novel I most enjoyed. These characters are all looking for something that can no longer be found, which I find intriguing.

DREW: I sense a theme here. Any other characters? [*He was still coming up with characters, however, and I thought it best to just let him talk without my comment.*]

GERD: Hamlet, of course, and Tristram Shandy, and who wishes that he hadn't created Ignatius Jacques Reilly living large in absurdity in New Orleans, or Don Quixote fighting imaginary windmills? There is Ahab, too, and Cormac McCarthy's Judge Holden, perhaps the most heinous character in literature but tremendously compelling. Too many to list. So, the short answer to your question is yes, there are many characters I wish I had created.

DREW: [*I hadn't read the Turkish, Nobel-Prize winning author Pamuk but had read John Kennedy Toole's cult classic novel. I thought about asking why there were no female characters in his mix except Molly but decided against it. This was particularly strange to me since Gerd's best original characters were all women, to my thinking. I might work in that question, I decided.*] Holden, Stephen, and Kemal Bey as contemporary Ulysses, nearly everyone else as Hamlet, so, is nothing original?

GERD: [*He shot me a glance that hinted at derision just as I remembered that I hadn't accounted for Molly.*] It's still possible to be original within a framework, I hope, just not without a bit of appropriation from all those who came before us. [*He looked as if he was trying to find some common ground for me.*] Like Aureliano, Garcia Marquez's character. [*He quoted a passage from One-Hundred Years of Solitude too fast for me to get it all down.*] Yet, they were all unique, too. We're all using the same clay, after all.

DREW: [*At least I had read Gabriel Garcia Marquez. Here Gerd launched into some observations about archetypes and Fisher King permutations as generating forces, but I knew that many readers would feel lost with the whole archetype discussion. I needed to bring him back to something slightly less abstract without insulting him.*] When you have this kind of memory, in which you can pull exact quotations from works instantly, do you ever fear that you may subconsciously draw on someone else's work as your own?

GERD: Plagiarize unintentionally?

DREW: Well, yes. Is that something you ever worry about?

GERD: Worry? No. T.S. Eliot addressed this idea repeatedly in his essays, his poetry, and in his Nobel speech in 1948, the idea of the poet, the writer as representative of those who came before him and his, "function of serving as a representative, so far as any man can be a thing of far greater importance than the value of what he himself has written." Now, I'm loosely quoting from his speech, but I believe he said, "When a poet speaks. . . the voices of all the poets of other languages who have influenced him are speaking also. And at the same time he himself is speaking to younger poets of other languages, and these poets will convey something of his vision of life and something of the spirit of his people, to their own." So, yes, and no, I both consciously and subconsciously incorporate some aspect of those who came before me. Awareness of the other is actually what gives a work greater richness.

DREW: [*It was this quality Gerd had of being able to remember almost verbatim the words of others that most startled* me, much more than the fact he could sustain 900-plus page narratives.] Does it always feel honest?

GERD: Honest?

DREW: I mean, does the incorporation of others' ideas into a new work feel like an honest attempt to create something original?

GERD: I think it is enough to create something worth saying. When you look at Eliot's poetry, he wrote exactly what he was doing, using the works of the classics to speak to his "own" people, whomever they may be. He was frankly honest about it. The key is cognizance. Eliot knew what he was taking and why he assimilated precisely those works, yet he also reshaped them into his own vision, in his own poetry. Even a cursory reading of *The Waste Land*, if such a thing is possible, will reveal hundreds of fragments from other words, and I love how he addressed the concept of fragments thematically, words and phrases of others, yet as a whole. The poetry of others coalesces into Eliot's poem masterfully.

DREW: Are you a fan of T.S. Eliot then?

GERD: Fan is not the word I'd use, but I appreciate what he contributed. I am not sure about the man but about the worth of his writing, I'm fairly certain of his legacy. I am also conscious of these words floating around that belong to other writers.

DREW: What lines are floating around for you right now? [*Out of the corner of my eye, I was distracted by a hatchling of spiders near the knotty pine ceiling; they were running up the wall and down around a window frame. I supposed spiders were constant in a lake house. I was not a fan of spiders, and I kept half an eye on them. Gerd did not seem to notice my divided attention, or he did not really notice me. There are two walls almost entirely covered by book shelves, a crude painting of a small, rural church from a long-ago landscape covered with snow. I didn't recognize the painting and wondered about its significance, or if it had any, but those speculations did not fit my line of questioning.]*

GERD: "I essentially am not in madness, but mad in craft."

DREW: That sounds familiar.

GERD: Hamlet to his Queen mother Gertrude.

DREW: Ah, it always seems to come back to Shakespeare.

GERD: In the Western canon, it comes back to Shakespeare, the Bible, maybe, Plato, or Dante.

DREW: What about female characters? I have to admit that I wish I had created your Bergljot and Antonia. [*I felt suddenly brilliant, remembering to flatter him here.*]

GERD: [*Showing more interest, he leaned in toward me for the first time.*] Which one, if you could have created only one of them?

DREW: Bergljot. She is the kind of woman I would like to be in love with, but one who wouldn't even acknowledge my existence. [*It was not lost on me that I might be in a similar position with Gerd in my presence or even with Angela if Gerd, too, was in the same room.*]

GERD: Ah, creating a character who might reject you if given that opportunity. I'm certain Bergljot would have nothing to do with me either, if given the choice. She had none.

DREW: [*I almost laughed at the prospect of a woman actually rejecting him. I also wanted to tell him that the real-life woman I was in love with was in love with him, but I was able to stop myself. Crying and pleading into a message machine revealed enough about me. I didn't need to mine any more sympathy.*] So your characters take on lives of their own? At what point do your creations seem to assume their identities for you?

GERD: When then begin deciding to move out of the house entirely, and it happens, probably to every writer. Faulkner was obsessed with his little girl with muddy underwear for years, but she left home and ended up somewhere in Germany, employed by a Nazi, hardly an end he could have wanted for this incredible child/woman he conceived, perhaps desired, as well. Characters move away from you, all of them, at some point—if you're lucky.

DREW: Caddy Compson? Faulkner's character?

GERD: Yes, Caddy, I think she may have seemed more real, more flesh and blood than some of the actual women in his life, likely the women from his Hollywood affairs.

DREW: Is Bergljot your Caddy?

GERD: No. No, I let her go almost immediately. To be honest, she scares me a little [*For just the second time, he smiled.*]

DREW: Could you describe your creative process?

GERD: [*He leaned back, looking comfortable.*] Catching water with your fingertips, then watching it fall into a narrow stream, becoming a river. You live in a character's head for a while. That's how you give them distinct voice, but you can't fully live inside another being. They always leave you.

DREW: [*I wrote down what he said even though I didn't really understand.*] So, you can't really know anyone?

175 | Socrates is Dead Again

GERD: Unless they're already inside you.

DREW: [*I wanted to ask Gerd about the women in his life since it was believed he was heterosexual, and women flocked to him, but he never seemed to be in the company of one woman for very long.*] But, like children growing up, they leave. [*GERD shook his head, indicating that Bergljot was not like his offspring.*]

GERD: Some are born fully adult, never having known childhood.

DREW: Can we talk about your short stories? You're known for your novels, but your short stories and essays are more widely read.

GERD: Short stories are the most accessible form of fiction. I would naturally expect more people have read my short stories. Essays, you need to have an interest in the topic first. Novels, well, it takes a certain tenacity, a level of education, and experience on the part of a reader to finish a long work, and mine tend to be very long. They are not for everyone.

DREW: [*I wanted to brag that I had finally finished his 978-page latest novel, but I wisely held back because it sounded too much like my achievement rather than his.*] Where did you get the idea for your short story "The Man Who Was Struck by Lightning?" I think it's my favorite short story. Or perhaps, your reincarnation story that starts out with a man walking into an Army recruiting office and setting off a flash bang grenade.

GERD: With the first story, I was rummaging around in my mother's attic where you find things: a portrait of grandparents, a lace collar, an article in an old newspaper. It becomes a sort of treasure hunt of the past, as you discover some secret, and this or that artifact presents itself, demands your attention. Once it comes into being for me, I follow the thread until I am no longer interested or the story arc has taken over.

DREW: How do you know when the story is complete?

GERD: There is no formula; you either have that sense of satisfaction because something clicks, or you're left with this empty feeling. You know it should end one way or another with a degree of certainty.

DREW: To come back to my favorite story, if I may—

GERD: The story concept belonged to my mother, really.

DREW: Is it something you could share? [*He hesitated, and I encouraged him with a nod of my head. I was patient and sat through the extended silence without fidgeting.*]

GERD: Ah, a fairly morbid tale.

DREW: Well, you have certainly created morbid characters that make us reflect on those irrational fears, but intriguingly, like Melville, perhaps. [*I felt suddenly brilliant for making an apt comparison that he most likely would appreciate. I'd read one of his essays on Melville in The New Yorker.*]

GERD: Melville and his "king of terrors."

DREW: The white whale.

GERD: More than that creature. Whiteness itself, that "changeless pallor."

DREW: [*I shrugged here as one who always struggled with Melville's Moby Dick and the concept that whiteness was representational of some abstract fear rather than the whale itself that Ahab chased into metaphorical, if not actual, hell.*] Why do you think it is so frightening?

GERD: All those "nameless things," according to Melville: "Though in many of its aspects this visible world seems formed in love, the invisible spheres were formed in fright the incantation of this whiteness, and learned why it appeals with such power to the soul; and more strange and far more portentous, the intensifying agent, stabs us from behind with the thought of annihilation—"

DREW: Melville?

GERD: That is Melville. Not a fish or mammal story after all.

DREW: What we most fear?

GERD: Annihilation or perhaps lack of recognition of the self.

DREW: The most important technique for a writer?

GERD: Metaphor. I recall a line in Colum McCann's novel *Transatlantic*: "The old days, they arrive back in the oddest ways, suddenly taut, breaking the surface, a salmon leap." When we reach "salmon leap," something almost inexplicable happens to the reader. Our thoughts are altered like the page. I can't help but think of Ezra Pound's "In a Station of the Metro," impossible, bigoted man but remarkable poet. Tranströmer has wonderful metaphors, too. And I like poet Mark Doty's remarks on metaphor, particularly his comments about the compression of language helping us conceive, then lead to understanding. It's noteworthy that a poet has written one of the best essays on that subject.

DREW: [*I knew he'd bring up the Norwegian poet Tranströmer, but thought I'd save that question about his Norwegian heritage connection for later in the interview.*] The

178 | Socrates is Dead Again

compression of language, seems particularly ironic since your own work is tremendously expansive.

GERD: Ah, but you have no idea how long each was before I started editing. [*He laughed.*] I hope the work remains open to various interpretations suggested by compression, capturing something of the indirection facilitated by the use of metonymy and metaphor.

DREW: You've been gracious in sharing your thoughts on favorite characters and techniques. What about plot?

GERD: [*He shook his head.*] Nowhere to land with plot.

DREW: Unimportant then?

GERD: You know what Shakespeare thought about plots. I suppose that I'm less interested in the vessel, as well, but a story needs a frame or frames even if they overlap in order to order to breathe and move.

DREW: If you had to choose only one plot from all of literature; however, would it be *Hamlet*? [Part of me wondered if he was just showing off with this litany of writers, but I was also curious.]

GERD: No, no. Which *Hamlet*? Shakespeare's? He admitted to borrowing his plots. *Hamnet*? Possibly Thomas Kyd's *Ur-Hamlet*? *Amleth*, Norse for mad? Too fraught with Freudian interpretation at any rate even if the language is gorgeous. Although I'm not that intrigued with the question [*I tried not to cringe here.*], one plot strikes me as an almost perfect absurdity: *The General of the Dead Army* by Ismail Kadare. If that plot had been offered for sale, I would have purchased it.

DREW: What is it about Kadare's plot that makes it compelling? I have to confess that I don't know the work.

GERD: An Italian general goes to Albania to dig up the buried Italian dead, in order to count the uncounted after the end of the war. Of course, the hopelessness of the task comingled with the politics of it overwhelm him. The dead are difficult to unbury. In a sense, it is a simple concept plot but symbolically layered, ridiculous, ending up quite beautiful.

DREW: [*I wanted to return to the topic of fame but with some trepidation.*] Since my last visit, you've been featured on the cover of *GQ* magazine, quite a coup for a literary writer. [*I initially had trouble recognizing him in that sleek black suit and narrow tie on the magazine cover.*]

GERD: [*He laughed generously.*] Or a curse. Set up by my agent and publisher and not something with which I'm entirely comfortable. Both Celestine and Harper have these little excursions lined up on my calendar, and remind me continuously that works don't sell themselves, a point I continue to argue.

DREW: Of course, but the fact that *GQ* wanted you is what surprises here because, you know, they typically feature actors and athletes: the likes of Brad Pitt, James Franco, Leonardo DiCaprio, Ben Affleck, LeBron James, Bill Murray.

GERD: I see you know your *GQ* covers. But you left out Anne Hathaway. Writers never entertain? And we do know something about style.

DREW: [*I refrained from correcting him in that Hathaway was on the British version of GQ, and I winced noticeably when he said that, realizing that I had named too many cover boys and none of the women, and my litany showed way too much interest in pop culture, which, after all, was becoming my specialty. I would edit this out of my article, except his comment about Anne*

Hathaway.] I didn't mean that we don't entertain. [*Again, I think I stumbled, including myself in this mix, but he didn't seem to care this time.*]

GERD: Writers and poets are entertainers. We could go back to the earliest story tellers, all poets.

DREW: [*I thought he was going to launch into a discussion on Beowulf.*] But your art, it is art with a capital.

GERD: Ah, literary hierarchy. I would be pleased if my work offered only amusement.

DREW: Your work is far more ambitious than "amusement" suggests. [*No, ambition was not the word I wanted to use here.*] Your novels are encyclopedic [*I remembered the adjective from The New York Times' review of his latest work.*], and they provoke.

GERD: Tranströmer, you already know I'm intrigued by his poetry, wrote in one of his poems from *The Wild Market Square*. [*Here, he quoted the poem verbatim.*] By this measurement, I'm simply trying to tell the story of one soul.

DREW: Would you mind addressing your fascination with mathematics, working it into your prose? I know that you have written about it previously [*in a published essay*]. Your father was a mathematician; am I correct?

GERD: Yes, he was a professor of mathematics who specialized in number theory. I often wonder what he would have thought of my writing. [*He appeared amused.*] As the lines in my novel move from the extra-diegetic, external narrative, to diegesis, in the stream of consciousness form, there is a mathematical system that begins to dictate the structure even as the inner logic appears to disappear. I suppose I enjoy paradoxical elements at work, and I have always had an affinity for math, particularly at the higher levels.

DREW: You considered majoring in mathematics, if I am correct?

GERD: No, but I did major in philosophy for two years and loved courses in logic. The play of antithetical forces at work continues to compel me. I am reminded of the Conrad Aiken lines from his poem "The Room" in which he suggests that creating is a process of designed chaos. I suppose I am always working against these mathematical forces in the language at the same time I am observing points of convergence.

DREW: I know you admire other writers, poets, artists, but what other well-known people do you respect or esteem?

GERD: If I could have been born in another time, in another body, I would like to have been Charles Darwin.

DREW: For his theories, for evolution?

GERD: More specifically for his ideas about variation and natural selection, for his careful observation, his drawings, those meticulous notes, his patience in seeing what everyone around him missed. Five years on the *Beagle*, five weeks in the Galapagos, sitting on what must have been wholly uncomfortable lava formations on Floreana [*Charles Island*], noticing the slightest of changes in tortoise shell patterns, the slenderest curve distinctions in the beaks of finches. That kind of patience combined with his brilliance made for some very intriguing revelations.

DREW: Anyone else?

GERD: [*Without hesitating*] Marie Colvin.

DREW: Th journalist who was killed in Syria?

GERD: There is a photograph of her writing her last notes in Homs, where she is leaning against a metal shell of a window with one boot balanced on rubble. Half a wall stands before her, pocked by shell fragments or bullets, scant protection from a ceiling long gone. The photo of her was taken by one of her comrades, Paul Conroy. I am not sure if I am brave enough to have been that woman, but I certainly wish I had known her.

DREW: She had an eye-patch, I recall, like a pirate.

GERD: A highly literate, moral pirate.

DREW: Her stories were mostly centered on the world's hotspots, if I remember correctly?

GERD: As a war correspondent, it's what you would expect. I've read her work, and the news became narrative in her hands, not a catalogue of the world's atrocities but human stories. They were real people who were affected, and suddenly Sierra Leone, East Timor were not distant places with faceless suffering; her lens focused on a specific woman, an individual child, a soldier wearing a dead rat pelt for a cap. We got to know them, making it that much harder to turn our backs. Even when the body of her work contains an indictment of mankind, we are left oddly hopeful because of the bonds she made apparent.

DREW: I guess I'm going to have to read some of her work.

GERD: Do. But it is getting late in the day, and I would be an ungracious host if I didn't offer you supper.

DREW: [*It surprised me a little that he chose a woman as one of the two people he looked up to, but I refrained from saying anything about that, fearing I'd betray my own lack of social consciousness and what he would surely misconstrue as anti-feminism, but I'm not really. Or maybe I am, but I try not to be.*

Angela reminds me of this on a daily basis.] Before we eat, I brought you a couple of bottles of wine. Red or white?

GERD: Ah, both, but let's talk about something other than writers for a while. I grow weary of the topic. You know what editors say about writers writing about writers.

DREW: You set the agenda; I'm along for the ride.

GERD: Then it won't be much of a conversation, and your ride will be over before it began. Suppose we talk about something that interests us both?

DREW: [*Jokingly*] How about the origins of the universe?

GERD: That'll work. Convergence of physics, calculus, and poetry, where we talk in metaphors about probabilities because the mathematics is too far ahead for most of us. We need linguist equivalents of echolocation. [*Gerd was already pouring out two glasses, handing me one of them.*]

DREW: To be honest, the only thing I know about the origins of the universe is that it was violent.

GERD: Then you know more than most people. [*He sat back in the chair, settled in, and took a whiff of the wine's aroma.*] Annihilation that bred new worlds, eventually life. Quite a paradox, no?

***

Everything felt different this time. I was starting to believe I was getting to know the man. And the interviewer no longer existed, rather we had morphed into two people having a conversation. No longer worried about questions, I allowed myself to listen and respond. Somewhere in the territory created after too much wine and loss of self-consciousness, we talked in the way I seldom talked, even to friends.

Twenty-three

Gerd Meticulously Cleans His 12-Gauge Browning

Jens Wahl never liked guns and had no intention of having one anywhere in his house, but his brother Kristjen was a hunter who had once bagged a white-tailed buck with one of the largest racks recorded in the State of New York. Gerd had seen the mounted deer head with its enormous rack on the wall of his uncle's house when they went to visit at Thanksgiving. The boy never forgot that imposing sight: glass eyes, worn antlers still looking like powerful weapons.

"He was over 220 pounds before he was field dressed," Kristjen said proudly. "You could easily fit inside the spread of his antlers."

"I could?" the boy asked in wonderment, thinking about his uncle dressing a deer with a jacket.

"Someday very soon, I will take you hunting with me," Uncle Kristjen told his nephew, patting the top of his head and messing up his curly mop with his large, rough hand.

"We're not hunters," Jens said, overhearing his brother talking to his son as he entered the room. "And don't smoke around Gerd. Secondhand smoke is dangerous."

Kristjen put out his cigarette in one of the many ashtrays in the old house. "Whether you like it or not, maybe your boy will be a hunter? Who knows? It's better he knows how to shoot than be ignorant of how to handle a gun."

"Why? If he's not going to shoot one?" Jens' tone revealed his agitation and annoyance with his older brother. "He is my son," Jens said, lowering his head for emphasis.

"Yes, and my nephew. I mean no harm, Jens. It's good for the boy to have another perspective."

"And that perspective he's supposed to have is yours?"

Kristjen laughed which put the boy at ease between these warring brothers. "I'm sure he'll become a professor not a mechanic, but don't forget he's his mother's boy, too. You don't need to worry so much. She's got it covered." Here, Jens stepped back from tension between them; he meant no disrespect to his brother. Jens nodded as if accepted his brother's conciliation, but Gerd saw his father turn away from his more physically powerful brother.

Jens did not need to win the argument with his brother. After all, he thought as he left his son, he had already won by the fact he had a son. Kristjen and Maureen could not have children.

Although Jens never consented to Gerd's initiation into hunting, the eight-year-old went out with his uncle the next

Thanksgiving while his father was attending a college mathematics conference. His mother had allowed the extended visit alone because she had wanted to travel to the West Coast with her husband.

Trekking over hills, and following tracks of deer, they looked for spoor. "Spoor means signs of their presence, tracks in the snow, broken branches as they pass," said Kristjen. The boy quietly noted bent twigs on brush and bushes, a cluster of pellets beneath a barren crab apple tree. "Deer scat," said his uncle, pointing to the mound of black, pebble-like scat.

"Poop?" Gerd asked, and his uncle indicated his nephew's wisdom with a pat on the back. "They look like little rocks." This tracking appealed to Gerd's inquisitive nature. The boy was not sure he wanted his uncle to kill the deer.

As they reached the top of the hill and looked out over the remains of a corn field, they surprised a doe. Downwind of the animal, Kristjen first raised then lowered his shotgun from his shoulder. "I never shoot doe anymore," he said, blowing out a puff of frosty breath. Gerd did the same. They stood making foggy puffs in the numbing chill without speaking as the doe lifted her head before bounding. "I'll bet your father would tell you the reason you can see your breath is that water vapor comes out when you breathe. It's made up of molecules that slow down when they hit the cold. They change form, called condensation. Did you know that?"

"No," said Gerd, continually amazed by his uncle.

"I'll bet your father doesn't know that I know that either." Kristjen laughed, his big shoulders moving. He stopped, and said, "Let's keep moving but quietly. The big buck is out there."

Climbing the hill winded his uncle, but young Gerd loved the exertion, wanted to break into a run but knew his uncle would disapprove. The grasses were nearly as tall has he was in places where the farm had not been maintained. Suddenly, just as he was thinking about the fact his father would not want him trapsing around the hills, Gerd spotted the four-prong buck before his uncle. He had entered the open field from the tree line above. In an instant, Kristjen brought the shotgun to his shoulder a second time, when a larger buck leaped out from the woods at the other end of the field.

Turning his rifle and aiming, Kristjen was about to fire when the large buck disappeared into the trees. The movement triggered the pronghorn, and both were gone.

"Almost," he said "Caught wind of us." Kristjen shook his head. "That one was a beauty, too. I should have been scanning the entire tree line. My mistake."

"Magnificent animal," said Gerd.

"Look at your big words," said Kristjen. "You'll be a scholar all right but one who knows how to hunt."

Although he went with his uncle on expeditions into the fields, Gerd never saw his uncle kill a deer. It was almost as if he did not want to shoot in front of his nephew. This was something Gerd only thought about in reflection.

Gerd became a scholar like his father and mother, but he never forgot how to hunt, the feel of a gun in his hands that Kristjen had taught him as a boy. Gerd thought about that day with Uncle Kristjen all those years ago when he opened the locked door to the cabinet that held his shotguns. His uncle only outlived Gerd's father by nine years, succumbing to a heart attack too young, his aunt told him over the phone. His mother was too sick to travel at that point and could not be left alone. Gerd never even attended the funeral of his beloved uncle. His familiarity with death at that point was complete.

Pulling out the 12-gauge Browning, Gerd felt the heft of the same rifle that Kristjen had used to kill a trophy buck in another era. His uncle had left him this prized gun, along with the antique wood and glass cabinet, and Gerd made it a point to take out his rifles once a year to keep them in working order even if he did not use them. Once his uncle passed away, Gerd had no further interest in hunting, only enjoyed watching his big labs in the chase.

Cleaning the shotgun was necessary, not a rite of passage, but Gerd approached it ceremoniously: his rags, brushes, cotton swabs laid out on the bench beside oils and grease he would use. He was careful and methodical in his approach, not reverential. It would not be a complete tear-down, but he had to make sure that nothing was in the barrel: no old powder residue, no wad build-up nor gunky oil that could lead to malfunction. Examining the gas chamber, choke tubes, and wherever metal-on-metal friction could occur, Gerd then swabbed the barrel, making sure the snake was clean before pulling it through. Using a rag, he twisted it slowly into threads before reinstalling the chokes and tightening screws, reassembling the hardware. When the gun's workings were cleaned, he oiled and polished the stock, then looked at it in its entirely for an instant. After surveying the matter, he sat back and pointedly watched his chest rise and then slightly fall with each breath.

It no longer fascinated him, this dynamic in which the act of breathing seemed almost miraculous, and then he lifted his head. He would have only one chance. His separation was complete; it only then required concentration and a steady hand.

Twenty-four

Angela Imagines Falling in Love

I have noticed Ian Frost before, but I believe that I've never really felt him his presence until tonight. I love Drew, but everything keeps changing. Drew is more confident; it was the Wahl interview really. Gillian told me that it should have been Ian's, though, as if the interview was somehow stolen. I like Gillian but not the fact she seemed to be taking sides against Drew because, for one thing, Drew is such an unlikely suspect, and Ian hardly seems like a victim.

Why am I looking at Ian? I know Drew loves me even if he is somewhat clumsy and occasionally inattentive. And, who am I kidding? Drew is incredibly immature, but I do love him. No one's perfect, not even the great Gerd Wahl whom I imagined falling in love with before he took his own life.

When I look over at Drew, he is tweeting on his phone again, just like every night.

Somehow, I know they are talking about Gerd. I still can't believe that man killed himself. I also can't believe Drew's luck and timing: to land the last interview with Gerd. Drew is walking around as if he's famous because he keeps being mentioned in connection with the late Gerd Wahl. They are linked in a way he never anticipated, in some way that I never anticipated either. One unexpected turn and everything changes for everyone. At least for those in our small circle. Less of me really. Being a nurse, I seldom hear other people at the hospital talk about Adrian Gerd Wahl the way Drew and his writer friends do. But while I'm not a writer, I am a reader, a better one than Drew perhaps. And I fell in love with Wahl's words if not the man.

The man of my imaginings, not the writer who shot himself, was my crush. That other Gerd Wahl would never have killed himself. The Gerd of my imagination would have serendipitously run into me on the subway and struck up a casual conversation that instantly turned deep and serious. We would have exited the subway car together with him changing plans and deciding to have coffee with me at La Colombe in SoHo; of course, we would end up in SoHo where I'd gotten an apartment after splitting from Drew. I would invite Gerd back to my place, and he'd follow me as if it was all part of a preconceived plan. We'd end up talking and making love and talking and then making love again because it was bound to become love. Later, getting married, we would decide not to have kids because that would alter our perfect rhythm. I'd secrete him away, keep the press and publicity at bay. He'd live relatively anonymously with me, but we'd live well. I won't say happily because that's somehow reductive. No reasoning being lives "happily" and certainly, not "happily ever after." But suicide is just so hard to accept. Death comes soon enough it seems to me. Perhaps because I work in a hospital where I see the dying and the effects of their pain and loss on the people who love them.

At night, this fictitious Gerd would read passages of his novels out loud and ask me to critique them, as he wrote, listening to my comments. I wouldn't tell anyone that I was editing for the great writer. After all, I wasn't looking for validation or any kind of credit. I just wanted to contribute. I would then pull out one of my own stories, and I had time to write since I had retired from nursing. Of course, he would listen and smile with pleasure.

What would he say here? I can't get his words right, not the words I imagine he would say because then they become mine, and he ceases to exist even as fantasy. We can never know another person completely even in our imaginings. Suicide is an act that is entirely alone and lonely.

It suddenly occurred to me that I might have this other life, this ideal, with Ian. I found myself staring at him across the room, noticing that his dark hair curled at the nape of his neck, his shoulders looked as if he had been carrying some unseen weight, his hands grasping air when he spoke, then his eyes met mine as if he'd caught me. Startled.

I don't think I was imagining this connection, but it's hard to be sure of anything. A charge. No bolt of lightning, however. I can't be certain, but I think he took a step toward me. I look at his eyes and catch that uncertainty, as if he's not quite sure of himself, but there were too many people between us. I looked at Drew.

Drew slipped his phone in his pocket and walked toward me all smiles, and I recognize my life again. Sorry, fantasy men, apparently, I have chosen Drew. I don't think I'm settling, but I have to be careful here because it is difficult to step outside for perspective. Okay, maybe I am settling, but he makes me laugh. Drew can be sweet. He takes my hand, and his is warm, electricity after all. I smile at him and realize he has no idea I ever thought of another man. Perhaps it's better if he never does.

Twenty-five

Gillian Hospitalized

Not entirely sure I wanted this baby until he was lost to me. How did I end up in the hospital? I was sitting at my desk, trying to figure out how Craig had messed up the accounting paperwork so badly while I was out for a couple of days' vacation, when I suddenly felt like I had wet my pants. That's what it seemed like, and I started feeling horribly embarrassed before I got nervous.

Then Ian yelled, "My God, Gillian. What's wrong?" I looked down and saw blood which then scared the hell out of me, but I tried to be nonchalant about it anyway because there had been something going on between me and Ian, and now there was something going on inside me.

"Oh," was all I said when I got up and headed for the bathroom. I only took a few steps, they told me later, before I went down, out cold. It turns out Ian and Shwetak lifted me up and carried me downstairs, hailed a cab, managed to squeeze me between them, and sent the driver to the hospital in record time. If this was wartime, and they were my rescuers, it would all be rather romantic, but it wasn't, and they had to know what was going on before I did which made it awful, and I wanted to cry for days and days afterward. I was too sad to be humiliated. That would come later.

When I woke up in the hospital, I was dressed in one of those funny hospital gowns with a thin sheet over me. I looked around and saw my clothes in a plastic bag. A nurse came in and looked at my chart. I was hooked to an IV, and I asked her what had happened. I think I was shivering.

"The doctor will be making rounds shortly. He will talk to you." She put a cup of water with a straw in it on my tray, pointed out the up and down button on the bed remote, and left. She wasn't so much cold as efficient, and right then, I so much needed more than efficiency. Warmth was what I needed. I grabbed the water and sucked the entire cup dry even though I knew I was being hydrated intravenously.

Yeah, I knew what happened, but I couldn't believe it. How do you lose a baby? Everything was going along fine even though I had no idea what to do if my baby decided to come out full term and healthy and crying and demanding me every single minute. Still, I wanted him. I wanted my son, it turned out. I figured that I'd make it up as I went along, and how hard can it be with millions of people having babies every year? I was pretty sure I could be a good mother even if I had no idea of what that entailed. I knew my own mother was not exactly an expert, and she managed, only breaking down and sobbing here and there when we were young, mostly because my brothers were fighting or had broken her coffee table or a lamp or the TV but only one TV and dad wasn't home again.

I hadn't named my son or anything, but I knew he was a boy, and he was already hearing every detail of my life before this happened. I started bawling uncontrollably, but it didn't help. There was a clock on the wall, yet I couldn't seem to focus on it, even to figure out what time it was, what time had passed, as if I had forgotten how to tell time. Apparently, I had already been in surgery where they finished cleaning me out. There was nothing left of him.

By the time Drew knocked on the door, holding out flowers, I had managed to calm down a little and was only mildly gulping air.

He looked stricken. For a second, I shifted my worry to him. "These are for you," he said.

"Who else would they be for?"

"Right. Sorry. I mean, I'm really sorry, honey. It's, it's. I didn't know about, I mean, I'm sorry," he said, still holding the flowers out.

I was still struggling to keep from crying again. I didn't interrupt him as I am sure he was conditioned to by now. "It's okay." I don't know why I felt the urge to comfort him.

"You know, this is one of the few times we are not talking about Gerd Wahl or writing. "

"Really? It's that bad?"

"Sometimes. I'm not criticizing, understand. Just seems that my perspective has shifted rather dramatically."

"Sorry. I guess I have been a little obsessed. And, I'm really sorry about, you know.

"Nice you came."

"Is there anything you need? Anything Angela or I can do for you or bring you?"

When he mentioned Angela, I brightened up. "Is Angela here?"

"She'll be here in a little while; she had just finished her shift and arrived home, but she's coming back in to see you."

I really wanted to see Angela rather than Drew, so it felt hopeful to know she was coming back. I experienced little guilt over the fact that Angela had just finished work and had to return. Despite my Catholic upbringing, I experienced much less guilt of late, and it felt wonderful, except what I felt over my son.

Drew finally put the flowers on my tray then swung the tray over the bed. I could smell the gardenias, and they made me feel nauseous. He stood near my feet, right under the TV. Looking above his head, he said, "Do you want me to turn on the television?"

"What? No. When did you say Angela was coming?" I wasn't processing things very quickly, but the thought of talking to another woman, particularly one who is a nurse, sounded exactly what I needed to at that moment. I wanted Drew to leave and produce Angela at that moment. I realized I had to spend more time cultivating women friends.

"Any minute, I think. I'm sorry, I didn't know," Drew said after an extended silence between us. "I mean, when did you know?"

I must have shot him the look that told him his question was stupid because he corrected himself immediately. "You don't have to tell me anything if you don't want to. I shouldn't have asked."

"Thanks." There was nothing I wanted to tell Drew right then. He stood there looking at me, and I stared at his flowers. This went on for way longer than it should have, but that is what happens when no one knows exactly what to do or say next.

"Is Shwetak here? Or Ian?"

"Uh, I think they went home a little while ago, but they were here through your surgery. You know they, Ian and Shwetak, were the ones who brought you here. You were out cold, went down like that." He clicked his thumb and fingers. "I think you might have hit your head. Does it hurt?"

"Oh." My head did hurt, and I touched the back of it, feeling around for dried blood or a gouge, but there was only a slight bulge. I couldn't think of anything more to say and neither could Drew. There was this second very long silence between us that never happened at work. I always had something to say there, was always in command of my troupe, but now, everything seemed horribly messed up.

"Okay, then," Drew said, finally getting the hint that I wanted him to leave. "I'm going to let you get some rest. I think you need to sleep unless the doctors told you not to sleep, with the concussion and all, unless it wasn't a concussion." He shrugged. "Sorry. Sorry. Don't worry about anything, I mean, anything else except, we'll take care of everything at work for you. You don't need to hurry back."

"I'm not worried about work," I said flatly.

"That's right. Good. Don't worry. That's good. No need. Don't worry."

I thought he was going to say, "Be happy," but fortunately, he didn't. He leaned over, patted my shoulder awkwardly, sort of kissed the top of my head, and then stepped back gingerly. I wanted to tell him that I would not break even though I felt broken.

"I'll be fine," I said, trying to remember to be civil. I was struggling with kindness and being polite in the moment. "Thanks for the flowers and for coming. They're pretty." He cheered up for all the wrong reasons, but I was glad that I could at least make him feel better before he left. Even from my bed, I could hear his audible sigh in the hallway. He must have been thinking, "Whew, escaped."

As soon as he was gone, however, I felt one-hundred times worse and started bawling again. I cried until the doctor finally showed up to tell me that I was doing well, and the fetus had naturally aborted. I was lucky, I guess, but I couldn't get my son out of my head, and my boy was not some bloody clot. My boy didn't have one thing wrong with him. I could go home soon, but that thought suddenly terrified me even though I said nothing. The last thing I wanted to do was go back to my tiny apartment and sit in the dark while I thought about losing my baby and how stupid I had been to get pregnant and fall for the same guy who hadn't grown up which meant that I hadn't grown up or changed much either. I had been a walking disaster, and now I was a bedridden one. So much for progress.

I must have fallen asleep for a while because it was much later when Angela mercifully stopped by. I had given up waiting for anyone to come in, and I was sure that visiting hours were over. When she came in, she didn't say anything, not even hello.

She flashed her scrubs to another nurse who looked in on us, as the other nurse nodded and left. Angela brought a warm blanket into the room with her and wrapped it around me.

"It's warm," I said stupidly.

"We have a warmer here," she said smiling and hugged me like I was her little girl. I had forgotten how cold I was. I had forgotten how good it was to have someone hold you in a comforting way, not just out of duty.

I spilled my guts to her, telling Angela everything that I badly needed to tell someone, about stupid Seamus who didn't love me but pretended to in order to fuck me, about Ian and Shwetak, about our mixed up almost romance, about tensions at work, about my little son who I would never meet even though I felt like I had known him for years already. Angela just listened, then she brushed my hair. I kind of expected to get some kind of lecture from her, where she told me I deserved everything that happened, but she didn't. I don't know what she was thinking except that she did not seem to be judging me.

All she said was, "Oh, honey."

At last, when I was spent from crying again, I said, "I loved him, Angela."

"You did, of course," she said nodding, somehow understanding that I was talking about my son who would never be born and saying the only thing I wanted to hear. I knew why Angela was a nurse, why she was so good at her job that didn't feel like a job but more like a calling.

She held me until I fell asleep again and came back in the morning when I woke. Somehow, she understood all of it. She held a bag with clean clothes for me, my own clothes from home, and told me that she would help me get up and walk around the hospital because it was good to get moving to start the physical healing process. I decided right then that Angela was going to be my new best friend, and I really needed a friend at that moment.

Twenty-six

Two Highly Articulate Writers

It's
I
She
You?
I never
Did you?
What?
You two?
No. You?
Oh, no, not me
Really? Then?
I don't know.
Somebody else, I guess
Oh
Well, that's it then.
It is?
If that's it, where is he? Both young men shrugged.

You love her?
Shwetak nodded his head.
Ian put his hand on his friend's shoulder.
And you?
No. Ian lied. *Good luck. She needs you now.*
You, too.

Shwetak accepted his victory gracefully, and Ian got up to leave the hospital, but turned at the last moment. *She'll be okay, you know. You both will.*

Yeah. Thanks. I mean that.

It's probably better if you give her some time alone though. Don't rush into anything.

Of course.

Take care of her.

If she'll let me.

She will. Give her time. Ian looked back at Shwetak who nervously tapped his right foot and rubbed his eyes aware that he had been crying before Ian showed up in the hospital waiting room.

You'll be fine, Ian said, not to Shwetak who was already out of hearing distance. *You'll all be fine.*

Twenty-seven

Inexplicable Universe

One morning, Henry started howling. I had already taken him out for his walk. Checking his food and water dishes, I saw they were untouched, never a good sign, but I wasn't that worried yet. I looked at him, and Henry lowered his head, his ears pinned back, only his eyes were turned up toward me, expressing what seemed like both shame and pleading. Within a few seconds, I was on the phone to the vet's office. "Yes, I'll hold, but this is an emergency. MY DOG MIGHT BE DYING," I screamed even though I didn't really mean it, but I wanted to get Henry in as soon as possible. In the middle of the call, Henry started howling again, and the assistant heard him through the phone.

"All right," she said. "Bring him in. We'll schedule you for 2:30." Henry licked my feet.

By the time I got Henry to the vet's office, which is no small feat in the middle of the day and traffic being what it was, he was bleeding from both his mouth and his rear. And he kept looking at me like I could fix things for him, making me all the more desperate. For some reason that I still can't fathom, Angela was prepared with two towels, and she wrapped him up on the way, comforted him while I drove. It occurred to me that I was lucky to live with a nurse rather than a writer.

"Somebody help him," I yelled, carrying my little dog past other waiting clients and their animals. Everyone was looking at me like I was crazy, and I was for a little while.

The x-ray revealed small, sharp splinters of bone had penetrated his esophagus and the lining of his intestines in several places. "I don't know how he could have gotten a bone," I yelled. "I don't give him bones!" But I was frantically searching my memory banks for the last time I had ordered chicken wings. I knew Angela hated them and never ordered them. Could I have killed my own dog? Trying to think logically in the midst of panic is impossible, but I determined that I hadn't had wings in more than a month.

"No," said the calm but not indifferent veterinarian, "Something more recent."

I was interviewing Angela, demanding to know how Henry could've gotten into chicken bones, and it was not even registering that even if I knew the precise time and day I took him for a walk, and he had chomped down a couple of bones by the curb in the dark, it would not have saved Henry. The vet worked on my dog while I texted work. Got Ian first then Shwetak picked up Ian's phone and wanted to know what had happened. Finally, Ian said he would tell Craig. "Do you want me to tell Gillian?"

What could Gillian do to help, I reasoned? Other than Craig, who needed to know I wouldn't be in, the others didn't need to know anything yet, but I told them the news was as important as the latest sequester. Angela sympathetically patted my arm then hugged me. I wanted to tell her I needed oxygen not an arm pat but decided it was better to say nothing under the circumstances. We were there for hours that felt like days.

The aging veterinarian tried surgery, he said, but the expression on his face told me everything else. I looked at him, and he nodded. "I'm sorry," he said at last. "We couldn't save him."

I wept like a little kid, lost it completely in that space filled with weird antiseptic and animal urine smells that agitated every living creature in the office except the fleas and ticks that were somehow immune even to the toxic pesticides in which we covered them. When I finally looked over, Angela was crying, too. We stood there sobbing in the room filled with uncomfortable people and jittery, barking, growling, mewing, yelping animals because we apparently set off a chain reaction. One of the dogs, a big Rottweiler, started howling in this piercing, almost human-like wail, and his owner got up and took him outside, giving us a look of disgust. I finally realized, like a man coming up for air, that I was upsetting everyone, and we went out, too.

That's how I lost my best friend Henry, inexplicably, unexpectedly, irrevocably. That's the thing about dogs. They love you ardently and unconditionally. Then one day for no logical reason, they swallow something that punctures their intestines, and they die on you.

Angela suggested we get some coffee because neither of us wanted to go home where Henry would not be waiting, hopping up the moment he heard the key in the lock, wagging his short tail, shaking the whole backside of his little body in excitement over our mere presence. Thankfully, we didn't talk for a while. I think anything she said would have made everything worse. I don't know how Angela knows things like that, but she does. She has timing down to a science. She knows even more than I give her credit for, and I give her credit for a lot. I can't believe how lucky I am that she is still with me.

On my second cup, I really looked at Angela, her beautiful eyes with black streaks around them, and I reached for her hand which she allowed me to hold tightly. For once, she didn't pull away and act embarrassed by my public display.

"I'm so terribly sorry," she said at last. She was crying silently, tears running down her cheeks and nose.

"Can't believe he's gone," I said, thinking about how she cried for me and Henry. I knew at that moment how much I loved her and wanted to marry her, but the timing wasn't right.

"Damn, just going to miss Henry so much," I finally said. "So much loss lately."

She turned her head slightly almost the way that Henry used to do when he was puzzled. "Do you mean Wahl's death, too?"

I realized at that moment I had not been very sympathetic when Angela was mourning for Gerd. It was not as if Gerd's death didn't get to me, too. In fact, I was pretty sure that I knew him better, liked him better, than Angela had, even in her imagination, and I really hadn't reconciled the fact of his suicide with the man who had allowed me to return to his home and talk with him, share dinner with him, exchanged stories until two or three in the morning when Gerd told me that it was really too late for me to start driving back to the city. I realized we never talked about suicide. Why would I have brought it up in the interview? But then, I wish I had asked him. I tried to imagine his response.

"Suicide is not an act of fear," one of his characters said. "It is a calculation."

Would he really be that cold about it? No, that was my projection simply because I did not understand. What Gerd did, however, was pull out a pillow, blanket, and sheet and tossed them on his couch, so I didn't have to try to drive home on that last night. I don't know what we were to each other, but it was more than acquaintances, more than work contacts. I wasn't sure at the time how I was going to work that into my article, but I knew that my life had changed because of Wahl, and now it had changed again with Henry gone. Yet, everything was conflated in my misery. Trying to separate the enigma from the pain.

"Yeah, I can't believe what is happening to me."

"It's not just happening to you, Drew. Death happens to everyone."

I think it was because Angela assumed that she felt more grief over Gerd's death than I did, that was what got to me and maybe that she found him far more fascinating and better looking than me, smarter, which he was. I'd been too possessive of Angela and worried about losing her. I didn't realize what I had, and now Henry was gone. I felt gutted, and all of the competition and jealousy disappeared. I didn't know if it was gone for good or the feeling represented a temporary truce, but there was something more powerful at work in my muscles, my memory, brain chemistry even.

Aware at that moment but couldn't articulate until later, I felt the dynamic between Angela and me had altered. All of the tensions and needs to make each other jealous, flirt with other members of the opposite sex, follow every really good-looking New Yorker down the street with our eyes, over in that instant. We started falling in love all again, the kind where everything and everyone else seems to disappear, and there you are, just two of you, the last human beings on the planet, and your heart aches. Little mutt Henry did all of that.

Twenty-eight

Julia's Fateful Decision

Water was restless, white froth spilling onto shore then gradually disappearing, turning inwards, arrival announcing nothing more than ripples and whispers, sounding like a creek moving over stone. In the half-circle bay, a reminder of last night's storm: mounds of foam piled as if a god had spit back at the world. That was it, God's spit, Julia thought. Watching those waves build and collapse, Julia anticipated their division into smaller sections before drifting out over open water where they dissipated.

Cabin had become writer's sanctuary; damp, shaded days were met with relief, coffee endlessly brewing, sighting a pair of loons, only in spring on their way further north, cause for awakening of perceptions, and she surveyed both dawn and dusk as one, sight lines measured, attributed, juxtaposed for color composition, hint of storms passing and those to come, full-blown weather making its entrance. There was anticipation suspended in the air of the house, and she could never get entirely comfortable with Gerd even in this almost perfect comfort. She tried to talk to him about it.

"What about living in Boston? You could write there, and New York is not far." She didn't say "with me," but it was clearly implied. Refusing to go there, she came as close as she could without proposing.

"Boston? No." He simply shook his head, making her angry without comment or a way to respond appropriately.

Used coffee mugs lay about in strange places, left in mid-sentence perhaps. On walls were maps of the lake's elevations as if he was a cartographer. What a strange thought, her lover as mapmaker. They had many conversations about the connections between a map's symbols and those found in languages. Gerd knew more about such things than many contemporary cartographers, she decided, and she loved listening to his stories, made up on the spot to explain complex symbology. Those were their best nights: when she could wrap her mind around his ideas and cuddle although there was still the hum of agitated state, never in complete repose. He was on to the next idea while she often felt left behind.

Books and magazines ruled the cabin or at least set its tone, its pacing, unruly in their mildly threatening piles, spilling over at various points, precarious in other instances, only a few neatly stacked. She never interfered with these configurations. It remained his cabin not hers, not theirs. He kept the place cool for his dogs who suffered in any kind of heat, preferring winter, nestled in their well-oiled coats. So, she was always cold in the cabin, reaching for her jacket or one of his.

She glanced out through branches of trees and down to water, the cottage built on a severe angle of the hillside above Skaneateles. Below, weathered and uneven, the dock needed work, boards pushed up by ice, splintered wood remembering movements of water before being torn by ice.

"Why don't you have a new dock put in?" She looked back at him, but he was reading, not even looking up when he spoke.

"Because this old one is grandfathered. New restrictions on building docks, so you have to take out anything new every year. Best to leave it as is."

Tall grasses had grown unruly around his door, signs that no one was living there full-time, but here and there were markers that indicated Gerd preferred wildflowers and grasses to cultivated gardens. Julia tended her own garden with meticulous care. *He would laugh at me*, she thought as she recalled snipping buds on her plants, positioning them in locations with the best sunlight, measuring exactly amounts of water given to help her plants thrive.

"How did it start?"

He finally looked up.

"The fire?" she asked.

"Electrical. Old wiring—rain drenched outdoor sockets, and we had 'an arc flash,' the electrician said."

She went over and put her arms around his neck impulsively, scorched smell in her nostrils. "You could have been killed. Look at all this paper. It would have gone up in an instant."

She detected him pulling back slightly. "Varg was on it. He wouldn't let me go back to sleep once he roused me."

The big dog nuzzled his master, and Julia bent down to ruffle his dark coat on that wide head. Varg indulged her then wandered off. Together, Gerd and Julia went out to look at the charring, permanently marked wood shingles that were shielding his cabin. Gerd reached for her hand unexpectedly, and they stood there looking like a domestic couple. It was only a corner of the house, but ugly black scars went from ground all the way to roof. Varg nosed around the underbrush nearby and produced a low growl as if still warning of danger.

"Not Viktor, too?"

"No. He and Viggo would have let us burn before waking," Gerd said, suddenly laughing with great affection. Viktor was rolling on damp ground nearby, coating himself in odors of some small creature's decaying remains. "But we're all alive, thanks to Varg."

"Still, it frightens me thinking about it." As Varg returned, Julia knelt and threw her arms around his thick neck, the big dog's coat longer than she remembered, hair wrestling with burdocks and windswept remnants of a day in open fields. "Our savior," she sang into his ear, and he twisted his head to lick hers. "Where does he go when he wanders off?"

"He never reveals his secrets."

They smiled in the dark and went inside to make love unhurriedly. He kissed her shoulders, neck, her breasts slowly, moving her clothing rather than taking it off, and she felt the silk on her blouse kiss her skin as much as his lips. Then she grabbed his thick hair in her closed fists. When he chose to make love, Gerd was passionate and attentive, gently brushing Julia's light brown strands from her face with his fingertips. They finally settled back in shallow sighs. And it occurred to her as she lay there in the darkness of his cabin, the best night of her spring had been one after Gerd had nearly died.

Yet, lately, he had grown increasingly more distant, she thought. Still, he kept to rituals, to his routine, solitary writer even in her company. He sat writing with his back to her. She pulled on a heavy wool coat and went outside. Julia watched Gerd from a lit window where she could she he was still at work.

In the morning, when she woke and reached for him, he was not there. Opening the cabin door, she spotted her lover casting a line off the dock, filament invisible to her and trout below. The early morning scene should have been one of peace and contentment, but there was something deeper, more elemental that pushed out everything else, eventually pushing her away, as well. Not for an instant did she think that he was mentally ill, but she couldn't help him find the source of his persistent discomfort either. No, discomfort wasn't the right word. Much deeper than that. Maybe she was overthinking it, she reasoned. Perhaps he had just grown tired of her.

She had done everything she could, even attempted against her better judgment to be domestic. He spoke very little that morning. Seemed far away. Only after trying to get him to talk to her, cleaning up dishes, putting away clothes he left around the cabin did she write a note and leave it on his old roll top desk, not knowing when exactly she would be back. He had been out in his boat all morning and into the afternoon alone with only Varg along for the ride. It was more than that, of course; she wanted some kind of commitment from him, and he had not the slightest interest in that kind of symbolism. Her irritation came as much from her surprise about wanting a traditional role, her need, as from his reaction. When she asked him when he would be coming to Boston next, he shook his head, as if that was not even in the realm of possibility.

He didn't call her in the car on her trip home although he must have heard her old Pontiac pull away. She would be damned if she would call him on the way back. Either he wanted to be with her or he didn't. When she got back to Boston hours later, she finally gave in and called him, letting the phone ring repeatedly until she hung up. Even at that point, she didn't know if she had left him or simply allowed herself to be driven away. Some part of her wanted to punish him; she would make him plead for her return, she decided. But he never did.

Twenty-nine

Gillian Decides to Self-publish

FADE IN:
INT. OFFICE MID-MORNING

GILLIAN
Why are you looking at me that way? It's not as if I've stolen state secrets or something.

IAN
I'm glad you're back. We, all of us, missed you.
And who cares about state secrets, just personal ones?
But are we talking FBI, CIA, or F-ing Homeland Security?

GILLIAN
Did you think I was gone forever?

IAN
No, but you obviously do a lot more around
here than anyone gives you credit for because

Craig was having a nervous breakdown last week.

GILLIAN
Craig but not you?

IAN
Okay, I missed you, too. What have you been doing, anyway? I mean, besides healing?

GILLIAN
I'm publishing my novel. This isn't some hasty decision. I have thought long and hard about this.

IAN
Self-publishing?

GILLIAN
Oh, please. Don't go there right now.
I told you I'm going the self-publishing route and that's all you have to say? How about some excitement for me? I will have a book out.

IAN
What do you want me to say? Endorse it?
You know a traditional publisher won't ever look at work that has been self-published. It's a dead zone.

GILLIAN
Hardly. Good God. Why don't you throw in some brain-eating zombies while you're at it?

IAN
There simply aren't thousands of readers out there waiting for your work to appear on the Internet. Self-publishing sounds like self-empowerment but can be a waste land.

GILLIAN
How do you know? And thank you for your dismissive and pessimistic appraisal of my next adventure.

IAN
You know I like your work and want to be supportive, but I don't want you to get your hopes up, find out that it isn't what you thought, become disillusioned.

GILLIAN
Isn't that what life is all about? I've been disillusioned before. Never mind. It's really not that bad. Ian, you have to realize not all of us are in your literary bracket or have the indulgence of literary purity.

IAN
My bracket? Purity? Really? That's what you think?

GILLIAN
Stop. It's a compliment. Writers, like you,
with agents who submit to traditional publishers and
actually get published. Why does it matter
to you what I do with my work?

IAN
Look, I'm just reminding you how the business
operates. I don't want to see you scammed.

GILLIAN
The business is not considering my work now,
and they weren't before. Do you have any idea
of the odds of me publishing a work through what
you call traditional publishers, even the small
independents in my lifetime?

IAN
I've told you that you have to try getting an agent.

GILLIAN
Who will dismiss me and my work with as
much pomp and circumstance as any asshole
publisher. And wake up, darling Ian, those houses
you revere are disappearing like passenger pigeons.

IAN
I thought you'd compare them to dinosaurs, at least.
Pigeons? Because I've an argument for the dinosaur.

GILLIAN
Which is? Do tell me about the successes of the dinosaurs.

IAN
That they were far more resilient than most people realize, and, most probably far more enduring than the human race will be. And while some publishing houses are closing, new ones are opening up. Are you sure you're not throwing in the towel too soon?

GILLIAN
A cliché from a writer like you? And you should know I hate professional prize fighting while you're mixing metaphors on me.

IAN
Acceptable short-hand under the circumstances.

GILLIAN
I'm simply not as high-minded as you. I want readers, and I'm not willing to wait until I'm 70 or never, for that matter. Don't you understand? I want this, and there is now a way to put my work in the ether and into print.

IAN
High-minded? Sounds like an insult when you say it, and you have every bit as much integrity as me.

Who do you think I am, anyway? I'm just saying
your work deserves a better opportunity than
swimming with billions of bytes.

GILLIAN
Ian Frost. You remind me of the cooler version
of John Updike. You know, "Writers may be
disreputable, incorrigible, early to decay
or late to bloom but they dare to go it alone."

IAN
God, I'm all that? And I'm early to decay?
How can you even stand to talk to me?

GILLIAN
Well, I mean you're like that last part of Updike's
quote, not the decaying part. Maybe I should have
said, like Adrian Gerd Wahl.

IAN
Quotation.

GILLIAN
Good God. What? You're correcting my grammar?

IAN
Sorry. It's quotation. You know "quote"
is the verb, and it's not grammar but usage
and spelling. Updike accepting the

MacDowell Medal, where he said that, I mean.
And, I think I'd rather like to be compared to Updike
who lived into his 70s, than to Wahl.

GILLIAN
See? Who knows that weird, obscure stuff about?
writers but you? The MacDowell Medal? Now I have to look
that up.

IAN
Hey, you're the one quoting Updike, and the one
who came up with questions, and I'm reasonably
sure that it's verbatim.

GILLIAN
It is. I wrote it in my journal last night. Otherwise,
I would have had no idea. It's not like I've memorized
everything Updike had to say. At least you're brave,
and I see you go it alone on a daily basis. I'm not brave.

IAN
Utter nonsense. Who's braver than you? Talk about going it
alone. You were about to have a baby, didn't ask any of us
for help either. Didn't tell us anything.

GILLIAN
That's not bravery. It's biology, and I don't
want to talk about it at the moment.

IAN
Okay. But you were brave or maybe even brash
the first day you walked in here and basically
demanded a job. By the way, I've seen pictures
of Updike at my age. Do I really remind you of him?
Geeky. I guess, I need slightly larger glasses.

GILLIAN
Yours are plenty big enough, no double-entendre
intended.

IAN
See, this is why I love your filthy, brilliant mind.

GILLIAN
And yet, you manage to insult me on a daily basis.

IAN
You're my sparring partner.

GILLIAN
Hey, I was thinking about that sexy cool writer
Updike when he was young, not a 70-year old.

IAN
Good recovery. I'll take it, but stop and think about
waiting a little while before self-publishing.
What's your hurry?

GILLIAN
I'm tired of waiting for life to happen. I think it's time to find some readers. It's not heresy, you know. I'm not selling my soul, just some words.

IAN
No one's saying that. I don't want you to regret it later.

GILLIAN
Thanks for your concern. I'm less likely to regret self-publishing than most of the things I do. And, besides, I don't want to be one of those writers pining because all her best stuff is collecting dust on a shelf, unnoticed and unread. I'd rather deal with a few scammers any day.

IAN
What I intended to say but botched is that, your stories are good and funny, and they'll find a readership if you give them time. You're younger than the rest of us.

GILLIAN
Is this age discrimination? You keep reminding me, but it's not desperation, Ian. I'm ready, and my stories are willing. I want to test these waters, and don't tell me to watch out for sharks.

IAN
You'll find them. They're everywhere.
GILLIAN
When I was home last Christmas, sitting
on the floor because my brothers and father
had confiscated couches and chairs, it occurred
to me that I was PREGNANT, and I sat there
surrounded by family, but what hit me hard
was not how loved I was but, perversely, how
alone I felt.

IAN
I'm sorry. You're not alone, you know.
You have me and Shwetak and Drew and

GILLIAN
No, writing groups, writers collectives,
we're all part of this era but really alone
in this experiment called life.

IAN
What is it you really want, Gillian?

GILLIAN
What I really want to know right now is,
have you seen Shwetak?

Thirty

Drew Becomes an Unreliable Narrator

[Date: June 17, 2013; Interview Continues]
I finally stopped thinking about myself and what this second interview could do for me, how it could advance my career, and I wondered about the man Wahl. What was he feeling as well as thinking? After the first two bottles of wine and a dinner of cold chicken and green salad, he brought out four more bottles, all reds, which we opened one after another with little ceremony. From the cabin's screened-in porch, I had a perfect vantage point to look out over the lake below and across the horizon to watch the setting sun bleed an array of reds and oranges into blue overcoat of that wide sky. Water painterly, taking on these colors and spreading them over its supple canvas. For those minutes, I felt entirely like a poet, content really for the first time in a long while.

"C'mon, we're going to get happy," Wahl said as he set the wine bottles in a tote and handed me a fishing pole before we headed down to the dock. I didn't want to tell him that I'd never fished before. Dangling the line over the edge of the dock, I hoped he wouldn't notice that my lure barely touched the water.

"I want to ask you something," I said, "but I don't want to annoy you or anything."

"I'm not that touchy, but I can't guarantee a response if I don't know what you're going to ask. I'm probably not sending you on your way this time of night and in your current state anyway." I didn't tell him that I'd driven much drunker than I was right then [although not as drunk as I would become] but recognized his wisdom and was grateful that I didn't have to try to sober up quickly, open the windows, sing loudly, slap my face a few times, before looking for a motel in an area with which I was unfamiliar. If worse came to worse, I could pass out in my car until I sobered up.

"You know that other writers envy you, including me. We see you not only as someone who is tremendously successful in an occupation, I know, not the right word exactly, but it will do for now, an occupation with little chance of success for most, but as someone who seems to have it all together, producing really great work. If I want reassurance of the primacy of man, I pick up one of your essays, and if I want to believe in the creative powers of humanity, I read one of your novels. I'm not trying to ingratiate myself here, just being honest. You have something the rest of us only dream about. I guess I mean that your work has real substance and worth. What does it feel like to have reached that pinnacle? This is not for a magazine article, but for me." I think he could sense the genuine curiosity in my tone because he didn't seem too upset with the meandering question this time, didn't find the flattery cloying.

"That was a long set up for a question." We laugh too easily. "Americans, in particular, have this fascination with monetary 'success,' which is in many ways unrelated to accomplishment. It is our particular perversity that accomplishment is largely measured monetarily."

I am nodding my head but can see him only in outline in the growing dark as he continues to cast his line far out over the water. "I think Beckett's word play, in both the name of his character Lucky in *Waiting for Godot* and in Lucky's monologue, works on multiple levels to cause us to examine ideas, but among them is this concept of good fortune as opposed to a 'fortune.'" He paused. I kept my mouth shut.

"I don't know if I really want to get into this, but my mother's family had money. I was brought up in a household where comfort was the norm. That circumstance was nothing I accomplished or deserved, simply the peculiarity of my birth. It wasn't until years later, after my parents were gone, and I was drawing on trust funds, that I started to realize my relative affluence afforded me opportunities to uniquely examine things without the immediate need to profit from that literary reconnaissance."

"He says eloquently while supposedly inebriated," I said, smirking.

He laughed, perhaps at his own expense, then continued. "In other words, I didn't have to make a living through my writing. That is tremendously freeing. Not every writer has that unearned advantage."

He paused again for a longer time and neither of us said anything. One of the things I learned from my earlier experience interviewing Gerd was to wait and listen, not grow impatient with extended silences. He did not disappoint.

"It's too easy to mash everything together and call an inward experience from an outside perspective, the 'pinnacle of success,' when much of the experience is actually destructive and diversionary. If you're referencing fame, it's a like a drug, and you can never get enough. You could split your veins and brain open for this chimerical, apocryphal artifice, and it would still be begging for more." He stopped again, checking his line, reeling in and sending the line out again.

"Maybe leaving fame out of it," I said at last. "Separating out fame, there is recognition and appreciation for what you do."

"Even that recognition can be both affirming and debilitating. Sometimes, there is nowhere left to go but down. It's not as enviable a position as you might believe although I imagine there are plenty of writers who wouldn't mind trying it for a little while, assuming they interpret these words as complaint, which they are not."

I couldn't help jumping in there. "I guess I'd be part of that multitude who would like to try it for a little while, to see if it feels as good as I imagined."

"It's never as good as you can imagine. Nothing is as good as you imagine."

As I sat holding my pole stupidly, I watched him expertly cast into the darkness, hearing only the slightest disturbance from the movement of filament flying out over the water until it snapped down at last by gravity, the weight of the lure causing it to hit the surface with a slap, startling a fish below into striking it. Gerd yanked back reflexively and began reeling, his pole bent with unseen weight. Even the dogs that had been sleeping nearby came to the edge of the dock to look into the water, expectant. My head was already dizzy from too much wine, but I leaned over, watching for a shimmer in the dark to indicate a fish nearing the surface, but about eight feet out, a big fish splashed out of the water, tossing off the hook. The line slackened, and the pole regained its original posture.

"Lost it," he said. "A nice trout, too." Viktor and Varg looked up at him as if questioning his decision to release the fish this time. Then, their senses awakened, they seemed to shrug and wander off into the dark, following their noses on the trail of some small animal near the shoreline. Viggo was still sleeping and dreaming, his legs trembling and running in that other place which does not exist yet feels so real and distinct even a dog's limbs must respond to it. Solar lights near the end of his dock allowed us to see only the immediate vicinity. Although Gerd's face was in shadow for most of the evening, I felt like I was seeing him for the first time.

"How could you tell it was a trout?"

"I could feel him," he said. "I knew I was going to lose him, too."

"How?"

"The way he struck. His fight through the line. I knew he wasn't hooked well."

The idea of fishing in the dark was kind of unsettling, and I would have been nervous about a hook in my face if I had been with anyone else.

Gerd shook his head and examined the lure in his hand as if the lure had been at fault. We sat back in two worn Adirondack chairs near the end of the dock and finished off a bottle. "You don't fish much, do you?"

"No, as a matter of fact, I've never fished. I just tried to look like I knew what I was doing."

"Too bad." I had to agree with him. I knew at some point earlier in the evening that I could get used to all of this, as my ambition dissipated, and I essentially stopped interviewing and began listening and talking. It must have partially been the wine, but I asked him at one point if he had ever been in love.

"Too many times," he said, shaking his head slowly. "And you?"

I told him about Angela and how she sometimes made me feel incidental. He didn't dismiss my complaint or credit it either, merely nodded as if he had experienced the same thing. Even though I was being far too honest, I managed not to tell him about Angela's infatuation with him. I should have pressed him on his "too many times," but my inebriated and contented state failed the journalist in me. If I hadn't had too much to drink I would have followed up on his comment about his lovers. Who were these women? The public demanded names and ages. Another missed opportunity, but right then, I didn't care about the public or their demands.

Gerd looked up at the stars. My eyes followed his. Clouds had finally disappeared, and the stars were magnificent. Positioning my head and neck on the narrow back of the chair also made me a little dizzy, but the view was worth it. "You can't really see the stars in the city," I told him as if this was a fact he would not know. "This is why people become astronomers," I said out loud although I had meant only to think it.

"Orion's red star cannot be held," he said quietly. I wasn't sure if I was meant to hear him.

"I don't know those lines. Are they from one of your works?"

"No. Not his lines exactly, but they recall Fred Dings' poem 'Redwing Blackbird.'" I knew a lot of poets, but I'd never heard of Dings. He exhaled deeply as if the thought of holding stars exhausted him. "The other stars, the still living ones, are discreet witnesses to man's overreaching utterances, revealing only his solitary unimportance."

"Dings' words, too?"

Just a drunken clutter of my words."

Here is the part that is lost to me. I think I either passed out for a short while or we were silent for a long time, but when I heard one of the dogs growl, I came to attention. I looked out across the lake to settle my queasy stomach. A beam of light here and there from the opposite shore reflected on the water like a lighthouse's beacon, as if guiding maritime pilots home. "Is this where you write most of your work?"

"I write wherever I am, but this is where I think."

"Of course," I said stupidly. I wanted to stay out there all night, but the mosquitoes began tormenting me since I hadn't had a drink in a while and I began to be aware of my body again.

He must have noticed me ineffectually swatting air. "We'd better go back inside or they'll eat you alive."

"Who knew they could be so voracious?" My words started rolling around inside my mouth rather than coming out fluently. He seemed indifferent to the mosquitoes, either immune to their blood sucking capabilities or somehow protected from their

233 | Socrates is Dead Again

poison. Of course, that made sense in my drunken state. Even mosquitoes, the most dangerous insect known to man could not touch him on a beautiful July night.

As I stood up, he became solicitous, "Go slow now. Don't fall in. I'm afraid I'm not in any shape to rescue you." Much earlier in the evening, we had both jumped in the water to swim, well before those last several bottles of wine.

"And there is no one around to rescue both of us."

"Not even your dogs?" I asked in some kind of slurred speech.

"Definitely not Viktor; probably even beyond Varg's amazing capabilities." I could hear the dogs moving in darkness but could not make them out as they were a little way off now. Either the wine or fatigue made me indifferent to noises in the night, however.

"I'm a good swimmer," I managed to get out. Despite my inebriated state, I remember finding my way up, with some difficulty, over rocks and tall weeds, a few with thorns, to large stone steps leading to the cabin by following him. From his right hand, a beam of light shot from a flashlight, guiding us. Even though the trek was arduous in near blackness if we stepped too far to either side, it was as if everything in my life had suddenly become much clearer. The dogs returned from wherever they had ventured and followed us up slowly at first then raced each other, nudging one another out of the way to get through the cabin door, knocking against screen door, nearly wrenching it off its hinges.

Gerd disappeared for a moment and came back, tossing me a blanket and pillow, indicating that the couch was mine. It was no small gift. The couch must have been stuffed with down; it was ridiculously comfortable. Viktor had already leapt up on it. I knew the difference between Viktor and Viggo by then, even when drunk. Varg was easy with his dark coloring, but his master motioned with one finger pointed to wood plank floors, and Viktor reluctantly complied, his ears and tail lowered. I don't remember anything after that until I woke in the morning with blankets tucked up around my neck, smells of fresh brewed coffee and warm bread in the cabin. One of the dogs started barking as I stirred.

"It's a way back," Gerd said as he gave me a cup of coffee.

Somehow the comment surprised me. I don't know if I expected that I would move in with him or that we had become such fast friends that all the decisions from there out would be mine, but I recovered enough to thank him, turned and petted Viktor's head for the kindness of sharing his bed and started to get my things together to begin the journey home.

"Shower is the lake this morning," Gerd said more cheerfully, handing me a bar of soap and towel. When I looked, I saw that his hair was wet, and he seemed like he had been up for hours. There were no bags under his eyes, and he looked sharp. When did the man sleep? Although I had no intention of jumping in that frigid lake with a clear head, I also had no intention of deliberately disappointing his expectations. I took soap and towel and headed down to the water with the dogs racing ahead of me, Viktor nearly knocking me off my feet. By then I was sufficiently awake and knew enough to avoid getting tripped up by their exuberance.

Jumping in couldn't be that bad, I decided, as I knew Gerd must be watching from up in the cabin. I did a clumsy dive off the end of the dock, hitting both my right foot on something and my belly flat on water's hard surface. For several seconds in which all sense of time and place disappeared, in fact, in which all thoughts, memory, understanding dissolved, except the sensations driven by extreme cold on submersed body, I hardly remembered who I was. When my head popped up, I yelped, screeched, and laughed, frantically trying to make my way back to land. There was no ladder on the dock, so I had to swim to the shore. How could lake water be that cold? The dogs had returned to the end of the dock, drawn by commotion. By the time I reached the shallow water and stone bottom, I was adjusted to the change in my environment, and I reached for soap, bathed quicker than I had ever done, dove once more to rinse, and then climbed out. The lake must have been fed with springs. I expected bath water and got the Arctic.

    Heading up to the cabin, I started laughing foolishly again, and it occurred to me that Gerd and I had talked for hours after we had ventured down to the lake the night before. I remembered almost none of it at the moment, praying my recall would return. I wasn't panicked, but I kept wondering how I could have been so inept a second time, allowing myself to get drunk. Much of that gap of time I wanted to fill in was lost along with the philosophy, concepts about writing and life that had been sifted into night air, stars, and black waters.

    He would not begin again. When I reached the cabin, Gerd was still pleasant but now more formal, even aloof, handing me my bag, along with a plate holding a breakfast biscuit, wishing me well, turning his back to me. We were done.

Thirty-one

Shwetak Confronts His Parents

If Arun and Pooja were alive today, I could not ask their permission to marry Gillian. Maybe the only advantage to becoming an orphan was being able to fall in love with a red-haired girl with a big mouth who is not Indian and not a practicing Hindu. My parents would almost certainly have arranged a marriage for me with some quiet girl from across an ocean, and I would have respected their wishes, probably learning, in time, to love this dark-eyed, much younger girl who would do everything to please me and never use profanity. She certainly would not have been pregnant before she met me. She wouldn't be writing books and stories and giving advice to everyone about things she knows and things she doesn't know much about. And she would revere me even if I did nothing to earn that reverence.

Maybe this girl my parents arranged for me would be named Aarika and be known for her beauty, and I would have to constantly defend her honor against other men, maybe getting killed in the process because my beautiful wife was desired by all who saw her, or maybe she would be named Harshini and be happy all the time, or maybe she would not sit quietly as Arun and Pooja promised but lead loud protests against female feticide, empowering herself and other women around India by organizing against and writing about this illegal practice. Maybe I would get killed defending her in India from my more radical brothers in the RSS because she had convinced me that I belonged in India, not America. Maybe she would decide to live with me in America and be happy, as her name suggested, for a while then demand a divorce from me because she wanted her space and freedom, and she liked this the empowering part of this culture. Maybe she would demand half of everything I own in this country even though I don't own very much except my car which would be a shame to sell. And I would embarrass my parents with the break-up of my marriage which was, in a way, their marriage, too.

In all of these seemingly perfect scenarios, I am unhappy. This is because I was raised in America, not India, and I have fallen in love with someone my parents would never have approved of.

Instead, I'm in this terrible position of having a pain in my stomach and my head, thinking about this crazy American woman whose name means young at heart, but it may mean immature because the interpretation is various, and this young woman has already been with another man and carried his baby, lost that child, and asked me ridiculous questions. She certainly does not revere me even on days when I seem wise or say the most appropriate thing. She makes fun of me sometimes and seems not to understand what part of the world my parents were from or very much about my religion even if I still practiced it.

Ah, Arun and Pooja have been spared this indignity but made to suffer another. Thinking about how they died should quash any notion of a superior being existing. Considering how these two very good people met their ends is enough to make me a nihilist even if I wasn't already heading in that direction.

If I could have this life in America and bring them back I would. If I could bring them back but not have choices, would I do so? I have to say, "yes. I would return them to life at any cost to me." But that makes me sound like an unselfish man, and I believe that I am quite selfish and irreverent and, probably, unwise.

This argument about the impossibility of returning the dead to life is truly ridiculous and unsound, I am fully aware, but I intend to marry Gillian, and there is no one to stop me from asking her except me, and I seem averse to preventing this impractical union.

"Gillian is a fine woman," I would say to my mother and father, then study the frowns on their faces. "I like the fact she writes well, perhaps even better than me," I would tell them.

"What does writing or writing well have to do with anything?" Arun would ask while Pooja shakes her weary head.

"What does my son think he is doing?" my father would say with dismay.

"Such is the life I have chosen," I would tell them. But I love my parents, and I would add, "I wish to make you proud and happy, so please bless my marriage to the woman I love. I truly think you will come to love her, too."

Arun would look at Pooja, and then they would turn to me and say, "Whatever makes you happy, son, is what you must do." Of course, that is not what they would have said at all, but I can create this unreal scene because they are not here to protest. And, what is much more strange; oh, excuse my English, I meant stranger: I am most happy about this unlikely prospect.

Thirty-two

Ornal Feels Less Alone

Ellison and I were fighting again, and I told him I was leaving but not leaving him for good.

"Go," he said as if he meant it, but I wasn't entirely sure what he intended; I know he didn't mean for me to never come back. "Now!" he added, but after that, I had to get out of our apartment for a while or I would want to kill him; I needed to get outside, even of myself. Admittedly, I'm not always the easiest person to live with, but then two artists of any kind under one roof present a few challenges, and you'll notice, I'm not addressing race nor feminism, two minefields that we manage to successfully walk across on a daily basis. I was trying not to provoke everyone in the world, and it is still an uphill battle, in part, because I believe the world needs provoking, needs to move out of its self-satisfied slumber of its racist, misogynist, ignorant character.

I walked several blocks, much further than my routine stroll around our area, all the way to Justice Avenue in Elmhurst. It was strictly an observational walk with my mini-journal in my pocket. Odors directed my navigation from Middle Eastern to India and back again from familiar restaurants. A shoe repair shop looked closed and boarded up and made me look down at the shoes I had chosen. Heels were fine but the leather looked worn, and my left big toe was starting to feel constricted.

Then I made a decision to embark upon a much longer journey, into the city, at least another borough. After I got off the bus and then a subway stop, a few blocks later, I decided to step into this unexpected little tea and book shop with an Asian feel that, not surprisingly, I had never been to before. Some mom and pop little, out-of-step establishment that was trying to establish itself; you could tell it had opened relatively recently but already had a few steady customers. They were in the process of decorating and catering to their customers in a solicitous manner. Probably not long before it closed, too, I thought. Check. These places come and go so quickly you could lose your way if navigating by the businesses. Have to remember this. Write down the address. The place wasn't chic, but it was intimate and dark inside even on a bright day.

Customers were seated at little round tables, and they were gesturing to each other in private conversations. A few individuals sat alone, and I could tell that they were protecting space around them as certainly as if they had set up screens. The environment was not entirely Asian, and, like I said before, I was more than a little surprised to find an Asian tea stop that also sold books. Apparently, others who wandered inside were equally surprised. Tall shelves stood against the walls, shelves lined with teapots and texts of various sizes, and music was playing unobtrusively in the background, kind of like being in a spa, only with books, and everyone was dressed in eclectic clothing. All right, it wasn't that much like a spa, but I instantly felt a tremendous sense of ease in this funky place. I wanted to tell Ellison, but then I remembered we were fighting, and he wouldn't want to hear from me at the moment.

The line of people standing and ready to place an order was fairly long, a good sign in that these appeared to be regulars who were willing to wait. I didn't get the taste of the usual frustration associated with long lines. I was thinking about Ellison again and why I loved him in spite of our pronounced differences. Were other people in line thinking about someone they loved, or a person she or he hated? Were they just thinking they wanted a cup of tea that would warm throat and then belly?

On one of the shelves, I spotted Wahl's most recent tome. He is still everywhere, I thought. The man is dead, but the writer lives on. My mind space was now also cluttered with images and thoughts about Gerd Wahl and why he killed himself. I wondered how many times I would come back to the absurd and question why, when I thought about death or deaths, everything around me felt more alive? There is this bizarre and wonderful children's book about a duck and death, and I kept seeing the dead duck floating peacefully away.

Scanning the room, I noticed two women at a table near me, their open laptops, back-to-back and touching like lovers. The woman closer to me had short, cropped hair, even shorter than mine, and it was dyed blonde. I could tell by her roots which were growing out gray. I knew she was older but couldn't precisely determine age, somewhere in the 50-60 category that I would certainly keep guessing at and not likely win any prizes at one of those little county fairs. I loved her big, dangling earrings of blue stone, however, and on her left wrist, she wore a matching blue bracelet that slipped up and down her skinny arm as she tapped keys. She paused and held her finger to her lips when I leaned over to see if I could tell what she was writing; it looked like dialogue. It was dialogue. Maybe a screenplay, but then, no, the formatting wasn't right.

Across the tiny table from this woman sat another elderly woman. Their knees had to be touching. The other woman had her long white hair wrapped up in a band of some kind and twisted around itself again, looking less like a bun than tissue paper squeezed and scrunched. A yellow scarf was wrapped around her neck all the way to her chin, hiding her neck completely, like Katherine Hepburn in her later years. I would have to remember that trick. I could see her face better than the woman who was closer to me, and the white-haired woman had a long face with a pointy chin, rather severe. Her eyes were small and intense behind the dark frames of her glasses; she wasn't attractive, but I rudely couldn't stop staring at her because she intrigued me. These two women were engrossed in their writing tasks; it was as if they were the only people in the tea shop. I longed to be that lost in my work in the way they were. I realized that my journey across the city had led me to this place; this is exactly where I was meant to be and for this reason. I felt the fates or perhaps the Muses at work. Would I write about this pair who didn't speak or gesture or even look at one another, but whose clicking keys seemed so perfectly in sync?

Someone walked by holding a pretty cup of raspberry herbal tea that was very strong. I could still detect fruit odors after the cup crossed the space between us. Raspberry tea woman looked about my age, and she sat against a wall, pulling a book from one of the tall shelves she could easily reach beside her. It was as if the subject matter was unimportant, but the feel of the book was what she craved, and I understood her need. In that short time, I was already at the front of the line and ordered a Moroccan Mint tea that was pleasingly both bitter and sweet, I thought, like my relationship with Ellison. A table conveniently opened up next to the two women with laptops. I sat beside them, felt as if I was joining them.

The one with the short hair looked up at me, seeming to stare, but I could tell she was concentrating on her words and not seeing me at all. She was well past me and into other lands.

I couldn't resist. "What are you writing?" I wasn't provoking. I could hear myself arguing with Ellison and explaining to him that I was just being curious.

"Me?" They both asked.

"Yes. Both of you. Is that dialogue you are working on in a story?"

"Oh, it's part of a novel," said the blonde.

"How's it coming?"

"It's finished really. I'm organizing now." Blue-earring woman was becoming more animated, and she remembered her tea which had grown cold, I expected, from the slight wince on her face when she sipped it. I wanted to ask her how she could be finished if she was organizing which sounded rather like she was pulling together notes, and nowhere near done, but I decided to try out my new line of tact. Ellison would have been proud of me at that moment. I don't know why I considered his opinion of me as if I was the child and he the parent. I even irritated myself.

"Are you writing something together?"

They laughed. "No. No." They both answered. "We come here to encourage each other," one said and the other added, "So we don't stop or give up."

"Is it working? Both novels?"

"Oh, yes," said the blonde. I could tell the other woman had decided to let her friend answer most of my questions either because the blonde had better answers or the white-haired woman was trying to maintain her creative concentration.

"You're in the editing stage?"

"It's done; I'm putting it together." I couldn't quite figure out what she meant by that since I envisioned these words in chapters out of order that she had suddenly decided to force into chronology. She was adamant about that facet, however, giving me essentially the same answer she had already stated. I liked her resolve if nothing else.

"What's it about?" I hated this question when someone asked me but found myself asking it anyway.

"It's a paranormal romance, but there aren't any vampires or werewolves," she was quick to add.

"Delightful," I said, sipping my tea, deciding to leave them alone to create their masterpieces, but I continued thinking about paranormal romances, one in which I was sure I was engaged with Ellison. "We have enough vampires running around," I couldn't help adding.

"Precisely," she laughed.

"That's what I told her, too," her friend finally said without looking up from her computer.

Since she had decided to join our conversation, I asked her, "So, what's your novel about?"

"A kind of dystopian vision of our future, about where our environmental decisions are leading us. It's very dark."

"Ah. Did you have to do a lot of research?"

"Oh, yes. I'm still fact checking some of the details to make sure they follow scientific principles, but I can't reveal more."

I almost laughed at that statement but stifled it. As if I was about to steal the vagueness of a paranormal romance or dystopian environmental calamity. "Titles chosen yet?"

They looked up at each other and smiled. I assumed it was some kind of private joke that I would have let drop.

"We actually helped each other with our titles," said the blonde.

"We chose them for each other," said white-haired woman.

"Was there a method?"

"Of course. We list words that most often appear in contemporary titles."

"Published works."

"Then looked for those repeated multiple times."

"Then, from those, we chose ones that seemed to fit."

"Such as?" I was really curious at this point because I always have a hard time with titles, but Ellison said he finds them easy. In fact, he often starts his work with a title as if the naming begins the entire creative process.

"Redemption, ruins, chaos, vacancy, shadow, realm"

"Not 'Snooki?'"

"Oh, no," the lady with the long face said.

"Well, maybe they would sell faster if we added that name to our titles." Then they laughed.

"You create titles with words that seem to have a proven allure?"

"Exactly."

"Very methodical of you." I was trying to imagine how any of those words were going to work together.

"Are you a writer, too?" asked my favorite already, the blonde.

"Yes. Any advice for me, other than your method of choosing titles?"

"Oh, you're young," said the wispy-haired, elderly sprite. "You should travel."

I meant writing advice, and I thought it was funny she essentially told me to get lost.

"Yes, go everywhere," said my new blonde friend. "Don't worry about money or jobs. Go live on a shoe-string; oh, do people say that anymore?"

I smiled. I hadn't heard anyone say anything related to shoe strings since I was a very little girl, and my grandmother used that expression. "And then?" I asked, playing along. "What do I do when my shoe strings run out?"

"Ignore all that. People can live on surprisingly little. And then, when you're old"

"Like us"

"Write like hell."

"Don't let anything stop you."

"Not publishers"

"or paid or unpaid critics"

"or your favorite aunt or niece or"

"the guy who lives in your apartment below you who told you that he's a writer, too,"

"and that the stuff you're writing won't sell and even if it would, it'd end up"

"embarrassing you if it ever got published."

They were finishing each other's sentences rapidly, part of a practiced routine, it seemed. Maybe they went from tea shop to tea shop with this comedy set. I nodded in encouragement and they smiled, but I could tell they wanted to get back to writing "like hell." I wished them luck and said good-bye.

They grimaced in response to something on their pages, smiled at me sweetly, then returned to typing away on their laptop keyboards as I walked toward the door of the tea shop.

"Oh, wait. Your name?" asked the blonde, waving at me.

"Ornal," I shouted back. "Yours?"

"Helen." She pointed to her friend, "Ellen."

"Good-bye, Helen and Ellen," and I waved, turning once more as I imagined them following me, giving me more good advice or bad advice, my new rhyming friends.

Tracing my way back to my apartment after subway and bus stops and mindful of the ways in which you could wander into an area of Queens that is cut off, I looked at my feet and how they were rebelling against the shoes I had chosen to wear before walking that far, friction setting up between my heel and the back of my black shoes with plastic overlays that were cute in the store and my closet but not as practical as I had assumed before I set out. I had been in the midst of writers in a shop across the city and then heading home again like Odysseus finding his way back to Ithaca, my day-long journey taking years which made me think about not Odysseus but Homer or whoever created him since even identity was surrounded in uncertainty. I was thinking about writers and all of the other cafes and dwindling book shops people wandered into as far away as Chicago, Istanbul, London, and Sao Paulo, every city in the world, and all the little towns, and out in the country, in every country, rapping keyboards, tiny lights beneath their strained wrists, words appearing and disappearing with keys, symbols and signs indicating something redolent.

These two women I met were connected not only to each other, I decided, but to me and Ellison and Ian and Marshall and Scott and Tom, no, not Tom. Maybe Ian wouldn't mind being connected to Tom, I reframed my malicious thought, for once pitying the purposeful isolation of Tom or perhaps envying him. And suddenly, I wanted to get back to Ellison right away.

When I opened the door, I expected Ellison would run up to greet me, hug me, wishing he had never been angry with me, but he was sleeping, and I had to wake him in order to tell him about my odyssey across the city. He got up without saying a word and handed me an envelope. I read it and almost cried. Then he hugged me, and we broke open that red wine we had been saving. Three of my poems were about to be published.

"They want all three! It's official, darling: you're a poet."

I started to protest that I was one before being published by a prestigious magazine but thought better of it at the last second. "Yes," I said. "Let's toast to writers."

Thirty-three

Last Time in the Cabin

Julia returned to Wahl's cabin a few weeks after the reading of his will in which it was revealed that Gerd Wahl left his dogs and $30,000 to a neighboring farmer, his book royalties, stocks, and his condo in the city to an aging aunt, but his Skaneateles cabin and all its contents went to Ms. Julia Alexander. The solicitor raised his eyebrows at her name. Although she had kept Gerd's key, Julia did not know whether she would be able to return to his house.

    An insurance agent contacted her about unoccupied home owner's insurance, and she finally decided she needed to act. Unsurprisingly, emotional paralysis had provided no answers. She needed to find out, what exactly? There would be no statements of admission, no confession, no steps that led up to what happened waiting for her in the cabin, but she still went expectant and dreading possible discoveries. Scorched wood outlined that corner of the cabin which had never been repaired after the fire, she noted, when she walked down the bank from the narrow road. At the door she hesitated, unable to unlock it immediately. Before going in, she changed directions and headed down to the water, stood on the dock, and looked out over Skaneateles; it was a windy day and whitecaps threatened a few small boats skimming its surface. Julia was surprised to see fishermen out on the water in such wind. Their little boats bobbed and seemed to disappear behind water walls before reappearing again. She knew little about fishing. Although she had been told by the lawyer that the Labradors were no longer there, she half expected Gerd's dogs to come bounding down the bank, turning her head in anticipation. Gerd had given her the farmer's phone number in the event anything ever happened to him. He must have made his decision long ago, she thought.

When she finally worked up courage and resolve, she faced the house, turned the key and went in. Taking shallow breaths, she began the slow examination of first the expansive open room, touching his artifacts, wondering which of those vestiges of his life he had last held and what secrets they contained. Even the most ordinary objects seemed imbued with new meaning.

Scraps of paper drifted next to the bed as she opened the door, as if torn from a journal. Unintelligible words lay on the pages, but she didn't know if he was simply playing with inventive language, attempting to coin new terms, or descending into a place from which he would not return. Perhaps they were a code of some kind. He loved puzzles. She took an armful of papers to the porch coffee table and began to examine the letters, moving them around to see if any arrangement gave her a clue. On one scrap, she read the strange "coined" words:

guelantive

ricendent

exlit

thetical

She tried rearranging the letters in each word as if he had left a jumble for her, but quickly gave up that silly idea. There were other, recognizable words and phrases on the page, as well: fables of poetics

detaches detached detach---------------ing

That last one, detaching, seemed ominous. How unfair she was being, she suddenly realized. *Imagine if someone picked up every scrap of paper in my house and tried to determine its significance and what I had intended?* But she could not stop looking. There was a short, handwritten paragraph that looked like possible lines from a story:

Wind tells the roof it is there by grace alone.

She liked that line. Perhaps she could incorporate it into a compilation of Gerd's unfinished works. Did she now have that responsibility?

Whalen smelled rain, heard it, before it began to soak through his shirt and faded jeans, his house shingles having disappeared before cloud burst, downpour seeping through rafters until bouncing off pails and pans set out below, musical even to untrained ears. He was not surprised by the storm's ferocity, just the pleasure he felt from its fury.

Initially looking for other pages to continue reading what seemed to be a story in progress, she could find none. It ended abruptly. After walking around the words and rereading them, she could make no meaning from his made-up words either. Not his words, not his will, nor his will to carry through with such an

253 | Socrates is Dead Again

annihilative mission. Only the words "detached" and "detaches" seemed indications of his state of mind, and there was, of course, a character with no roof who had submitted to the storm. Why hadn't he called her? Why hadn't he answered her calls? She would have turned around and driven all night to be with him. He had to have known she left him only in frustration, not anger.

Picking up pages again and folding them, she tucked a few in her purse before moving around the cabin again. His felt fedora hung on a rack on the wall beside his bedroom door. A black wool stocking hat and a Yankees baseball cap were layered one on top of the other on the arm of a chair. She picked up the fedora, lifted it to her head, then set it back down and cried. Not hysterically. It hurt too much to fully let go. It almost made her laugh to think about her restrained crying. Gerd would have found it funny, she thought. His fedora would not go home with her, too much of him to take in every day.

Although she knew she had to go through his closet, it did not seem possible yet. One of his plaid shirts, worn through at the elbows, hung over a bedpost near where his head would have rested. Was that the shirt he had on the day before he woke up with the determination to end it all? She grabbed the shirt impulsively and stuffed it into her bag. It was the least valuable thing he owned, and she suddenly loved that old shirt she had asked him to throw away many times before.

There was still the rest of the cabin to go through, and she moved out from his bedroom, walking carefully around the site where he had shot himself: dark wood floor discolored even after repeated cleanings by a professional crew, and when she finally allowed herself to look at that spot where he had died, she stood over it unable to move. Although she could not see him or even imagine him there, she felt his presence and finally allowed herself to collapse. Curling into a near fetal position, she lay as if entwined with him. If only she had not left him alone.

He must have known she would feel this way. It was not like Gerd to be cruel, but then she began to wonder if she had known him at all. Perhaps it was exactly like him to, at least, be indifferent. What must he have felt about her to have exacted such revenge? Had he loved her at all? What was it about her that allowed him to care? From the first time she met him, she knew he was extraordinary even before she discovered his fame. Although she once asked him what he saw in her, his terse response offered no real insight.

Recognizing that no one was going to rescue her, she finally pushed herself to her feet, exhausted, too spent to think what she should do next about the cabin or Gerd's possessions, and then she walked out. Her lungs drew in sharp, late October air. There were the dogs, she remembered again, and she headed up the hill on her way to the neighboring farmer's. It was not as if she expected answers from this farmer or Gerd's big dogs but, perhaps, some kind of relief if only in the form of distraction, and she wanted desperately to see those Labs, ruffle their short fur.

Looking like he had been out in the sun baking for twenty years, Jake walked toward her wearing his leathery skin as emblem. He might have been a good-looking man when he was younger, Julia thought, but bent from heavy labors, his hands calloused and cracked, he appeared much older than his 57 years. His whistle for Gerd's dogs was powerful enough to be heard a mile away. Viktor raced for Julia once he spotted her, running then colliding into her, nearing knocking her down even though she had braced for him. Viggo circled around them frantically, leaping and panting from his exertions, anxious for her attention but willing to wait.

"Where's Varg?" she asked patting Viktor's wide head, half expecting Gerd to come over the hill toward her, as well.

Jake shook his head. He didn't speak for a moment, and Julia's eyes widened. She felt her stomach flip and the bile rise in her throat even before he got out the sentence. "He got hit by a car some time back, right before. Mr. Wahl didn't tell you?"

She hadn't known about Varg's death until Jake Harris stunned her. "No." Julia ignored Viktor and Viggo for a moment as they licked her hand, rubbed against her legs, nudged her, recognizing that her attention had radically shifted.

"When he brought these two that last time, I offered him a cup of coffee like I always do, and he always turned me down, but that last time, he said, 'yes.' We went up to the house, and he tossed a fat envelop on my table."

"An envelope?" she asked, after once again ruffling Viktor's fur and bending down to greet the animals properly.

"Yep. Had the dogs' papers, certificates, licenses, breeding information, vet's number, that kind of thing, all in order."

"He always gave you an envelope, when he left his dogs with you?"

"Every time when he said, 'In case something happens, you need their paperwork.'"

"Nothing was different that last time he came?"

"Well, he only had the two dogs with him, and then he brought that big envelop inside, setting it on the table rather than handing it to me outside as he usually did. I didn't think nothin' of it at the time, though." Viktor's attention was drawn off by a movement in the field, and he raced away, followed by Viggo.

"When did he tell you about Varg?"

"It was a few minutes before I asked him where the other dog was, and he said, 'Hit and run driver. Killed instantly.'"

She wouldn't let herself mourn Varg then and there.

"Did Gerd tell you where he was going?"

"Mr. Wahl talked about a trip, but he was always traveling, what with being a famous author and all. I didn't think no more about it, 'cept to tell him how sorry I was about Varg. I knew that big chocolate was his favorite; mine, too. He always gave me a little extra for feeding 'em, so I didn't think about looking in that envelop right away. I mean, it didn't occur to me to look. I expected him back in a few days."

"When did you know?" Julia hugged her arms across her chest as if preparing for the blows.

"I didn't open that envelop until I heard about it, about his death, on the news, and when I finally got around to looking, there was $10,000 sitting right there on my kitchen table. It didn't hit me right then, but later, I knew something was different that last time he came. Thinking back on it, I imagined he was pretty torn up about losing Varg. Believe me, I wished I'd a said a little more. Wish I could've done something different."

Julia looked away from the farmer and followed Viktor and Viggo with her eyes until they became smaller and smaller in the distance. "They look wonderful: healthy and happy with you," she said.

"Yep. Like to run, those two. Good dogs; no trouble, never. Just have to tire 'em out." Neither one of them knew what to say next. Jake rubbed his gray whiskered chin and shifted his hand to his right shoulder where an ache had set in. He messaged his shoulder and neck for an instant. She looked out over his fields and then down to the lake where there seemed only emptiness and sharp wind over cold waters.

Bowing his head slightly, Jake said quietly, almost a whisper, "I'm terribly sorry about Mr. Wahl. He was . . ." There were tears at the corners of his eyes, but she couldn't tell if they were caused by sorrow or the bite of winds. The two of them continued to stand there, neither one able to move, both reluctant to speak. Nothing could seem to fill that chasm. She wondered if Jake knew about the additional $30,000 Gerd had left to him in the will. It wasn't her place to tell him.

Growing chill caused her finally to shift position. When she reached up and hugged the surprised farmer before leaving, Jake awkwardly and tentatively patted her back. "Don't want to get your pretty dress dirty with these old farm clothes." She waited.

Say anything, she thought. *I'll listen*. He stepped away from her and looked down toward the lake. They both stared in that general direction. Jake rubbed the back of his neck again. Even the dogs sensed something wrong. "Going to ice up before you know it."

Thirty-four

Envy Welcomes Relief of Despair

When I have a few minutes that I'm not using productively—who am I kidding here? What part of Tom Hayes' existence has anything remotely to do with productively? As soon as I sit down to write, consciously make the decision that this is it, this is the time and space to discover some prose magic, a plain of dead space opens up like a desert, and I am mired in similes or metaphors of which I have no understanding. I stare it at for a while, without even knowing what "it" is, expecting or hoping some creature will walk across frozen gases and look up at me, yet with all the turmoil in my head, nothing but silence continues to negotiate the page.

    I figured that once Gerd was dead, I would be free of him, his influence, envy, the hatred for someone I didn't even know, but he continues for me, a ghost paralyzing something inside. If I ask Marshall what he thinks about Gerd, he has nothing but praise and seems unaffected by this snake of envy twisting itself inside me until there is the long, thin shape of despair. This is what I could not tell Marie, what I could not tell my parents, what I could not tell my friends. It is slimy and petty and unavoidable. If one thing had gone my way, everything would be different now. I could have been the one with the book contract, agents calling me, bugging me to meet my deadlines which would not be difficult at all because everything I wrote would fall out like coins. Writing is not difficult if someone is asking you to do it, or if that someone values your words before you have even written them, and tells you that people want to read what you write. Your audience is impatiently waiting for your brain to release the page.

More likely, I'll become another Jack Torrance typing the same sentence over and over and over until they break down the door and find me toothlessly laughing with an axe in my hand. Where is my fucking Xanax? If Scott took it, I'll, forget Scott. The glint of reflected light off a nearby window travels the short distance between buildings to blind me temporarily.

"I'm going blind," I could say, and they would be sympathetic, but not for this kind of blindness. And then I see it, beneath the bed, pushed nearly half-way across that dusty expanse, and I drop down, my belly skidding on the floor to reach for it. I'm licking dust for a little pill to quell the panic.

Thirty-five

Ian Exhorts Marie to "Hold on Tight"

I'd seen Marie only a few times though I'd known Tom for years since the days we roomed together. Tom always told us that Marie kept to herself.

"Believe me, Ian, she is not the type to socialize," Tom said.

I got the idea from Tom that she was a little unbalanced. He'd met her shortly after leaving Iowa. None of us knew her well, except that she was quiet, pretty, beautiful, a little unusual, and "annoyingly complicated," according to Tom. But I have to admit, I never took much stock in Tom's assessment of people. I remembered thinking I liked complicated when he told me. There was also something he said about her parents dying or her father, some tragedy figured into it, and I couldn't quite believe that Tom was entirely matter of fact about her parental loss. Tom never brought Marie with him to any functions or get-togethers. For those reasons, it didn't really surprise me when he said that he had broken up with her. I actually wondered if they had ever been together. Maybe she existed only in his imagination, and the woman he pointed out to me was a stranger.

Then Tom called out of the blue and wanted my help to pick up his stuff from his old apartment because, "Marie won't let me in anymore," and I told Tom, "You know, I don't do that kind of thing." There is nothing I hate more than brokering a couple's fights and relationship, especially one that has ended. My old roommate promptly reminded me of the time back in our Writer's Workshop days when he coaxed an inebriated and highly inappropriate professor out my bedroom without anyone noticing or at least without a major scene.

"This is it then," I finally said. "No more interest on this debt. Paid in full if I agree to do this." The only time I've ever asked a favor was in grad school, but to Tom's credit, he managed to usher Professor Dickhead out, avoiding further embarrassment for me and a possible arrest for him because a botched, attempted rape of a student never goes over well. So, I owed Tom.

I ended up standing in the hallway outside the door of Marie's apartment and waiting before knocking, hoping she wouldn't open it. That way, I could at least tell Tom I'd tried, then turn around. I actually started back to the top of the stairs when I heard the lock click, and I turned to look back.

"Oh, hello. You must be Ian," she said as she opened the door and stood there, her hair wet and messy but lovely; her large dark eyes clear, and her lips so pretty but a little pinched. "I recognize you from a photo and that one time with Drew Levin. Tom told me you were coming. I was expecting you."

"You were? I guess Tom never bothered to introduce us," I said.

"He did introduce us once."

"I'm sorry," I stupidly responded.

"We were at a party, I recall, Levin's apartment, and Tom introduced us to each other."

"Yes, I should have remembered." I realized now that the night Tom pointed her out to me, I was fairly inebriated and had managed to confuse things. It was also more than a little crowded in Drew's place, and we were all pushed up against one another, but Marie held her position.

"Tom told me you are a good friend. It's kind of you to pick up his things. Not the sort of favor most people will do for someone."

I was still standing on the landing.

"Please come in."

"I don't know," I said, feeling guilty that I had no such feelings of friendship for Tom, only obligation. "I'm afraid I'm the one who should be sorry for disturbing you with this errand." I was already losing track of how many times I had apologized to her before I walked in her door. I didn't expect to be nonplused, but I was, stupidly so. I've never had a problem with women until recently when I badly misread first Gillian and then Angela, even if only momentarily. What was Marie thinking? When had I become terribly inept at reading signals?

"Drew told me you are a good guy. In other words, you come with highly recommended credentials," she laughed. I was trying to decide if this was sarcasm and whether she felt the same about Drew as she clearly did about Tom.

"Drew told you?" I may never entirely forgive him for the Adrian Gerd Wahl interview. He'll be gone from our magazine after his feature on Wahl comes out, no doubt. I happen to know Drew has already gotten offers from other magazine editors who are merely anticipating his feature story. I'd been feeling sorry for myself quite a bit lately. I guess I was showing my vulnerability when I walked into Tom's old place. Her laugh? I wasn't sure if she was laughing at me or with me.

"Yes, I needed a second opinion. Drew Levin. You work with him, don't you?"

"I do, at least for a little while longer. I didn't know he knew you, too." I always thought I was the one connecting my writer friends.

"It's okay if you don't remember Tom talking about me. It doesn't matter anymore. Tom left some things in the apartment, but he really doesn't have much. I packed it all in these few boxes for you."

Trying to stop staring at her, I looked over and saw four large cardboard boxes neatly stacked by the couch on the opposite side of the room. Tom's life in four boxes. Nothing in the apartment looked as if Tom had ever lived there. Marie had thoroughly excised him. I liked the place immediately. There was nothing pretentious anywhere, and it was neat and clean, stylish and smart. Marie looked stylish and smart, too. Was I imagining myself living there? I think I shifted from one foot to the other.

"Is that all he has here? Those four boxes? Nothing else?"

"That's it, I'm afraid, or in this case, it's rather good you don't have a lot more to lug down the stairs. One on the bottom is pretty heavy, though. I can help if you need me to." She sighed as if that was the last of Tom, and she really was finally rid of him.

Needing to stall, I asked, "Do you want me to lift anything else for you? Anything you need help with? I mean things to move for you?" I wasn't even sure what I meant by that last remark, just guess I was offering to move heavy furniture for her, things Tom would have taken care of if he hadn't been such an asshole. Was I really looking for an excuse to delay my departure? I liked being in her presence for some reason that I could not yet fully comprehend. Oh, hell, of course I could. She was gorgeous and exciting. The whole scene was surreal. Almost as if I was in a movie, and someone forgot to tell me. It wasn't only the weird sexual tension in the air. It was like she knew the script but had forgotten to give me a copy.

"Move things?" She stared at me. "No, not really, but thank you for offering." She was smiling.

There was no reason at all for me to stay any longer. I stood there stupidly for a few more seconds, taking in the unfamiliar, while returning her stare, wondering if I had anything of interest to say that might prevent me from exiting. Maybe I was even thinking about asking her out for a cup of coffee. I realized later that we must have stood there a long time looking at each other. "Look, would you be interested if we . . . ? I wonder if you might like to . . . ? I don't mean to be presumptuous but . . ." I couldn't finish what I wanted to ask.

I'm not a particularly impulsive person, at least most of the time. I didn't expect what happened then, but when I finally gave up trying to come up with an excuse to linger and leaned over to pick up a box, Marie threw her arms around my neck, and I drew her in. I don't remember every second of what transpired next. No, I do, but I'm not sure I want to share it. We were taking off each other's clothes, kissing every inch of exposed skin. Her beautiful mouth was warm and wet and luscious. I hadn't kissed a woman in that way in a while. In another instant, we were climbing all over each other; I didn't even know until then that I was desperate, desired her more than I could have imagined.

In the morning, I hadn't left, and she was still warm and touching my face. I slipped my arm around her beautiful naked body, and she held my hand as if she would never let it go.

"You know, Tom's boxes are still in the living room."

"I'll take care of them," I said before kissing her again.

"No hurry."

Thirty-six

Marshall and Scott Rescue Tom

As soon as they left the hospital, Marshall started in on Tom. "We're not doing this again, not ever. Got it?"

Tom crawled into the backseat and curled up in defensive posture. "I know. I'm not asking you to," Tom said, staring at his hands that rested on his legs as if those hands held some kind of mystery.

"No, you have to cover more ground than, 'I know,'" Marshall warned.

"I don't blame you. You can kick me out. I'll find my own place. Don't worry about me," Tom sat up straighter but pouted.

"Slow down, Marshall said. "We don't need any more drama. Nobody said anything about kicking you out."

Scott turned his head to look in the backseat at Tom who was again slumping over as if trying to disappear. "You're going to be fine, honey."

"We're not tossing you to the streets, so you can't use that excuse to go back to," said Marshall.

"Back to being a user? I need my own place. Once I get on my feet and get another job."

"You do, and you will," said Scott sympathetically.

"You'll find your own place soon but not until we know that you're not taking Xanax, and you've got some visible means of support. No more excuses, by the way. Bastard."

"What?" Tom put his hands on the back of the front seats.

"Not you, Tom, this jerk ahead of us who keeps stopping and starting. Damn tourists," Marshall added.

"But you're done with Mr. X and dope," Scott said. "It's poison, and we are not going to let you kill yourself."

"It's not. You don't know."

"It is."

"It won't be easy." Tom was thinking it would not be possible.

"Where'd you get that stuff from anyway?" asked Marshall.

"Kid on the street," Tom said.

"Do you know that they mix all kinds of crap in it when they sell heroin like that? Who the hell knows what they put in it. You're lucky you only had a seizure and that you're not dead."

"Yeah, I'm real lucky."

"Stop with the sarcasm. At least use something less harmful like a little weed," said Scott.

"You heard the doc. You do that to yourself again, you have another convulsion, and you hit your head. Suppose it was in the street, and no one spots you until morning?" Marshall asked.

"Imagine if we weren't there? It frightens me to think about it," said Scott, shuddering. Tom tentatively fingered the stitches on the back of his head. He was sore all over as if beaten.

Marshall sighed. "Okay. Today we begin a new regime. We help you look for a job, and we set up a schedule for you to exercise."

"Exercise? What the hell?"

"Nothing insulting, Tom, but you're getting a little gut there," Scott emphasized the word gut.

"Thanks for noticing."

"And then a time for writing. Discipline. Damn it. What's the holdup for this time?"

"It's someone unloading." Scott rolled down his window and looked out. He motioned uselessly for them to move.

"What's the point? Stop that horn!"

Scott turned almost completely around in his seat. "The point is you are going to start living and living healthy. You will take this step-down drug the doctor provided and not return to Xanax or cheap heroin. Got it?"

"I've got nothing. No one and nothing to write. Fucking empty. Maybe it would've been better if I."

"You're full of shit right now. Listen to yourself. You're hardly empty. Yeah, with your life events, you have nothing to write, nothing at all," said Marshall sarcastically.

"He's kidding, of course," added Scott, giving Marshall an exasperated, scolding glance.

"You're really a professor?" Tom said sarcastically. "They let you talk like that?"

"Low blow, Tom," Scott jumped in, with his hand extended. "You have no idea how patient Marshall has been with you."

"An adjunct, and yes, we curse all the time. Newsflash, so do the students. And you've got to develop a bit thicker skin.

Really? Letting Ornal get to you like that? She's harmless. Moving out on Marie when—"

"Christ, let's not go there. I can't do that one right now," Tom groaned and held his head.

"Oh, I don't know about that," said Scott. "I think Ornal can be rather formidable even if she is a tiny fireball."

"All right, not harmless, but what she said about the emperor having no clothes"

"What she said was fucking insulting," Tom yelled, suddenly leaning forward again and animated. "I hate that bitch."

"None of us have any clothes in the final analysis."

"Oh," said Scott excited. "Did you read that nasty piece about Kafka in *The Atlantic*?"

"What?" Tom was growing increasingly annoyed with Scott.

"*The Atlantic* writer,"

"Joseph Epstein," Marshall added.

"Well, Mr. Epstein, whomever he is"

"He's been writing for 50 years and is pretty well-known and in more than a few circles, either hated or admired," Marshall corrected.

"All right, all right, but I don't like his assertions about Kafka, at all." Scott turned his head to inform Tom, "Mr. Epstein wrote this piece, essentially about Kafka being overrated.

"I'm not following you. What's Epstein got to do with that Ornal bitch?"

"Essentially, Epstein claimed Kafka was the emperor with no clothes which reminded me when you were referring to Ornal."

"I get it. So, he's known for causing controversy," Tom said.

"Thought you'd never heard of him?"

"Never said that. You did."

"That's how critics earn their reputations. And that's how they work; they provoke."

"If that's the case, why can't I be a critic?" Tom cracked a smile for the first time in a while.

"He has a very good view of himself, Epstein, I mean," added Scott. "And I think what he said about dear Susan"

"He means Susan Sontag," added Marshall.

"I was going to explain that," Scott said, slightly annoyed.

"Sorry, go ahead."

"His comments about Susan's work being all about self-promotion seem to be projection to me, every bit as true of Epstein's 'art,'" Scott raised his eyebrows for effect as he turned again to make his point.

"Okay, so, why are you, why are we talking about this critic anyway?"

"C'mon, Tom, we know you get this. If even a literary giant like Kafka gets this treatment from a critic, even after death, even after being part of the established literary canon, is attacked in order for some literary theorist to cement his name into our consciousness, then this arena of literary fiction lies in a latitude where you need to proceed with both a good compass and a very tough hide," Marshall said, looking into his rear-view mirror to read the expression on Tom's face.

"That was god-damn eloquent," said Tom. "Really. I'm not being sarcastic."

"And you know what Iris Murdoch said, right?"

Tom shrugged, meaning that he had no idea. "Didn't she go fucking crazy or something?"

"She had dementia, poor dear," added Scott.

"A bad review is less important than whether it is raining," Marshall said.

"In Patagonia," Scott chimed in. "I loved that dear woman even though she went mad."

"She wasn't mad. She had Alzheimer's," said Marshall.

"We've already established that. Don't get me wrong. I like Murdoch's work, but she couldn't remember anyone at the end. Mistook her husband for a hat," Scott said.

"Murdoch? Are we still talking about Iris Fucking Murdoch?" asked Tom amazed at the direction of the conversation. "I think you've switched to"

"That dear man Oliver Sacks. No safety nets once you're published; why hurry?" Scott asked.

"We're discussing writers' insecurities in the face of the publishing industry," Marshall said.

"We are?" asked Tom, somewhat amazed.

"We are now," added Marshall.

"I don't want any nets, safety or otherwise." Tom leaned back against the seat again, looking out the window at a man panhandling who approached their stopped car before Marshall sped off at the last instant.

"Precisely. And the reason we are fighting traffic on the way back from the hospital where you had to have stitches because you were popping pills to prop yourself up demonstrates our point," Scott scolded him.

"And in case you think we are forgetting about this incident, we're doing a thorough house cleaning when we get back. Every last pill gets flushed," Marshall said.

"No stone unturned," Scott said with enthusiasm.

Tom groaned.

"If you're staying with us, you're done with the pills." Marshall put his foot down quite literally, speeding.

Tom put his hand to his head. "I've got nothing."

"You know, life is not about finding a subject to write about," Marshall said emphatically, honking his horn at the car turning in front of him.

"It's the journey, dear boy," Scott adjusted the passenger mirror and checked his hair. "Oh, dear, I thought I looked put together. The fantasies we concoct for ourselves." He sighed.

"Not for me."

"What's not for you? Tom, do you honestly think you're the only person who has gone without fucking for a few months or the only writer who has ever had writer's block or struggled to produce even a word? Maybe this sounds cruel, but I think your best strategy is not to write for a while. I mean, do not even attempt to put your pen to a page. We'll hide every pen in our place, just like the Xanax. Maybe then, you'll figure out something to write about."

"We will?" Scott looked over at Marshall with evident surprise.

"Then I never write again? That's what you're suggesting?"

"Oh, I get it," Scott said. "That's not what he means," Scott interjected because he was frustrated with Tom.

"He knows what I'm talking about," Marshall said.

"He means you should take a vacation from the unnecessary tension you have created in yourself and produce a new kind of tension: one that is productive," Scott said.

"How?"

"If this guy doesn't move his truck, we're going to be all day getting back."

"Look, someone's coming now. Oh, he's ripped," said Scott, his left hand out.

"I'm not jealous, Scott. And, Tom, if you don't allow yourself to write when you think you should or even when you desperately want to, the desire will become so overwhelming that the dam holding everything back right now will break, and for a while, at least, words will flow."

"Let me get this straight: I don't let myself write in order to write?" Tom folded his arms over his chest in defiance.

"Paradoxical but, yes, something like that." Marshall turned the steering wheel sharply and they swerved out of the way of a kid running across the street. "Now, that was suicidal."

"You don't understand." Tom whined.

"Good move," Scott clapped. "Oh, I think that's brilliant, Marshall." Scott said.

"Thank you, Marshall, of course I don't because I'm not a writer."

"Stop whining." Marshall was not in the mood to listen to Tom complain any longer.

"You're writing for students," said Tom.

"As opposed to real writing?" Marshall shook his head.

"Let's dispense with the sarcasm, everyone," Scott said, hating the tension.

"Shut-up," Marshall and Tom said simultaneously to Scott.

"How did I get to be the villain in all this?"

Marshall then reached out while driving with his left hand and took Scott's slender one in his own large hand. "I didn't really mean that."

"Then what precisely did you mean?" Scott asked, pulling his hand away.

"I suck at it," interrupted Tom.

"Not at all. I've read some of your stories that you conveniently leave around the apartment, and they're not bad." Marshall looked into the rearview mirror again to check to see Tom's reaction.

"You've read my stuff?"

"Their placement looks like an invitation."

"I haven't read them," said Scott, "but I will if you'd like. Actually, I've read a few, but I could read more."

"No. It's, it wasn't an invitation. I'm a slob. What do you mean, not bad?"

Scott nodded in agreement. "I will second that assertion. You already know you have talent and the tools, but you're a little side-tracked right now with this obsession with publishing and fame."

"If I don't publish, how is anyone besides the two of you going to read anything I write?"

Marshall jumped back in. "You know exactly what we're talking about, but I will spell it out for you since you're being obstinate, Tom. You're too wrapped up in acquiring fame before you actually write."

"The fuck I am."

"Try writing and not worrying about other people's reactions." Marshall began again. "The purpose, what you really care about or should care about, has taken a back seat."

"And he does not mean literally, but we're punning," said Scott brightening.

Tom rolled his eyes and directed his statement at Marshall. "I'm not wrapped up in getting famous."

"You most certainly are. Ever since we started talking about Adrian Gerd Wahl," Marshall and Scott said, nearly in unison.

"Maybe I am. What's wrong with that?"

"Everything, dear boy," Scott cautioned. "Oh, watch out for that lady. Look, she's not even looking. Here she comes right into the street!"

"I see her," Marshall leaned on the car horn again. "Oh, god, now I've given her a heart attack."

Scott turned his head and watched her pick up her bag and successfully maneuverer to the other side. "She's fine, just don't look back. Kidding."

Marshall looked in time to see the elderly woman give him the middle finger. "Lovely. You don't have to suffer for your art. Suffering comes to each of us quite naturally and inevitably."

"Well said, Marshall," Scott patted him on the arm, realizing he had forgiven his lover for earlier slights. Marshall smiled.

"That I know," Tom added, turning his head slowly to test the extent of the damage, and suddenly grateful that Marshall and Scott had taken him in. He didn't want to say it, but it came out anyway. "Thanks. Both of you. Really, thanks."

Thirty-seven

Ellison Embarks

I was in the middle of reading a Natasha Trethewey poem and thinking about the narrative structure when Ornal burst into my study. She likes to call it our second bedroom, reserved for guests who never arrive. Neither her parents nor mine have forgiven us for having the audacity to live together. Of course, they are unlikely to be forgiven by us, either.

"You have a letter," she said in that excited manner that gives everything away instantly.

"I get lots of mail. No one writes letters anymore. Are you sure it's not a bill?"

She handed me an envelope from a publisher. By then, I had gotten used to form rejections, but this envelop was thicker than the rejection missive typically indicates. I opened it slowly, trying not to build up hope.

"Hurry up!" she yelled, dancing around.

"Give me a second." I took my time not out of fear but to delay what would certainly be the inevitable. When I pulled out the letter, however, there were additional pages, and even the most cursory glance let me know it was a book contract.

"Oh, my God!" Ornal grabbed me.

"Hold on. Let me see what this is exactly."

"When is the last time you checked your e-mail? They usually e-mail."

"A week ago, I think."

"No one waits a week to read their e-mails."

I read the letter and felt first joy and then the overwhelming sensation of a long journey ahead of me. I always assumed that a publisher's contract would secure things for me, set me on a journey in which everything previously denied would be opened up, and nothing but satisfaction would emerge, but then I realized I felt circumspect.

"What's wrong?"

"Nothing. It's that there's so much I have to do now. Set up a blog, an author's website, and help market, promote, sell myself in order to sell the book. There are several pages here devoted to my responsibilities for promoting." I stopped flipping instructions, feeling weighed down.

"I'll help you," said Ornal. "It's going to be wonderful."

"I know," I said with a hint of trepidation. Ornal is the most helpful person I'd ever met, but she somehow managed to make things more difficult whenever she stepped in. "Maybe."

"What do you mean 'maybe?'" she looked offended.

"Poor word choice. I should say, I am not sure where to begin, and I am just wondering out loud. How about 'complicated'?"

"I love complicated." And she did.

Thirty-eight

The Published Novel

Imagining I had hit on something unique, enough to draw attention, my work flowed. Words rolled out, clearly making their way. At times, my novel almost wrote itself. Marie read it and loved my work, couldn't stop complimenting my writing, but then, Marie is in love with me, and I am in love with her, making her a terrible critic in this situation. I could probably come up with pure garbage and wouldn't be sure she would not still sing its praises. This, of course, makes me love her move. She might even be worse at analyzing my work than me.

By now, however, I would like to think I have learned to create some space, at least after a sufficient period of time has passed, enough to provide the distance to actually tell if something I've written is any good, and this is good, I think. All right, I'm not sure, but then I'm as sure as I have ever been about something I've written. What I do know is that I keep coming back to it.

Sunday morning is my absolute favorite day and time of day. Marie is still in bed because it is the one day of the week she can sleep late, and I make breakfast for her. I was never a good cook, but I learned to make pancakes, waffles, and omelets for the woman I love, not all at the same time, of course. I told her that two jobs were too much, but she said she would quit one when she got a raise in the other. I think she is pleased that I pay my share of the rent, too, unlike Tom. Anytime, there is a comparison to Tom, I'm going to come out ahead.

I'm trying blueberry crepes this morning, and I have to get the pan hot enough, just the right temperature before I pour the batter. I've even become scientific about this. Like I said, I never made breakfast before moving in with Marie, but somehow the whole idea of hominess is much more appealing now. I routinely make meals on the rare days when we can take our time in the morning or evening. I hear her wake and enter.

We sit at this little table in the alcove and read the paper, write, or comment on whatever is going on in the world. And I am embarrassed to admit it, but even the world's disasters become fuel for our intellectual wanderings in conversation about life, about our writing.

If I had to end my life right now, it would be okay with me because this is the one scene that was missing in my life, where the woman I love is sitting across the table from me, close enough for me to touch her long, slender fingers, and we're talking about something we're both interested in, and one unplanned day is stretched out before us like a blanket in a tableau.

While I am squeezing orange juice, because I have decided to really spoil her with fresh squeezed on Sundays, I have the book review section of *The Times* open. I hardly wanted to think about my new novel until I got it out to a few agents or independent publishers to test the waters. I was in the middle of this process I call the business end of writing when I saw it: *Into the Other Dark.* I was scanning the *New York Times Sunday Book Review*, casually, to see what was there. It was the first review, and my eyes widened involuntarily. *Into the Other Dark* found a sympathetic reader in that particular *Times* reviewer. Plot summary, although cursory and only a paragraph in length, stopped me from all activity, even the autonomic activity of breathing for a few seconds. There it was: my novel in someone else's head and now on their pages and on a sheet of the *Times Review*.

When I could breathe again, I opened my laptop, first crepes burning, and searched for the author's name. This writer of my book had grown up in California but attended Florida State, graduating with not only an MFA but a Doctorate in Creative Writing. A compulsive scholar, it seems. There was no point of convergence in our bios, at least one that I could see from the outline of his life and travels; nowhere that we had crossed paths. He couldn't have stolen my story idea, but then I realized with equal horror that it would look like I had copied his. My perfect morning was ruined: felt like the whole building was falling from under me. Quakes are not known to happen in New York, but I experienced the tremor.

"What's going on?" asked Marie who was scrapping burned batter from the pan. Then she was standing behind me, wrapping her arms around my waist because, by this time, I'm also standing, still holding the paper.

I handed her the *Times* review, pointing to the offender; I couldn't speak yet.

She was quiet for a few minutes, rereading it. "It's only a plot, Ian. Nothing to panic about."

"And the 'innovative narrative,' and its structure, and the character's motivation and psychology. I'm surprised we came up with different names."

"Oh." Marie was not going to give up on my work that easily. "You know what they say about plots? There are only"

"I know the 37 basic plots, but this is mimicry almost scene for scene. How is that even possible?"

"Did you ever meet this guy? Go to school with him? Maybe meet him at a workshop, send him your complete manuscript?"

"No. I've already Googled the guy's life. We weren't ever in the same state at the same time as far as I can tell."

Marie, thankfully, didn't pass it off as nothing or as simply coincidence and remind me to move on with my life. She got the tragedy or at least the hopeless absurdity. "I'm so sorry, Ian. This really is awful, but there must be something you can do? Maybe make some changes in revision?"

"Revisions of the plot, characters, and structure?"

"I don't know what to say," she said defeated. "You're such an amazing writer. It's not as if you will use the same words. Your story will be unique to you because it has your voice."

I said nothing and she stared at me. The fact she was trying so hard got to me.

"I know you tried to make a lovely breakfast." The fan was still on in the kitchen, clearing away smoke. She ended the impasse.

"No, I burned your crepes. But I'll try again." We were silent while I prepared near perfect crepes and served them.

"Lovely and delicious." I appreciated the fact that she noticed even if I was no longer hungry. "You still have to eat," she added.

"Not this morning or maybe for a while." I tried joking, but food got pushed around on my plate. Still, I determined not to let this unbelievable situation paralyze me. At least I could still drink coffee.

"You've got to submit your journals as story," I said suddenly.

"What?" She was eating my plate of crepes, too, because I had pushed it aside.

"I want you to submit your journal as an experimental novel, now, before someone else does." I had never felt such a sense of urgency, and I wanted her to start typing her entries immediately. "I mean, before someone else submits an idea similar to yours."

"I don't know, Ian." She looked uncertain. "They're really just musings. The conflicts are sporadic or often untraceable."

"Trust me on this, please. I will help you key them. We'll start today."

She could see how agitated I was and wanted to do something to help me. We began typing her manuscript before 10:00 a.m. that Sunday. All of the negative energy that had gone into my momentary paralysis was redirected into polishing Marie's manuscript. My action didn't change anything for me in terms of that sense of loss, but somehow doing this for her made me feel better. All right, it did change something. I was a damn good editor, and I can't think of another writer I know who deserves recognition and readership more than Marie.

We worked on her manuscript for several weeks, when Marie looked up at me one afternoon and said, "Ian, incorporate the idea of the unexpected, stolen plot into your novel."

"Huh?" My mental processes were focused on Marie's fiction, and I was not immediately sure about what she said. Everything felt like mush as if the sudden turn of events had reduced me to, well, I couldn't even come up with an apt simile or metaphor, such was the chaos rolling around my head.

Pulling her chair closer to mine, she said, "Write the incident about the parallel work into your work, as if you and the other author are echoes of each other."

"I think that's been done, too." I couldn't tell her that it was a terrible idea because she was excited. I let her go on about how to create this doppelganger, but by the time she was finished outlining it, I started to think that maybe she had something. I played around with the concept for a couple of weeks before scraping it, at least in the short term. Apparently, there was a film about that concept, too.

Several weeks later, I checked the reviews again, couldn't find out enough about this other writer who somehow, without knowing how, scooped my novel. By then, other reviewers were also appearing, the ones with nasty critiques that started with lines like, "From opening obscurity cloaked as overly long sentences to the closing mixed metaphors parading as gaudy poetic gymnastics, X's new novel is so much meaningless hyperbole." Reviews got worse from there. I started collecting everything critics wrote about his work, reading voraciously, thrilled, then intensely agitated, before becoming defensive.

"It has become all too hip to write about someone else's work in a way that deceives the reader while simultaneously insulting the writer," I yelled to Marie who was still in the bathroom after showering.

I pulled out a review to show Marie when she appeared. "Just listen to this: 'X seems to think that writing a novel means belching out sentences so derivative, so overly constructed readers will contemplate his constructions rather than decide it was never worth their time.' It's almost as if the early acclamation brought out the anger in this latest crop of critics, raptors scraping in ever more vengeful circles, pecking at the nose and eyes until there was nothing left but bloody holes. Look what they have written about X's novel!" I said with indignation. In a way, it felt like they were writing about the pages filed in my bottom drawer.

"Ian, my darling, it's not you they are criticizing," Marie said.

I grew increasingly protective and less discerning. Suddenly X was becoming my favorite author. I had left Gerd Wahl behind and lost all ability to be analytical or neutral. Then I allowed my honest response to come out. "It should be!"

Marie leaned over me while I sat still hunched over the computer and glanced at the latest reviews. "Don't worry about him," she said softly enough that I had to turn. "He is fortunate. When they hate you, they really hate you, drawing us in," she added before breaking into a laugh. "Just look at us trying to defend this writer we don't know."

"No, really," I protested. "It's awful and unfair. I fucking despise critics."

"Of course, they are awful, but X is one lucky bastard. Critics made him one."

"What?"

"Oh, Ian, that's when you know you've made it. They're writing about his work. Do you know how amazing it would feel if someone started writing nasty critiques about my works or yours in literary circles? To have people talking about your stories even if they are criticizing? I can't help feeling that it's still a man's world, though, even the literary world, but we should all want that horrible review at some point because at least it means they are paying attention. No, more than that. They are obsessing to the point that they must spew venom. I can't imagine anyone ever obsessing about my work."

"I do. Your writing is brilliant, and they will write about you; I'm obsessed already. I will write about your work." I started thinking about becoming an independent editor that day. Time to leave that magazine. I realized I wasn't hypothesizing. Her work was that good. Better than mine, and I didn't mind admitting it. "Something I have to confront about myself is why it took me so long to realize it."

She lowered her head but I could see the emerging smile. "Are you going to write something nasty or obscene about my novel?"

"I will get everyone riled up, accuse your work of everything under the sun, and they can never forget it or you."

She said without irony, "Oh, Ian, of course, they'll forget. In time, they forget everyone, even the great Adrian Gerd Wahl."

286 | Socrates is Dead Again

Thirty-nine

Social Networking on Immortality

Tweeting on the anniversary of the death of Adrian Gerd Wahl #Wahl

> @MARSHALLL · July 12, 2014
> Would dead writers have tweeted? Our topic. Anyone reading?

> @marierollins · July 12, 2014
> Replying to @MARSHALLL
> Parodies or serious commentary? Anniversary of Gerd's death. Momentous.

> @ThunderRoad · July 12, 2014
> Wahl was too long-winded. Who can get through a 1,000-page novel or wants to?

> @MARSHALLL · July 12, 2014

Replying to @marierollins
Both. Check it out. He's been gone a year. I remembered.

@ELLISon · July 12, 2014
Finished Richard Wright's Black Boy: "I would hurl words into this darkness and wait for an echo." Heard myself. Heard Wright and an echo of Wahl.

@GillianHottie · July 12, 2014
Replying to @ELLISon
Wright's sentence is not 140 words. Clipped. A year already? Anyone still reading Wright? Still reading Gerd? Not meant as insult. How long does a "legacy" last?

@Morethanenough · July 12, 2014
Just finished Wahl's novel. Well, quit halfway through. It made no sense. Can't figure why anyone is tweeting about this dead guy.

@ELLISon · July 12, 2014
Replying to @GillianHottie
Yeah, Wright and a few of those other dead guys and women more than relevant.

@Toms · July 12, 2014
I pretty much hurl my words into darkness daily. #Gerd

@DREWLEV · 1:02 AM · July 12, 2014
Replying to @ELLISon
It's as if Richard Wright prefigured Cloud computing; the ether of nonexistent existence.

@ScottH · July 12, 2014
Replying to @ELLIson
You didn't quote ending: "words to tell, to fight, to create . . . to keep alive in our hearts this sense of the inexpressibly human." Thought it relevant.

@GillianHottie · July 12, 2014
Virtual existence. We're all immortal in the ether. Yet none of us is immortal. What would Gerd have written as tweet?

@Toms · July 12, 2014
Replying to @GilianHottie
Gerd wouldn't have tweeted. If he did: suicide as sin or act of hero?

@DREWLEV · July 12, 2014
Replying to @Toms
Why is suicide a sin? Or an act of heroism? While we're discussing sinning, "My name is Ozymandias, King of Kings, /Look on my works, ye Mighty, and despair!"

@Ornal 12 · July 12, 2014

Replying to @Toms @DREWLEV
Speak for yourself. Shelley? What famed writers would have tweeted? Hemingway, certainly.

@Toms · July 12, 2014
Replying to @DREWLEV
Shelley or Gerd? Gerd caustically fits hollow shell of our times better than Wright, though equally dead. But Gerd too long-winded for our era.

@DREWLEV · July 12, 2014
Replying to @Toms
Gerd had something to say of importance which continues to make him relevant. This brings up the question of immortality? Is this what writers wish or hope to gain?

@Ornal · July 12, 2014
What we are all searching for—some meaning in this shocking, sad, and mundane absurdity called life.

Forty

One Day in September Feels Like Another Until

Endings

At some point, a story ought to get around to how it ends, I decide. Marie and I talk about how to wrap up where our characters are, where they will stay fixed in location at least until another reader opens the book, and everything is set in motion once more. A story needs an ending, but I couldn't see even a denouement in sight except for Gerd's story because death has a way of finalizing every possible trajectory. Up until then, we could go in any direction unanticipated or planned because even a carefully designed existence will take some unexpected detours.

Like yesterday, there was a guy who walked in front of a city bus. "My God, Ian, look what happened today!" Marie came in, nearly crying. Newspapers stated he was 36. He would forever be 36, and his parents would outlive him. No one seems to know why he suddenly stepped into the street, but it is difficult to believe reporters at these events, armed as they are, looking for witnesses who will attest to some facet that no one else observed, but this guy who isn't much older than me, with all of the frenetic energy, waited for the last possible moment, giving the driver no time to react. There would be no disciplinary action taken against the poor devil who had only been on his route about 20 minutes before all of that happened, and the bus driver's life was altered along with his passengers and the pedestrians who were thinking about work or buying a new shirt or where they were going for dinner that evening when there was suddenly a man lying in the street, blood spattered and body crumpled. The guy driving would be known as the man who unwittingly hit the suicide. The 52-year-old driver had become the beginning of that other guy's fame and the end of it simultaneously. And for a day or two, people talked about the guy. They asked questions and searched on their computers for every tidbit of information they could find on this otherwise anonymous man. Why had he stepped off the curb? What led him to that point of no return? I recalled reading something about Randall Jarrell, the poet, walking into traffic in Chapel Hill, but it was tough to classify Jarrell's act definitively as suicide, as long as there was a possibility of an accident. We don't want to believe that anyone willingly checks out. Unlike Gerd. Nothing tenuous there. Gerd Wahl involved no one else in his act, yet here we were involved. Was this really an ending? Yet the mystery of the man and his life continues.

  Adrian Gerd Wahl might have commented on the artificialness of endings in one of his essays, I seem to remember someone saying or maybe I read. Only death extracts definitive endings, he would say as if he was an old friend who was leaving you with the bottle of wine and his new book as he walked out the door. Think whatever you like, he seemed to say because he no longer cared.

So, I'm thinking about endings and stories, and I'm drawn to a few that are almost perfect.

"Easy, you know, does it, son" was Nabokov's in *Transparent Things* as his Person is choking and burning to death. There, death again. What strikes the reader is the casualness of Nabokov's tone, the simple, slang diction juxtaposed with the horror you have to feel over Person's last moments. And what a great symbolic name, too. Right then, the tone hit me as reminiscent of Vonnegut's refrain from *Slaughterhouse-Five*: "And so it goes." But I'm not as drawn to Vonnegut's last line in that novel: "Po-tee-weet?" Original, yes, but not as riveting as "And so it goes" or "Easy, you know, does it son." It wouldn't have worked as well if Nabokov had written, "Po-tee-weet" while Person is burning to death. The informal address and, "you know," strikes me as odd precisely because we don't know. We don't know what Person is feeling or what death is until it's too late to define. Too late.

Last lines. Endings. There is James Joyce's Molly who has an orgasmic stream of conscious utterance, "Yes I said yes I will Yes" from *Ulysses,* but the interrupted half-thought ending didn't feel quite right to me after roughly 1,000 pages. Then again, maybe that is how it had to end because there is no final ending, Joyce implies. And there is the curious joy in Dostoevsky's *The Brothers Karamazov* with the devastated family yelling, "Hurrah for Karamazov!"

But for last, devastating lines from novels, I turn to Virginia Woolf's from *Jacob's Room*: "'What am I to do with these, Mr. Bonamy?' She holds out a pair of Jacob's old shoes." I feel the loss, the absence like cold winds that leave even your bones chilled. I hear the pun and think of leaves blowing around. "What am I to do with these?"

Isn't that how we all go? Someone in our family or one of our friends, holds up some remnant of our lives and says, "What am I do with this?" Of course, they probably give it to Goodwill or the Salvation Army or, with some reluctance, toss it.

There's some relatively new work that has that resonance: Yoko Ogawa's *The Housekeeper and the Professor* with a boy nicknamed Root and his mother the Housekeeper observing, "And I can see the number on the back of his pin-striped uniform. The perfect number 28." If I hadn't already read the novel, I would want to begin reading about such an end.

I've been thinking about what makes an ending, posits it, yet coaxes us to follow? Marie confessed to me that she has never finished *Moby Dick* even though I keep telling her that it's worth the relative struggle.

"I've started it four times," she said. "How many more times do I have to try? I had no idea it didn't start with Ismael but some bizarre catalog of information about whales and whaling."

But Melville had it right in the end, of which there are two, both lyrical, both enigmatic. From his Epilogue: "It was the devious-cruising Rachel, that in her retracing search after her missing children, only found another orphan. FINIS"

And the ending before it in Chapter 135. And who writes 135 chapters?

"[T]his bird now chanced to intercept its broad fluttering wing between the hammer and the wood; and simultaneously feeling that ethereal thrill, the submerged savage beneath, in his death-gasp, kept his hammer frozen there; and so the bird of heaven, with archangelic shrieks, and his imperial beak thrust upwards, and his whole captive form folded in the flag of Ahab, went down with his ship, which, like Satan, would not sink to hell till she had dragged a living part of heaven along with her, and helmeted herself with it. Now small fowls flew screaming over the yet yawning gulf; a sullen white surf beat against its steep sides; then all collapsed, and the great shroud of the sea rolled on as it rolled five thousand years ago."

You can't simply quote one line from Melville I told Marie. It is not his ending line but his lines. It is part of the whole piece of it, that search into the soul, the ending being the continuous search, five-thousand years of it. After reading this ending to Marie, she asked for my copy of the novel to try again.

Endings that we read but not necessarily live with; although I can still sense the sea rolling on as it has for millions of years. What of the endings in my small circle of writer friends? What of our endings? We are still making them up as we go until we can go no longer. That is where imagination comes into play.

I could state that Marie's journal/novel found a publisher willing to take a risk on an unknown, inventive, original voice, but that seems rather unlikely because publishing, even with the profusion of independent presses, is first a business, and there seems to be little about Marie's wonderful work that shouts moneymaker. But that is not an ending at all. What then becomes of Marie or her writing? Does she see herself as successful? Her book does or doesn't sell, or she begins to doubt that anything even happened, mixing wishes and dread with fact. Whatever the present circumstance, the next day brings unanticipated events or consequences, suggesting that I have no idea what happens with Marie, only that I love her and we are in process individually and together. I'm forever grateful to Tom for his indiscretions and inappropriate requests. Tom and I haven't spoken since I moved in with Marie. That is a kind of an ending. We no longer keep up even the pretense of friendship.

I don't know why we all didn't go into the young adult, romance, or dystopian genres, but that wasn't what interested me; what was the point? Even Tom couldn't bring himself to write a sexy, violent vampire or Goth Romance. Even Gillian decided to scrap her historical romance novel because she could not stomach it. I could speculate that Tom is trying his hand at a screenplay about a character living in New York City and writing a script. Oh, Tom. It is possible that he's doing well and living on his own finally, writing cleverly and well, but I don't really know. It's not as if Tom still loved Marie, but I understood how my actions were betrayal. I hope he is off whatever drugs he was taking for a while, though, but that would be naïve, too. Tom was always at his writer's best when he was drinking or high on something. I guess it didn't surprise me that he went too far with it all. Marshall and Scott sometimes offer a comment about Tom but seldom because they know we aren't friends anymore.

It makes me feel a little better or assuages my guilt that Tom found a couple of good souls in this city to semi-adopt him. Tom needs another set of parents, and I can't imagine a more understanding, indulgent, and forgiving pair than Marshall and

Scott. But that is not an ending for Tom either. Sooner or later, he'll wear out his welcome with Marshall and Scott, too. Sooner or later, we have to grow up and leave home.

Gillian still hasn't married Shwetak although he asked her at least twice that I know of, but I suspect that they are not quite right for each other even though they live together. Shwetak doesn't talk to me about Gillian anymore, particularly since she left the magazine, and there is some awkwardness, but at least Shwetak's job is more secure now that Drew left, too, and our little culture magazine hasn't folded yet even though we are primarily read online. We may go under next week or the week after that. Even our magazine's ending is uncertain or not an ending at all.

I guess the only endings I have to offer involve ambivalence. But when I think of Gillian who has few hits on her website for her self-published book and hardly any sales, I am stopped. She told me right before she quit working at our rag that she has yet to make a dime from *Part II*, but I also know that Gillian doesn't care because someone somewhere is reading her work even if it's only a pirated manuscript or an e-book for which she receives virtually no compensation. I ordered five copies of *Part II* to give it some action on the site, and it took months before one really cheap-looking paperback, filled with errors and type partially off the page, finally arrived. A few pages were also miss-numbered, and at least one page was never printed, a blank appearing in the middle of the book.

When I turned a page in *Part II*, the rest of the chapter was gone. It reminded me of Italo Calvino's *If on a winter night a traveler* without Calvino's artistry, wordplay, or mystery.

Missing evidence. Maybe carelessness and lack of funding. Gillian's mystery was about little more than cheap typesetting and sloppy printers found in some of the self-publishing industry sites. There was a different font used on several pages of Gillian's book. The type shifts move like her story should have. Colors on the cover ran and smeared, but at least I could read the title even though a subtitle was misspelled. That one must have hurt. She swore that it was right on her copy, but self-publishing printing operations seldom deliver page-proofs and corrections for their authors. Still, I didn't really see Gillian as a sucker. She knew what she was getting into and went roaring ahead. She seems proud of her work. Good for Gillian.

Afterall, she does have a book in print. A physical object she can hold, turn over, set on her desk even if she hides the bleeding cover and shows only its binding. She has tangible proof that she is a writer who won't disappear tomorrow or the day after although it will eventually disappear. When someone asks her what she is, what she does, she can state with honesty, "I'm a writer." Yet, this too, is hardly an ending.

I could relate a story about re-crafting my latest novel in order for it to seem less familiar to those who had finished X, the "next generation's Updike's" work, but instead, I abandoned my novel. Or, it is entirely possible that I will revisit my forsaken story someday and figure out a way that I don't seem like I'm plagiarizing another author's work when it was always all my own. Of course, if I'm honestly looking at what's my own, I end up with nothing on any page because every word I've ever written carries some influence of a writer who came before me, shaped by every writer I've read who preceded me. And I don't mean this in the grandiose way that T.S. Eliot meant it. But I don't think the situation calls for us to stop reading any other work ever again. Sometimes, however, I try not to listen to all of those voices who are clamoring around in my head, having walked these paths before. Even the dead do not necessarily have an ending when there are those of us to remember.

Drew and Angela are doing fine, I think, but who knows really what the next day will bring? I could draw conclusions based upon their conversations with me and each other, their body language, and be incorrect with every speculation. I would not be the first person to misread signs in a relationship that appears to be thriving when, in fact, it is about to collapse on itself. My parents were very clever about the way they held their contempt for one another from me before they finally divorced. Dad still prides himself on the fact that no one knew what was going on when he was living with a woman younger than his son while his wife was making dinner. He's not apologetic to her, to me, or anyone else. He did end their marriage and permanently altered the relationship with his only child.

Drew still calls and drops by on occasion, but we hardly ever see Angela. Just as well. I don't need any more complications. Drew says her schedule is always at odds with his. But the last time I saw Drew, he wasn't talking about Angela.

He said, "One day, Adrian Gerd Wahl had everything and then he was gone. It really does all fall apart." I guess we're still wondering about that, about Wahl, about the great and mighty fall not only from grace but into death. One day Drew Levin was a second-rate writer at a small circulation rag, and the next, he became a hot shot, in-demand journalist. I should be jealous.

More than the surprise of Wahl's death, because death is always unexpected even when we are waiting for it, was the fact that Wahl planned and carried out the end to his own life. One day, Adrian Gerd Wahl was the envy of the literary writing world and then he chose to stop. He didn't drop out of his social circles, move to Alaska or New Hampshire like J.D. Salinger, or stop writing, or refuse to talk to his friends and publishers. He didn't leave the country and set up a cabin on a remote island. He made the deliberate choice to stop living, not quietly or submissively but violently, horrifically, and without compromise. I don't like to admit it, but there is something that I find compelling in his act even if I am also angered by it. It unnerves me to think that maybe he knew something I didn't.

As the wonderful Margaret Atwood wrote, there is only one authentic ending: "John and Mary die, John and Mary die, John and Mary die," but that seems awfully bleak even if it's absolute and accurate. I will leave this entry in my journal with the following: Ian and Marie die. Ian and Marie die. Ian and Marie die, but not as of this writing and not for a long time, and not before loving each other well, at least from my limited perspective, maybe even having a kid along the way, and with Ian finally writing a really good novel even if it wasn't one he had pinned his dreams to, even if he never made a dime from it, and Marie publishes and is able to confidently tell people she is a writer when they ask what she does, and she can answer with some satisfaction before heading home and climbing into bed with Ian who has been waiting for her all his life, and making love all night or least once but in a way that suggests procreation not annihilation. I can only hope.

Forty-one

Ornal Takes on the World Again

Some guy was mouthing off to a kid who was wearing a green stocking cap minding his own business on the bus. I listened to him berate the kid for a couple of blocks. I couldn't tell if they were related or didn't know each other, but the angry guy decided to bully the boy, and it occurred to me that I had enough of him although I hadn't planned on being confrontational when I got on. I found myself suddenly letting go of a string of profanities that ended with something like, "Will you shut your fucking fat asshole mouth!" Then my stop came, which was a good thing because everyone was looking at me like something was about to happen, and I was taking a shortcut when the weird-looking big-mouthed dude with the scar that ran the length of the right side of his face, got off behind me and started following me. I knew immediately, as if it had been part of a script, that this wasn't his stop.

Like a scene in a movie, I got out my cell and called Ellison, and he told me to go into the nearest business: "Ornal, find somewhere with a lot of people around you and wait there," but

I was nearly home and didn't want to walk around my borough or wait for hours. I turned again to check on this guy's too rapid progress, and then I crossed the street and looked again. Muscled white dude was crossing after me, and I turned and grabbed my apartment keys, like any self-respecting woman, and said when he got too close, "Back off, asshole!" He laughed in a way that displayed menace rather than humor, moving closer until he was a couple of feet from me. I waited until he was less than an arm's reach when I pulled out my keys at the moment he grabbed for my arm. I jabbed multiple quick stabs at him with sharp keys into somewhere soft because I felt the keys resistance. He yelled out, then hit me full in the face with his fist. I didn't black out for some reason, although I'd never been hit harder. I fell back, landing on my tailbone. A teen on the street came up behind my assailant and told that bastard to leave me alone when the big scar of a man pulled a gun and shot. The skinny black kid went down without saying a word, and I knew that we were done right then because I'd been hit by my stepfather and a few other guys along the way, many times with the back of a hand but more than a few times with a bare fist, but I'd never been shot.

I didn't have a plan other than to fight like hell at the end when the guy takes off as if he'd killed someone, and I thought he had. Only the boy got back up, dusted himself, and held out his hand to help me.

"You okay, lady?" he asked like I was some ancient. I tried to sit up, but couldn't quite do it, felt blood spurting from my mouth and nose. The kid knelt down next to me and pulled out his cellphone, but I hardly knew what was happening until somehow Ellison was finally there, and I could hear sirens.

Turned out, it wasn't Ellison but still the skinny kid trying to protect me while everything started falling away. I couldn't even fix position of the sky with everything spinning.

When I woke in an ambulance, there was an EMT holding something on my face, and my arm was too tight, and the EMT was talking to somebody, not me, when I started yelling, "Where's Ellison?" only all that came out was some muffled group of trapped syllables floating around my bloody mouth.

"Calm down, stay calm," this young guy says to me as if I had to do what he told me, but I couldn't calm down or stay still because I didn't know where Ellison was or what had happened to him. And that kid. Was he shot?

"I don't want to restrain you, lady," he said gently, but with a tone that made me believe him. I stopped struggling.

"Is he alive?"

The young EMT shook his head, which I took to mean Ellison was dead. I couldn't process any of it, when he finally said, "My job is to make sure you get to the hospital safely. You've got a nasty cut on your head. Stay quiet. No one is dead."

"Not even the boy?"

"Not even a boy."

When they wheeled me out on the stretcher, I was looking for Ellison, hoping somehow that he made it. I started crying. After they admitted me, even though I was still in a hallway because all of the rooms were full, Ellison walked right up beside me. I started laughing and crying and telling him crazy things because I couldn't believe he was alive.

"But how did you? You were shot."

"What?" he looked surprised by my comment even though he was bearing signs of relief. I had to reassess. "I think you are a little confused. The doctor said you took a blow to the head, blacked out cold, pretty bad concussion. No one was shot."

"You mean you didn't tackle the guy, and he didn't shoot you?"

"Whoa. Now that is an imagination, woman."

"You're okay then?"

"Yes, I'm here. But we need to worry about you right now. When I got there, they had already loaded you into an ambulance. You were unconscious, and they wouldn't let me ride with you."

"What about the kid? The one who was helping me? I think he was the one who got shot."

Ellison shook his head. "What kid?"

"The skinny kid who got shot."

Rubbing his chin, Ellison said, "No one got shot as far as I know. That son-of-a-bitch coward stole your purse and hit you, really hard. And I'm afraid he got away with your purse. There wasn't any kid around you."

Apparently, I was knocked out, and the rest of the scene was some kind of hallucination induced before or after my blackout, and Ellison was alive and no boy died for me, for which I am forever grateful. I really had to try to keep in check this whole overactive imagination thing, and I had already promised myself to stop interfering in other people's troubles, at least for a while. I expected a lecture of some kind about why I had to keep my mouth shut around people I didn't know, and I thought Ellison would be furious with me.

He wasn't. In fact, he said something unexpected. "Let's do this: make it legal."

"What? Legal?" I still thought he was talking about the incident and some ramifications involving me testifying or something.

"Will you marry me, Ornal Aude?" Ellison got down on one knee in the Emergency Room hallway, and everyone was staring at us. He didn't have a ring or anything, and I told him before I never wanted to marry anyone. We were both too independent for that, but what could I say? It wasn't about being embarrassed, rather the thought of disappointing them all. I didn't want to hurt Ellison either, if I'm honest.

"Are you sure?" I wasn't sure myself. I bought a moment to think it over and then said something that surprised even me, "What am I saying? Yes, I will."

Strangers started applauding. One man with a bloody towel wrapped around his right hand whistled as they wheeled him into an adjoining room. "Good for you, two," he shouted smiling or maybe grimacing. "Now, somebody get me a god damn, fucking pain killer." A little cheer went up, and I wasn't sure if it was for us or for pain killers.

Some days are like that. You get your purse stolen and you're mugged, your shoulder, nose, and jaw are killing you, and the cowardly bully thief gets away, the one you tried to put in his place but only managed to embolden further. You're surrounded by accidents and gushing injuries and smells of sweat trapped in rolls of fat, oozing abscesses, antiseptic, urine, layers of unwashed clothes, clothing trapping cigarette smoke and some other shit which I haven't had in too long, burnt hair, and rotten eggs that aren't eggs at all but some gastrointestinal problem, but, damn, if you didn't see this coming: worst of all, you actually want something traditional. No, not traditional because Ellison will never be traditional and neither will you.

"We're actually going to do this, woman," he said gently, squeezing my hand while we waited for the X-ray technician. I guess I must have really scared him. Together, we keep inventing new emotional territory, but there we were: in love.

Forty-two

Searching for Meaning

Question is, why am I always up this late? Why do I know that my friends, most of whom are working full time and writing, will also be up at this hour, debating our irrelevance? There was an expectation that a particular text would reveal something I wanted to know. Twitter was open to too many voices I did not want to consider, filled with profanity for profanities sake, so I decided to text my friends. I typed up their responses in real time as if we had discovered something together, referring to myself with my name Drew.

Drew

Did Gerd Wahl feel utterly alone for the entirety of his career or just at the end?

Ellison

Gerd no less "alone in [his] narrow room, watching the sun sink slowly in the chilly May sky" than Richard Wright at the end. Aren't we all alone in the end? But do we really believe community has no ameliorating value?

Drew

Groping about blindly in immaterial "community?" We definitely a part of a community of writers, but are we not alone, as well?

Ornal

Whose groping? Do you mean group? We exist in a community. Stop being so pretentious. Human beings are social animals.

Drew

Perhaps Richard Wright and Gerd Wahl and millions of "dead guys" also exist with us in this insubstantial world and beyond. Just asking questions.

Ornal

What happened to Marie? Where are the other women writers in our community, or does this community of writers belong only to men?

Toms

What women writers? I want to go back to hurling insults, expletives.

Gillian

Alive and well, Ornal, hurling words into the void with you.

Drew

Endings? I text these abbreviated symbols, the idea feels done, dealt with in the way death closes options.

Marshall

How do we know death closes options? My ideas are taking shape as a result of, or inspired by, nebulous concept of group in the ether with friends. What is more insubstantial—the ether or death?

***

Angela was leaning over me when I woke, telling me something about a woman at the door. For an instant, I panicked, thinking someone was jeopardizing our new-found domestic bliss. Was Gillian here to collect on thoughts I'd had about her in the old days before I came to my senses? Guilt is the worst of our emotions, at least it seemed to me at that particular moment when I was still between realms.

"Drew, she looks pretty desperate, not mentally ill. I wouldn't have let her in if she seemed certifiable. Hurry up."

"What?" I was still struggling to find my way back after an extended nap. Something from a Tranströmer poem came to me, in which he expressed waking as a "parachute jump" from dreaming or sleeping. It had been a tough night the evening before, what with our celebration of my new job and successes and, oh, my God, last night we celebrated finding out we were going to have a baby! It would mean a proposal, but Angela said it was not a problem. She wasn't sure she wanted to marry. Still, I knew I'd convince her. If she wanted to get rid of me, she probably would have by now.

The night before started with her announcing that she had something to tell me, and me badly ruining her plans when I shouted out, "You got us a puppy?" with the same kind of spastic excitement I'd displayed as a 10-year-old.

"God, no," said Angela. "A baby." Matter-of-fact. She was straightforward in negotiations with her nursing supervisor about better hours, and it looked like she was going to get more of them during daylight and have a schedule easier to manage a baby with my help.

I landed with a thud. A baby? Really? Was I ready? We were going to have a kid, and I was going to have to be grown up for real. I wanted to tell someone immediately out of fear, wonder, pride, and panic. It actually surprised me that I was more excited than I could have anticipated. Damn. My kid. I knew change was coming but this?

"Can we tell everyone? My parents are going to want to know right away."

"Let's hold off, a bit," she said.

For some reason, I wanted to tell Ian. Ian was writing a new book, he told me. I could finally stop feeling guilty about taking the Gerd interview out from under him. Well, maybe not. He was still at that magazine going under like the Titanic, and I was, well, weighing multiple good offers. There was a letter on my desk from my new agent asking me to write a biography based on the Gerd interviews, and my e-mail was packed with queries from publishers rather than the other way around. Angela had taken three messages from other agents about call backs. It was strange how Gerd Wahl's death had opened up opportunities for me. Such an inversion, and now I would have to be responsible. No, I wouldn't tell Ian right away; I'd let that wait.

Celebrated. Wine first. Two bottles we'd been saving for my job change, but I broke one out for our kid in the making. Unfortunately for Angela, drinking in the first trimester is "verboten." I had to drink alone. She toasted with sparkling water. I didn't even know what having a kid meant yet; what it would mean in our relationship, in my time commitment, in my love and concern, and all my fears.

But first, celebration. We made love. Not all night because let's be honest about human biology for once. She woke me up, and I was grateful.

"Don't look for this every night," she said as she left me still in bed. "It's hormonal."

It was like the first few weeks of dating again before the doorbell rang.

"C'mon. Get up. Throw a shirt on. This woman has come a long way, and her name is Julia. I forgot her last name already. No, wait, it's Alexander, but she seems like she's searching for something, said she was Gerd's friend. Standing in our living room! Yeah, in our living room."

Pulling myself together and managing to get my own clothes on, I walked out, not a stumble in my step, to find this stranger already sitting on our couch, the new leather one we had just purchased. The stranger looked expectant, staring at me and anticipating answers to what I had no idea. Well, I had some idea. She obviously wanted something from me about Gerd. Even though Gerd Wahl had never mentioned a particular woman to me and certainly not one of his lovers, I was aware there would be people searching after they found out I had last spoken to him. That was a book in the making: all of Wahl's shadowy lovers. It would have to be a fiction, however, unless they came forward of their own accord, like this one.

Immediately, I thought that I could conjure up a better-looking woman for Gerd Wahl than the one sitting forlornly on the couch. Julia wasn't ugly or anything. I've already put my first impression out there, but I expected Gerd to be with only the most beautiful people, the ones he chose, ones who would not have the slightest interest in any of the rest of us.

I realize I'm staring at her before being introduced. As we made our awkward introductions, I recognize she is striking in a way I had not immediately noticed. High cheekbones and intelligent, soulful eyes. Long auburn hair was pulled back and up off her face but not severely. Her body is lean and rather athletic in appearance. I guessed she might have been a runner. The longer I focused on her, the more intrigued I became and began to sense what it was in her that Gerd might have been interested in, providing she was offering a semblance of the truth about their relationship.

"Hello," she said without extending her hand. "I know this seems a little strange. At least out there, but you were one of the last people to talk to him at any length. I read your interview. I'm sure a lot of people are going to be very interested, but I want something else. I want to know something very specific."

Okay. She was perceptive and fairly direct.

"I'm not sure I can help, but what do you want to know?"

"You captured him in a way I'd never seen in an interview in print before. I felt like I was sitting in the room with him, with both of you. And, this is significant because sometimes when I was physically in a room with Gerd, I didn't think my presence fully registered."

I must have nodded my head in agreement before I held up my hand, intending to hush her compliments, but then she had already moved in another direction. I was standing there with my hand up. Although I'd heard this flattery before, I never tired of it. "Thank you. What can I help you with?" She was already beyond those introductory comments, but I persisted, not really thinking I could help her. It was difficult not to speculate about what she might offer in terms of a relationship with Gerd that I knew nothing about. Those interviews had become my meal ticket, and I had no problem digging for more gems. This might work for both of us, I was already calculating.

"I guess I wondered about his honesty with you." Julia was holding her own hand.

Was she suggesting that I had made something up? There is that line an interviewer stands behind, but Gerd was dead, and I knew that I could have changed his wording to suit the situation and my circumstances; he was my story now.

Angela pulled up the footstool to sit on as I faced Julia, who was half sitting on our couch but leaning out so far; it looked like she would fall right off. "I think he was as honest with me."

"How did you? I mean, when did you two meet exactly? Twice, right? He invited you to return?"

"To tell the truth, the second interview almost didn't happen," I said, betraying more than I wanted, since she had brought up the subject of truthfulness. Angela shot me a curious glance, but I could see that Julia couldn't have cared less what did or didn't lead up to my infamous interview. It was not as if I was going to give her the history of my competition with Ian, the tenuous situation at a small, doomed culture magazine. Julia was here for something more and would not leave easily unless I provided it.

"I don't know where to start," Julia said, taking a breath that looked as if it caused her pain.

"I'm sorry. But your last name?"

Angela gave me a scolding glance.

"Alexander. I am, was, still am in love with Adrian Gerd Wahl, and I believe he was in love with me. I didn't think that I'd actually ever find you or be able to speak to you."

"Here I am and here you are," I said, trying to be helpful. I scratched the back of my neck because it itched but also out of sudden nervousness. Angela crossed her legs, and Julia stared at me. We were all silent. Uncomfortable wordless exchanges always last longer in life than in films, but for some reason, I felt like I was in a movie, and the director was waiting to yell, "cut" but couldn't bring himself to do it. We were going to have to continue in that stalemate for moments longer.

"Can I get you a cup of coffee or tea?" Angela got up as if on cue. We needed something or someone to break our curious inertia.

"I don't want to trouble you, either of you," Julia spoke with her head lowered. I had to lean closer in order to hear her.

"It's certainly no trouble. I'm going to make some tea for myself anyway. Let me get you a cup." I looked over at Angela, grateful. She always seemed to say the right things to put people more at ease.

"Well, yes, as long as you are."

"I have Earl Grey, Herbal Ginger, or Orange Peko decaffeinated."

Julia looked confused by the choices, but then answered, "Ah, something with caffeine, please."

We both looked at her, and she appeared more nervous, and I was thinking that I don't like tea. "The drive back to Boston," she said as if that explained everything.

So, she lived in Boston. One fact established. I wondered if she had driven that morning and what ungodly time she must have left to arrive on my door at this late morning hour?

After Angela went into the kitchen, Julia pressed her lips together and turned pale. I pulled back reflexively. There was something dangerously wounded about her. "I need to know something."

I thought, here it comes. She wants to know if Gerd said her name before killing himself, like Kurtz's Intended in *Heart of Darkness*, only I wasn't a passive or accommodating Marlow witness and didn't know if I could lie about it or even how I would begin constructing such a tale. Then I thought in that split second, maybe I could distract her, get her onto something that interested me, maybe even bring it around to something I could use. "If I can help, how did you know Gerd?"

"I don't want you to put any of this in another interview or a book or."

I shook my head. "We're talking, thinking things through, off the record." But she knew better talking with a journalist. Nothing intriguing was "off the record," and I was aware of her doubt. I recalled telling Gerd that our conversation was "off the record" to put him at ease, but most of what I was able to remember went into the feature I had written. Using every last drop of someone else's lifeblood is the interviewer's job. Much of what I imagined we'd talked about was destined for a book on him that I was already being courted to write. It wasn't concern over ethics holding me back; rather, the temporary paralysis imparted from not knowing where to begin.

There is nothing really off the record with journalists. If Julia had something interesting to tell me about Gerd Wahl, I was listening with a notebook in the back of my head. If it wasn't verbatim, then who would know besides the two of us?

"We were, I know he loved other women and they loved him, but we were together for a time. I don't think it was delusional of me to think this, but he was in love with me; at least, I believed he was."

"Do you mind my asking how you met?"

"No. I mean, I don't mind telling you. In Boston. We were attending a writers' conference." She suddenly transformed before me. Sat up straighter, smiled. "God, he was charismatic. We both ducked out of a seminar at the same time. He had his broad-brimmed hat on that would have looked funny on anyone else, too ostentatious, and his jacket collar was pulled up around his neck. I said something stupid which I don't remember exactly that I must have thought was clever. Looking back, I have no idea why I was so bold with him. It wasn't typical of me. He was trying to get away without anyone recognizing him, and he had no idea how successful he was initially."

"You didn't know who he was when you met?" I must have sounded incredulous.

"I know. It seems impossible now, but I had yet to read his work."

"What did you say?" asked Angela as she returned with the cups of tea, and I wondered if she was imagining what she would have said to Gerd if she had run into him accidentally. For an instant, I was relieved that Angela had never been so fortunate. I have no doubt that she would have chosen Gerd Wahl over me.

"I asked him if he was practicing going incognito which I thought was funny because I didn't believe he was anyone famous. I was telling a joke that seems ridiculous now. He said he went around like that, disguised, all the time. I don't know why exactly, but then I asked if he wanted to ditch the conference for an hour and grab something to eat down the block. A couple of hours earlier, I had seen this restaurant and thought I'd like to try it out. I really don't know why he agreed to my proposal or why I was suddenly brash, but I suppose it was because I didn't realize I was talking to the great Gerd Wahl. I suspect he rather liked being spoken to as if he was anonymous and allowing someone else to briefly take charge."

"And the meal led to?"

"Conversations which led to a walk to the Aquarium and beautiful fish, which led to, well, I was in love before I even realized who he was."

"He must have said his name to you?" Angela asked, a little incredulous, finally handing Julia the cup of tea she had stood there holding.

"Oh, of course, but he simply said, Gerd, and I heard Khurt, and I gave him my first name only because it felt like we were being casual and not necessarily trying to get to know each other. There was a spontaneity neither of us wanted to break. It didn't feel like a date but an escape and an adventure we were on together. I have no idea why I was careless. It's not who I am, but that was his effect on me. He made me feel like I could be anything or anyone, at least for a little while."

Although I tried not to show her, I was a surprised because I thought I would have heard or read about this woman if what she said was true. I certainly was not going to tell this Julia Alexander that she meant nothing to Wahl or less than she imagined. I recalled him laughing when I asked about a special woman in his life. Or was he laughing at me for asking the question? Gerd Wahl seemed at peace with having multiple affairs but largely unaffected by them. I suspected he was bisexual for no particular reason other than the fact that I have gay friends who were equally attracted to Wahl. Hell, who am I kidding? I was attracted to him, and I have no direct evidence of his sexual orientation, but it fit.

Julia didn't ask the question I anticipated, however.

"And, well, I know this sounds indulgent or ridiculous or, do you think he blamed anyone? I mean, did he talk about me? You see, I left him right before."

"Uh, no." What she wanted to know was whether or not she had anything to do with Gerd's suicide. It turns out that the man who had everything was left by a woman who was looking for something more, and now she wanted to turn back the clock, wanted forgiveness if not from Wahl then, maybe, from herself. "No, no. He certainly didn't appear to blame anyone. In fact, he seemed quite pleased with his life. I had no indication he was about to take his own life."

"I'm sorry, but I keep going back over our last night together. There was nothing that jumped out at me; still, I don't know anymore," Julia said with her palm cupping her chin then touching her fingers to her lips as if to hush spoken word. Her neatly pulled back hair was starting to fall from the barrette that held it in place. "I thought maybe he said something to you, and it might have appeared insignificant to you at the time, either that

I was responsible or that I was not, that he was angry with me or he had forgiven me. Although he wasn't judgmental like that, and I am horribly aware of how ridiculous I sound right now, and I'm sorry. I know there is nothing you could tell me that will stop this guilt I've been living with since then."

"You have no reason to feel guilty," I said, fairly certain of my statement.

"I do. You see, I wanted to punish him for, for not loving me enough, for his seeming indifference."

I got nervous that she would break down completely. I also knew she was going to a place from which it is difficult to return, but I didn't stop her.

"I keep trying to reduce something horribly complex to a statement, something I can comprehend or deal with rationally." She shivered.

It wasn't cold in our apartment, but I felt the chill, too. Something hard was expected of me, and I didn't know what was going to happen. With Angela staring at me, too, I finally said, "Listen. I don't know the particulars of your relationship, but no one is responsible for someone else's suicide." I'm not sure I believe that, but it seemed like the right thing to say at that moment. In fact, I could suddenly think of all kinds of situations where one person might be the reason another took his or her own life. And we all bear a lot more responsibility for each other than any of us want to admit. Maybe it really was Julia Alexander's fault that Gerd Wahl shot himself, but I suspected not. We are directly and indirectly answerable for and to each other for how we treat one another in this world, but I was not about to share this opinion with a woman so tormented.

"He made a painful, hard decision, but it was his choice alone," said Angela, who positioned herself next to Julia on the couch, putting her arms around Ms. Alexander's slumping shoulders. I suddenly wanted a cup of coffee, needing something warm in me, as well.

"I don't believe he saw the act as choice," Julia broke into Angela's rational explanation.

Angela persisted: "Suicides are seldom about a reaction to one person whatever that person has or hasn't done."

Julia understood it for what it was, however, an attempt to lessen her pain. She turned and hugged Angela, and then they were both crying. Julia crying was not that difficult for me, but when Angela started, I thought I would lose it, too. I couldn't quite figure out why Angela had let go, but then again, her empathy with others was just one of the reasons I loved her. Still, this intrusion into our recent celebration with my good fortune and the announcement of our baby bothered me. Part of me wanted to throw Julia Alexander out at that moment.

Angela always seemed to be an expert on things I knew nothing about. In those moments, I started thinking about how I could be responsible if something happened to this woman, and I changed my tone. "Well, he. . . I'm sure he didn't blame. . ."

Julia had already buried her head against Angela. Feeling like I missed something again, I tried to bring the conversation back, but no one was responding to my feeble gestures or words. Amazing the way Angela was able to enter into another person's emotional life so quickly, like some kind of wind that blows in and pulls you to safety before you know the hurricane has struck.

I thought about bringing up the idea that maybe Gerd knew something the rest of us didn't, that maybe suicide could be a rational act, not one of cowardice or bravery but acknowledgement of the tenuous predicament we face every day. I wisely said nothing for once.

"I'm so sorry I troubled you, both of you," Julia nearly whispered in a pinched voice, after calming somewhat. She gulped with that prolonged exhaling of air that sucks the life out of you.

Angela and I looked at one another and shook our heads, more out of amazement than any sense that we were refuting her claim.

"But," she said, still unable to leave. "Was there anything he said in your meetings or conversations, perhaps something that you didn't include in your published interview? I mean, could there be something in your notes, possibly? I don't know what I'm looking for exactly: just his actual words, not an analysis of them."

Now she had hit on the one aspect I wanted to hide. How did she know there were other notes, ones that had not yet found their way into print. There was a book in the offering, and I was not about to betray it for anyone. Yet, I shrugged as if I had no idea what she was talking about, and Angela shot me a knowing look without moving her head. My darling was well aware of the notebooks filled with Gerd quotations from the interviews.

"I can't think of anything at all that he said, I mean, anything further where he mentioned you or something that would indicate what he was about to do." I realized how awful this must have sounded to her and tried to alter it. "Honestly, he gave no sign that he was contemplating taking his own life. I felt like he was quite cheerful or at least optimistic that night, that his life was full and complete in a way that few human beings ever find. I realize now my assessment was a deception."

Julia nodded as if she understood but looked at me expectantly, uncertain as to whether or not I was finished with my explanation, which caused me to keep talking even though I had no idea of what to say next. "I just thought maybe there was a word or two you might not have noticed at the time that now seems relevant?"

"He appeared to be the man everyone imagined: generous, highly intelligent, gifted, and yet grounded or as grounded as any of us." I didn't tell her how often I thought of Gerd Wahl and his annihilative act that brought no healing balm or cleansing of the spirit, the ending of one life in an indifferent sea of billions. Suicide, at least his suicide, continues to unsettle. It would never make sense.

"Oh. Yes. He was generous and," her voice trailed off. "Thank you." Julia straightened up, and held her arms across her chest before dropping her hands again and getting up to leave. At the door, she turned around again, hesitating. "If you do think of anything, no matter how seemingly trivial or insignificant it seems, could you, would you let me know?" She handed Angela a card with her name, address, and phone number, and Angela tucked it into her pocket as if safeguarding the information that we would never use.

"Wait," said Angela to my complete surprise, after I had already ushered Julia out in my head. "Why don't you stay with us for lunch. It's getting on in the day, and you've come a long way. I'm not a very good cook, but I promise it will be warm and nourishing. Maybe something will occur to Drew during the interim." She shot me a look with one raised eyebrow that spoke volumes. Angela was always too generous on her days off from work.

"I don't know. I can't put you both to all of this trouble."

"I promise, it's no trouble. Please stay," Angela actually entreated her. "I've plenty."

Eyes widening, Julia said, "I'm unprepared. I've brought nothing for you, for us to share."

"Nothing but stories to share," I said, resolved to make the best of the sudden turn of events, and I suddenly recalled pulling out two bottles of wine at Gerd's cabin, the past imploding present, when he began to share in earnest.

Julia's look indicated that there were tales yet to be told. Angela took her coat again. "He could be wonderfully clever, you know," she said half smiling. "There was one time in Boston when." She stopped. "I'm sorry, but I guess I don't feel comfortable talking about what went on between us. Perhaps some things should remain private."

"Oh, that's fine," said Angela, but I really wanted to disagree here; after all, she had turned around and decided to stay, and I felt that offered a kind of commitment to or at least attempt to shed a little light on their relationship. She owed us that.

"Maybe later, only if you're comfortable," I added.

"The one thing I will say about us," Julia said at last, "is that I felt like I had more neuroses than he did. I don't know. He seemed distant and then warm, but still, the sanest of individuals.

No, sane isn't quite right, I guess I mean that he seemed to offer an understanding that made it possible for the rest of us to be in this world. And now he is gone."

When Julia followed Angela into our tiny kitchen, I wrote down her words. I liked leaving Wahl like that. It was kinder than anything I could have come up with to put an end stop to my time with him.

I replayed a scene in my head in which Wahl condescended to me during the first interview, and I remember thinking that I felt like a dumb kid again in the presence of a wise and stern adult. Yet, at that second meeting, he let go of that posture, and it had been comforting to me just knowing I was in the world with him.

We shared few stories. Julia became increasingly more reserved rather than the other way around. I started getting the uncomfortable feeling that she was hiding something. I know, projection. I was thankful, however, that Angela didn't get too personal with this woman who was yet little more than a stranger to us.

After Julia left without resolution, no salve for her wounds, Angela made her promise to come back and visit again. I began wondering who had been deceived more: Julia with her delusions about Gerd Wahl's passionate and undying love for her or me, believing that I knew the man who blew off his head a few days after I mistakenly thought we had become friends.

Forty-three

Gerd's Last Work

Sometime after Julia kissed Angela on the cheek, cast one last pleading look at me before heading out, I unearthed my treasured notebooks on the interviews with Gerd, pulling these wrapped sheets out from under my favorite Colgate sweatshirt, the one with frayed cuffs that Angela promised to toss. Hiding the notes in a drawer of my dresser, as if that would be enough to stop any burglar from theft.

"Who keeps an old college sweatshirt?" Angela asked. "Who would steal your notes?" I ask myself the same question. I was not entirely sure from whom I was hiding them, but it seemed necessary to guard those fragile notebooks. I hadn't read my annotations since the publication of the interview, but these last scribblings were reserved, left out of the magazine article purposefully.

Even at the time, I thought I might do more with them, but that form had not yet taken definitive shape. In asking me not to publish any aspects of her anecdotes, her few revelations about

Gerd, Julia only compelled me to want to bring this new mystery to light. I would write more about Gerd Wahl even if I had to invent it, and I had begun to think that I could create something that could be taken as his. I was dangerously convincing myself that we weren't very different in terms of talents and writing abilities, but then I returned from my fantasy and settled into thinking about ways to effectively steal his words and get away with it. After all, I reasoned, he would not need them anymore, and if I were to use them, at least his ideas were not lost.

Near the end of our conversations, because the interview became a conversation finally, I discovered the story arc for his unwritten novel. I read and reread my notes, as scribed in the fashion of a drunken man in all the effortlessness he could master. What was my next move?

When I asked Wahl about his work in progress or novels to come, he said he was stopped, that the story was nearly impossible for him to write, but that only made the project more compelling. I couldn't imagine anything impossible for a writer such as him, and I told him something to that effect. Even drunk and unfocused at that late point in the evening, I woke up my brain sufficiently to jot down a few of his statements. I can't, however, be sure of his wording, but I know, or rather have some degree of certainty that I have captured the essence of his comments. Who would refute my calculations, anyway? Then again, I had become as unreliable a narrator as any reader can have. I actually wrote that phrase in my notes as fair warning to my future self. UNRELIABLE NARRATOR! Even less so as an interviewer, but who was left to question those assumptions?

Here was Gerd telling me about reimagining the tale of *Moby Dick,* not as parody or facsimile, nor even as prequel but like Jean Rhys *Wide Sargasso Sea* in that the narrator's glassy eye would stare into *Jane Eyre* with its hated, crazy witch in the attic and extract her, bring her fully formed as protagonist Antoinette Cosway, a Creole trapped in the 19th century institution of a stifling, English upper-class marriage. I told him I had read Rhys' short novel and liked the way the author both reimagined a character from another work and made that character live, caused the reader to sympathize with a character we had only briefly glimpsed in revulsion in Bronte's text—woman as merely flint for conflict, not even as important as a foil. It was as if I expected Gerd to compliment me for reading Rhys when he appeared to have read everything ever written, but then, he was the one directing the conversation and could turn it to his advantage, I realized only after blundering into his trap.

I think I recall asking Gerd if he was imagining his unfinished story from Ahab's perspective rather than Ismael's or perhaps, the far more difficult task of taking on the retelling from Queequeg's point of view or, even more extreme, from Ahab's "dark shadow," the symbolic, expert harpooner Fedallah, but Ahab would be the best, I continued, as if my advice had any merit to him. I concluded Ahab would be the voice.

"No, no," he said, scoffing at my limitations. Even drunk and laughing, we were both aware of an underlying derision. "Much bigger," he said suddenly serious. "Fedallah? Never Ahab. Melville captured him too well. Wouldn't touch him."

And it hit me suddenly. I nearly shouted, "The white whale! You're going to retell the Melvillian story from the narrative position of the whale?"

"Ah, close, but not quite," he said obtusely. "Not the whale exactly but from the perspective of, as Melville wrote, 'the vast whiteness,' the embodiment of representation of that creature in its multitudinous ubiquity."

I was lost and told him this more or less. I couldn't discern if it was the wine or the immensity or obscurity of the topic, but everything rapidly turned fuzzy. In fact, I had been in some danger of passing out completely. I tried fixing my gaze on a life preserver that had been tossed on the dock. Focus, I told myself, or I'm going to miss something really important.

He was patient as you would be with a child. "That's the problem, of course, but perhaps, I don't know yet, if it's solvable." He smiled slightly, barely slurring his words.

I literally slapped my face the way I would have if I was driving home late at night and falling asleep at the wheel. "Instead of Melville's perfect opening line, 'Call me Ismael,' we would have something like, 'Call me Moby Dick and other names, like great mass of flesh or death, shadow, or shape-shifting form and vast whiteness, depths, evil, and unsolvable mystery.' Kind of a long-winded opening," I teased, having awakened and temporarily lost my reverence for the great man in my inebriated state. I had also lost my planned and practiced reserve that had worked quite well into the evening.

Huffing in mock disgust, he cut me off, good-naturedly for once. "That would be truly awful." We both laughed. "And Melville's work does not begin with that infamous line, 'Call me

Ismael,' but rather a fabulous, winding etymology of the word *whale* and its permutations in literature and in the minds of men. Unfortunately, Melville's expansive opening is cut or edited out of most editions of his text. We teach readers to be lazy, it seems."

I sobered momentarily around the potential defamation. Here is where I confess that I never finished *Moby Dick*, only started it and skimmed it several times. "I didn't mean insult," I feebly attempted to defend myself even though I could tell he wasn't really insulted. "I'm not sure what you mean exactly? How you could pull off a narrative that defies singular point of view, perhaps that defies concept of human narrative."

"Precisely, the problem," he said, suddenly pleased with me again. "The idea, and this is floating around at conceptual stage, is to offer narrative perspective of the limitless, this 'headless phantom.' In this inversion, the story and search would have its beginning and perhaps its ending simultaneously."

"Which is it?" I said lightly, having lost all common sense with the alcohol working on my brain.

"Both: unraveling of narrative, of time, and the serpentine nature of beginnings and endings. The story as character in the story."

"Not string theory," I protested.

"Scarcely."

"All right but search for what? If it is omniscient or limitless, as you said. It must already know everything."

"Omniscience could be the problem, that is the conflict: to know all, yet try to see something as small as the struggle of an individual man or woman from the point of view of the limitless, particularly when that limitlessness is not benign."

"Evil?"

"No, just not part of a human moral equation."

"God," I said quietly, somewhat awed at the prospect of trying to create such a voice with any kind of humility or verisimilitude. I furiously scribbled as he spoke.

He sighed out of frustration with me. "No. Not God with a capital 'g.' Too many personal and cultural images of man *with white* beard, 'quaquaquaqua,' of course, 'outside time without extension.' No, this perspective would entail that Leviathan more ancient than man or his symbols or writing or organized through man-made structured religions."

I must have looked puzzled because he looked amused and simply said, "Beckett, *Godot*, Lucky's monologue, the question."

I'd probably read *Waiting for Godot* years ago but didn't exactly remember Lucky's monologue. I only recalled that I didn't find it as amusing as everyone else seems to have found it. "You have had as many glasses of wine as I have," I stated thickly, "but you still manage to quote verse and text accurately from a seemingly endless array of books." I'd wanted to ask him about this talent earlier but reserved the statement for a time when I had fewer inhibitions.

"Too much time spent with books. You'll have to check the accuracy yourself, but certainly not endless—this just what interests me."

"Seems everything interests you." I think he laughed, but I can't be sure now. At some point, I briefly passed out, and I noticed later that my notes descended into a scrawl that was finally illegible no matter how I tried to make meaning from them. Gerd would have nudged me awake, finally, and I recall something to this effect: that we should probably get some sleep. He was oddly practical like that at moments. I remember now feeling ashamed that I had most likely slept through all or part of his explanation as to how he would accomplish or even attempt to achieve such an artistic feat. It was mortifying to think of him expounding on the impossible task ahead of him, and me—with my mouth gaping open—sleeping on his dock as only the stars took in the immensity of his ideas unless his dogs were even wiser than they appeared. Maybe in the dark, he wouldn't have noticed that I had fallen into temporary sleep.

Yet, I must have asked him at some point, "Where would the conflict be if this being or entity or vastness—whatever it is or was—existed beyond all our human boundaries? And how could a human conceive and give shape to a voice beyond the range of our conception, even from our most brilliant minds?"

And he would have answered, but I cannot quote him. I approximated his response from my vague notes, taken after the fact: "An internal conflict—in attempting to see and feel and know that helpless human drowning in the seas from that vast, wide-angle of the multitudinous' wanting to know exactly the emptiness, the feeling of being lost, of one single yet singular life."

I closed my notebook. What surprised me after I left Wahl and arrived home, I found several sheets in Wahl's script. Since I didn't recall him giving them to me, my first thought was that I had stolen them in a drunken state, but then I didn't remember taking them either. For several days, I expected him to call and ask for his pages back (they were little more than notes, an outline), but he never did. Finally, assuming he, too, was drunk that night, I decided he had mistakenly or otherwise given them to me. I told no one initially about these last notations from my interviews with Gerd Wahl, but after Julia left, I took them out and set the pages on our coffee table—the little stand that had sufficed for dining, storage, and decoration—waiting for Angela to notice them when she got home from work.

Before falling asleep, however, I started writing. I could give Gerd Wahl voice again, imagine why Wahl had made the decision to obliterate himself. But there was still no entry to that experience, and I recalled our earlier dialogue in which he reminded me of the arbitrary nature of our stories, shifting with each telling, even memory unreliable. "Precisely why I'm worried about losing a story; the idea of trying to recreate one is next to impossible."

At some point in my scribbling, I passed out on the couch where Angela found me in the early morning.

"What's this?" she said. Angela was surprised to find me wearing the same clothes as the day before. I said nothing, allowing her to peruse the pages slowly. I wondered why she looked as if she had suspected something all along. Flipping a few pages, she then picked up a notebook for closer examination and began reading. "You? When did you? Why didn't you? These are Gerd's words? Julia asked you—

I shrugged. "I would have shown her these notes if it would have done her any good, but she is looking for something I don't have, can't give her even if I wanted to."

"How do you know that?"

"Because she—"

"She would have wanted to see this, to read his words, if these are Gerd's and not yours. They're not yours, are they?" I could sense Angela's disappointment and distrust in her tone, that lower pitch she reserved for concern, even anger, but there was also a hint of confusion. "What are you going to do with?"

"Maybe."

"Maybe what?"

"Maybe they're mine. I don't know with any certainty. I was drunk." I never cut Angela off, and I was cutting her off. And I didn't really know what I was going to do with them, but I had the suspicion that I would somehow try to use his words to my advantage. What good would they do him now anyway? Would he have wanted to murder me? Perhaps, but I was safe on that score. An image opened up before me. That scene of me crying into Gerd's message machine was still raw and humiliating even after the passage of time, even if there were no other living witnesses to it.

"You don't know if they're yours or not?"

"They were notes from the interview. What I do with them is up to me."

"So, you are going to try to publish this—as?"

"No. Not in this form."

"What then?"

"It was my interview, Ange."

"She loved him. They were his words, Drew, not yours. This isn't your handwriting." Angela looked tired, and I remembered that her pregnancy was probably making her even more

333 | Socrates is Dead Again

exhausted. I got up to hug her, and she took a small step back. It was enough, her statement as gesture.

"We were talking, sharing stories."

"Who? You and your friend you had just met, Adrian Gerd Wahl?"

"Let me get breakfast started; it won't take but a couple of minutes," I said, trying to make up something to her. It was the least I could do, I realized. I could be good in the kitchen when I wanted to be.

"I know that." She must have noticed my confusion because she added, "I know it was your interview. But it was her life. You could have shared these pages with her. What harm would that have been? She needed something more, and you had this to offer." Angela was not one to give up easily, particularly now that she thought of this Julia Alexander as some kind of lost soul. But then, again, everyone was under Angela's care, including me. I didn't expect I would ever see Julia again, and really, if Gerd had loved her that much, would he—I don't know where I'm going with this line of defense because even I find this reasoning cruel. Sometimes I know when to keep my mouth shut. Sometimes I don't.

"They're my notes, Ange. He gave them to me. And it's our lives," I said, motioning to our son or daughter yet to be born. "Trust me on this. I will honor him and respect her, too."

I realized she didn't know if I was talking about Julia and Gerd or our son or daughter. While she hesitated far longer than I wanted her to, she finally gave in and let me slip my arms around her. It was going to be okay. Once again, thank God, Angela had chosen me.

Forty-four

The Accident

Julia was angry that Adrian would not engage with her about the idea of him moving to Boston.

"I don't understand. You could write in Boston as well as here, and it's closer to New York, to your publisher than this location." He shook his head slowly. "What is it? What are you thinking right this minute? Please, tell me."

Adrian shifted his stance and looked away from his lover before speaking. "Not a body. A whole person," he said. "A baby, not a baby, a toddler. A pile of wounded rags rolling in the night. A thud. Bump, bump, bump. Again. Sound suggesting nothing more than inconsequential refuse. Nothing but something. Turning back. No need to turn back, but in the rearview mirror, a bundle that looked like nothing and yet more."

Obtusely—that was how Adrian began relating the accident, and she didn't know exactly what he was talking about. "A baby?" She wondered what that information had to do with a commitment decision. "What baby? What happened?"

"You won't find much about her," he said after a moment as if catching his breath. "Something horrific—a baby, struck by a car, alone at night."

"Was this a hit and run driver? The baby was alone?"

"Not a hit and run. Alone, though; she was utterly alone. The driver was alone."

"But her parents"

"Her mother wasn't home. She had gone out that one time, she said, because it was, 'hard to be cooped up in a house all day and night for months, baby crying.' And she couldn't find a babysitter, she said."

"You spoke with the child's mother?"

"No, but they tacked her to the wall in the news. Quoted her in order to demonstrate her callous, criminal behavior. A short article appeared later with emphasis on the mother's crime rather than mine. The child's mother probably wasn't a whole lot older than I was at the time. When it happened, my mother was dying of cancer. I was speeding. I left out that part of the story to the cops. No street lights. No house lights. My headlights bouncing off falling snow. Everywhere dark except the narrow path ahead forged by high beams defused in the storm when the car struck her."

She noted he didn't say "my car." His way of separating himself, she thought, realizing he was the young man in that car all those years ago. This was not one of Adrian's stories but his life.

"Garbage bag in the road or something that had fallen out of a truck that had passed me. I don't even know why I stopped." He waited for a few seconds. "But I stopped, pulled over, looked

336 | Socrates is Dead Again

in my rearview mirror, got out, and walked back. I must have known before I knew. My mouth dry."

"Oh, no."

"I had to know."

"Maybe? Why was she?"

"Then I saw her little face. I picked her up and carried her body to the nearby house; she weighed almost nothing; I remember thinking: *this is all life weighs.* It was almost as if I held nothing in my arms at all. A single life weighs nothing and everything at the same time."

"But what could you have done?" Julia moved a step closer to him, but he leaned back a little further.

"I could have seen her and swerved, jammed on the brakes quicker, wrapped the car around a tree, anything but strike her."

"I don't know. I don't think you could have done anything else. How could you have even seen her at night?"

He pressed his lips tight before stating, "Almost not there."

"Oh. I'm so sorry. It's terrible. What happened when you got to her house?"

"No one was there. I walked in an open door, the portal she had passed through moments ago. I must have flipped on a light then lay her on a dirty couch before I found a phone. I called the police, and waited with her, staring at her face. She looked like she was sleeping—a thin stream of blood at each corner of her tiny mouth."

"My God, how long were you there—sitting with her body?" Julia felt her hand reach out and touch air, the distance between them having somehow grown.

She thought he might not continue. Never had she wanted to hold him more than in that instant, yet something held her back. It was her lover. His expression and tone drew a barrier between them, a wall stronger than her love. "When the State Police arrived," he continued, "I told them everything—at least as far as the obvious aspects of the toddler being struck, and they tried to find her parents. I could tell they were angry but, strangely, not with me. It took the cops hours to locate the mother, the baby's father long gone, and then arrest the woman for criminal negligence. Imagine that scene: 'Your baby is dead. Struck by a car. We're arresting you. Turn around,' as they cuffed her. She was probably screaming."

"Did they? Did the police charge you with anything?"

"They never even gave me a ticket—nothing. Told me there was nothing I could have done—told me to make out a statement, even offered to drive me home after I filled out the papers. I said my car was still running, hadn't even been damaged. Imagine. I must have looked like a train wreck to them, snot and tears smeared on my face. Drove back to my house, crawled home really, checked on my mother who was sleeping—still sleeping. She was in her bed for another couple of years before dying. Everything seemed unnatural."

"But all this time? Why are you thinking about this now? You can't blame yourself. What could you have done?"

"I didn't exactly blame myself; I never faced it." He looked at her directly and with incredulity at her incomprehension.

His pain. She felt it, witnessed it, yet she left him.

***

Months later, Julia was driving home from her futile trip to see Drew Levin. An impulsive odyssey she once believed might give her something back: some words from Adrian. Her hands clutching the wheel, she realized she could have confessed to Drew this story of the accident. It was so long ago, she thought. How could that ancient incident have played any role in the fateful decision of the man she loved? Her eyes blurring, headlights coming from every direction, she experienced the highway to Boston as infinite; as if stretched out before her, timeless.

She never told Drew and Angela. Of course, she thought about telling them. Why hadn't she told Drew Levin about this consequential accident in the life of the man she loved? There was another story to tell about Gerd Wahl, but one she could not narrate it seems, though she imagined that Levin would have treated Gerd with respect.. And what if she was wrong? When was he narrating fiction and when was he telling his truth? How could she offer ambiguity to strangers? Perhaps, it was the intimacy she was ultimately afraid to reveal?

Julia's lover kept notes on news stories, on the morbid, as well as the sublime. It was entirely possible that his tale was a disturbing item he couldn't let go of—but then why claim it as his as if it was something he had read? And there were words which contradicted her apology directly.

That summer night—all those endless months ago, she left Adrian with a purpose. She wanted him to miss her, ache for her, realize that he had made a terrible mistake in not taking her in his arms and declaring his eternal love. All she wanted was for him to put aside his projects, his dogs, his theories, his publishers and editors, his vanity and ego, his past, and see only her for once. When he couldn't answer, when he couldn't tell her just once that he loved her right then, that he would give up anything for her, she felt something snap.

"We both made choices," she said out loud to no one, only the hum of tires on the road as companion. Then she wondered if what Adrian did seemed like a choice to him? She didn't know anymore. Julia had given him the chance, and the man turned away. She left him, and in leaving, Julia knew what she could not bear. Shaking as she drove, Julia Alexander knew that she wanted him—and wanted him to suffer. This is what she would carry.

Forty-five

Alone at Sea

Tucked into one of his notebooks, Drew Levin folded found pages of notes in another hand. He struggled with the words, then labeled them: "Found narrative of Adrian Gerd Wahl:"

"IIIIIIIIIIIIIIIIIIIIIIIIIIIIIIIIIIIIIIIIIIIIIIIIIIIIIIIIIIIIIIIIII IIIIIIIIIIIIIIIIIIIIIIIIIIIIIIIIIIIII as hierarchical position in the English language: first as is important; actor, agent, seemingly beginning everything yet unaware of bias. Homodiegetic narrator in the midst of it. Trapped self. Ego. Psyche. Focalized. Aggressive language centered on I. In the beginning, there was I. Beginning and ending with no boundaries. And then, unexpectedly, ego is temporarily and deliberately set aside.

"Listening to a fan blowing forced air, sound of the sea at night, he climbed out of his clothes like dead skin, sloughed off every vestige of his waking life, walked down to the dock where he stood facing blackness, deeper than night; wind moving tiny hairs on his body, each one distinct, independently felt, every motion sensed, every noise swallowed by his opening mouth before he dove into the cold dark. Fool that he was.

"When it began. Four and one-half billion years ago, alien to all that Earth would become, there were pseudo machine sounds made by rock breaking, volcanic greenstone, nothing—even rock—to survive this apocalyptic conception, even air a conflagration.

"Hell, not as conceived by men, but as inception until zircon from basalt dismantled, kidnapping hitchhiking asteroids before their preservation in sediment—stories in these grains embedded in rock—only much later to be read; platinum arriving violently on tail-end of meteors, those last voyagers from distant stars, divisions in stone and ice followed by fire, explosion, sounds concussive. Much later, with implications of animate cacophony, seemingly metal teeth clicking and gasping in agitation, blurring. Inarticulate voices of even the inanimate now indistinguishable. Intense heat then cold inimical to life, and yet, existence creeps in at this almost unquantifiable pace.

"Only a billion years later, crackling ice crawling, fire, then burble of water rising in spaces again, voids created by absence while life begins: generative, as something starts swimming, eventually navigating. Seas suggesting this pulse and wash of lamentation. Supereons followed by eons, eventually epochs and ages descend, the tumult emerges out of water, then phyla diversify across land mass, insects gnawing and winged in din; eventually birds screaming in disquiet; animals rasping; mutation, variation, transformation humming and wailing nearly deciphered, yet still distorted as other mouths appear: accidents, murders, revolutions, stirring and pushing against currents, this electrical charge building.

"Sound shadows because scale was too enormous to be as finite as an organism, with such shape and precision, moving across indistinct domains, until conceiving borders layered and overlapping, not boundaries after all but, nevertheless, something of demarcation.

"From there, not genesis because it was not causal and not entrance, from above and beneath and between, an arduous journey of separating distinct sounds, moving from one land mass and ocean to another, then smaller still, until cities could be heard bellowing in bedlam. Closer still: confetti of human voices, languages drowning in whirlpools of sound; lyrical gyres with grating ones, as simultaneously descending and ascending through opaqueness.

"Only with practiced stillness, with concentration, could it be heard like impulse: cramped animation, exchanges in multitude, mountainous volume loosed yet somehow still choking. Below were myriad sensations of scramblinglaughing runtingnashissshadowsymphony yet turnihilisticlamorashellyin gulprotestumult. Until there was abundance and then antithesis: one depth sounding, scanning in opposition, contrast to water, pressure beneath surface, bubbles forced, rising and releasing, again submerged. Pulling back and leaning in—wave after wave after wave after wave.

"Abundance and antithesis: until struggling could be discerned, air pushed out, ripples of sea water displaced, slapping, floating, moving, swimming—sobbing that was not sonorous sea. Ages condensed, concentrated, an infinitesimally small biological disturbance at surface.

"And then an arm, long, sinewy, and slender, attached hand, fingers extended toward sun and moon before submerging as diving bird, only with greater desperation expressed in unnatural curl of bent joints and tendons, now locked straight in terror, those hands thrust upward out of water, skin brown and leathery not from age but exposure to weather and salt water. A voice small and weak—almost not recognizable as anything—when another chord was struck, released from oval cavity through which sound came bursting out, water spit, sudden but not sharp ingestion of surrounding air, followed by quick awful silence then less rapid release and intake again of breaths expressing fear—inarticulate expression of terror—after all this time, horror, encountered, and forever, surprising.

"Recognition getting closer: struggling discerned, air pushing water, sea molecules displaced, yes, slapping, floating, moving, swimming in sea swell. And ages passed in singular, present tense, an infinitesimally small disturbance at the exterior, now determined by flailing limbs on icy cold waters.

"Not sight or sound after all but awareness of solitary gasping, as process is retraced and revealed before each new apprehension, sharp and painful in this long journey by the great other to acknowledge, to understand, to know intimately, this one man alone and fearful in vast sea.

"When, at the moment of evolving perception come distraction. A volcano erupts on the other side of this small planet, rock transforming into violent liquid, jarring; thousands of moaning voices echo simultaneously, animal squeals and cacophony of final notes, water boiling; land giving its slow, agonizing, choking sighs, hissing as water becomes vapor, all clouded again: layers upon layers obscuring. And in that calamitous diversion, shifting from near comprehension of one voice to thousands, to millions, to billions, one individual is unseen, unheard, slipping beneath churning surface."

***

I closed his notebook. Gerd Wahl had been trying to create story from a perspective that was impossible. How to narrate from the point of view of a non-human entity or non-temporal being when we are pitiably human, even if he was one of the brightest representations of such creatures? And what could I do with his fragments, with the nearly unworkable language left? He hadn't so much given these lines to me as released them into oblivion. I was pretty certain I didn't steal them; even drunk, I had some ethics. He had placed them in my notebook on purpose.

Wondering whether Wahl might have once intended his solitary man to survive and swim in the ocean, I recognized my folly. Of course, he planned to have his character slip beneath the waves anonymously. I thought of Gerd's suicide, his last disappearing act. Or escape. Not, however, undetected or unnoticed by the earthly creatures around him even if not by anything larger, noticed by some obscure cognition.

I should have been intimidated, overwhelmed with the weight of his words but did not experience that kind of fear. Unlike Gerd, I didn't know better, didn't acknowledge that there was no way to continue. While the rational mind suggested drowning lay ahead for me, for all of us, as well as for Gerd's incarnation of contemporary Ismael, I picked up a piece of paper ready for my own contortions. Perhaps I would write something worthy of this unexpected gift. I had to try. Then again, it might be Ian or Marie who is anointed as Author, but I was going to give it everything I had. And then? Then I began to write.

***

Across the city, with Ian in the next room making coffee, Marie tucked her tongue behind her top front teeth, twisted her lips into a shape that could be taken for crooked smile or grimace after finishing the last line of her novel. With some trepidation and the irrepressible hope of a young writer, she hit the key "send."

About the Author

Author and educator Nancy Avery Dafoe writes across genres and has won multiple awards for her work, including the William Faulkner/William Wisdom creative writing competition in poetry. She won first place in the international short story competition from New Century Writers, among other awards. Dafoe has twelve published books, with her thirteenth book coming out later in 2022.

In addition to her published books, Dafoe's fiction, poetry, and nonfiction works appear in several anthologies, including *Lost Orchard* (SUNY Press) and *Lost Orchard II* (PWP); *NY Votes for Women: A Suffrage Centennial Anthology* (Cayuga Lake Books); and numerous journals and magazines.

Dafoe has taught English and writing in a variety of settings, including high school, community college, and workshops. Her editing/writing consultation business website is found at dafoewritingandconsulting.com. She is currently second vice president of the National League of American Pen Women, Inc. (NLAPW), a former Central New York (CNY) Branch president, and lives in Homer, New York.

CPSIA information can be obtained
at www.ICGtesting.com
Printed in the USA
JSHW021553040922
29980JS00002B/7

9 781950 251100